**Triple Crown Publications
presents**

IN
CAHOOTZ

The Sequel to Hoodwinked

By Quentin Carter

Compilation and Introduction copyright © 2006 by
Triple Crown Publications
4449 Easton Way, 2nd Floor
Columbus, Ohio 43219
www.TripleCrownPublications.com

Library of Congress Control Number: 2006908232
ISBN: 0-9778804-3-5
ISBN 13: 978-0-9778804-3-0
Cover Design/Graphics: www.MarionDesigns.com
Author: Quentin Carter
Typesetting: Holscher Type and Design
Associate Editor: Cynthia Parker
Editor-in-Chief: Mia McPherson
Consulting: Vickie M. Stringer

First Trade Paperback Edition Printing November 2006

10 9 8 7 6 5 4 3 2

Printed in the United States of America

Acknowledgements

First I would like to thank the almighty for blessing me with the gift to speak through a pen.

Next I would like to thank two very special people, my mother and father, Lois and Charles Williams. You two are truly a blessing from God.

My very supportive family, my brothers, Fuzz, Brad and Dewayne and my sisters Joey, Cheron and Denisha.

All my children and their mothers, who shall remain nameless due to too much arguing about whose name should've gone first in my last acknowledgements.

A special thanks to the lady who made it all possible. Vickie Stringer, you are truly a beautiful person. Thank you. I can't forget the hardworking staff at TCP that always keeps this whole thing moving. God bless you all.

My closest homies outside the cage, Skatterman, Lil Jay, Veto, Chiefa, Boo Dewey, Mike, T-bone, Dagwood, Rico, Winnie, J-Ron and Rich.

And inside the cage, Lil D, Jarret Jackson, Monie, Josey Wells, Big Corn, Big E, J. Juice, Ray Duck, Mitch B, Gordon Mitchel-Bey, B. Warran, Geno, Jimmy Johnson, Jesse James, Smooth, Big Jeff, Big Hamp, White Rich, Smallwood, T-Nott, Twin, Paul Reed, Will Gary (Blac), Beno, Rico, Al Thomas, Stuffy, Shane, Keith, pete, Trudy, Chris, Ty, Shakur Nur, Abdula, Big Jude, J. Lambort and The Blac One.

And to my fans, thank you for all the letters of praise and your comments on Amazon.com. Y'all are starting to swell my head up. Thanks to all of you, Tukey Tosh has made it back on the shelves for a second run. I hope I didn't disappoint you.

Oh my God! I almost forgot. My friend and wonderful editor, Cynthia. Thank you for cleaning up and involving me in the editorial process of my work.

Remember, every story has been told, it's the way I tell it that keeps the reader turning pages.

King Author

Please send comments to:

Quentin Carter
13685-045 J-Unit
Federal Correctional Institution
PO Box 1000
Sandstone, MN 55072

Chapter 1

Traffic was light for a typical Friday night in Kansas City. Ordinarily the streets would be filled with tricked-out whips and half-dressed tricks looking for a place to kick it or a baller to chase. But tonight the streets were quiet. There wasn't a whip or a trick in sight.

The usually-crowded Friday night streets were the only reason why Peko had left her apartment with three thousand Ecstasy pills in her trunk. She had planned on blending in with all the traffic, but that night, there wasn't any.

Her sister, Tiki, who was riding shotgun, did not seem to share her paranoia. She sat in the passenger seat singing along to Ciara's "*1, 2 Step.*" Twice, Peko contemplated turning around and going back home, but she knew that her cousin Tukey would be mad if she missed that money.

Sitting erect in her seat with her seat belt fastened, Peko made a left turn off of Gregory onto Cleveland. Tiki looked over and noticed the apprehensive look on her sister's face. She turned down the volume on the radio.

"Gurl, yu straight Perry Mason tonight," she said, chuckling. "Perry Mason" was another way of saying paranoid. She took a half-smoked blunt out of the ashtray. "Smoke some of dis and loosen ya ass up some, gurl."

Peko frowned. "Unt unh, rude gurl. Ya bet not fire dat shit up while us riding durty, mon."

Tiki rolled her eyes as she sat the blunt back inside the ashtray. She was sitting back in her seat when she saw something that disturbed her. A dark blue Ford Crown Victoria was parked on the side of the road with the lights out. Tiki made out the word "Police" written on the driver's door as they rode by.

"Oh shit, gurl! Drive like yu got some sense," Tiki commanded while looking straight ahead, trying to make herself look inconspicuous.

Peko didn't have to see what her sister had seen to know what she was talking about. Her heartbeat increased, but she didn't panic. Her tags were legit and they weren't likely to pull over two women for no reason.

Sergeant Cody Brown glanced up after he heard the rose-pink Dodge Magnum stroll by on big chrome rims. He caught a glimpse of the two women trying their best not to look in his direction. Since it was the weekend, he was ninety percent sure that they were either drinking or had a bag of weed in their possession. Normally he would've ignored them, but he was bored and there wasn't anything else for him to do on that dead Friday night.

Cutting on his headlights, he pulled out onto the street and began to tail them. Through her rearview mirror, Peko saw the patrol car coming up behind her fast.

"Shit! Here his punk ass comes," she warned Tiki.

"Me see him." Tiki reached inside the glove compartment and pulled out a chrome .38. "We not 'bout ta go tu jail."

Peko shot her sister a hideous look. "Gurl, what ya planning on doing wit' dat?"

"Like me said, we not 'bout ta go tu jail," Tiki said seriously. She let down her window.

"OK, OK!" Peko said. "Just wait until we for sure dat him is gonna pull us over."

Tiki nodded her head in agreement.

Cody ran their tags through the computer, but came up with nothing. *Oh well*, he thought. He would just have to make something up. Surely they had something illegal in the car, even if it was something petty. He cut on the lights on top of his car, signaling them to pull over.

Immediately, Peko hit the gas putting a huge gap between herself and the patrol car. The evasion took Cody by surprise. Before he realized what was happening, the high-powered Magnum was a block ahead of him.

"Shit!" he exclaimed. He hit the gas in an attempt to catch up.

He was about six car lengths behind them when he heard a gunshot. Cutting the wheel, he swerved a little to the left, but continued in pursuit of the fleeing vehicle. The next shot that Tiki fired went through his windshield, barely missing the side of his head.

Peko made a quick right onto 67th Street and her car spun sideways. After she regained control, she took off toward the zoo. Once again, she gained about a block's distance on him. But she knew that he wouldn't go away, and sooner or later, the ghetto bird would show its face and the chase would be over.

"We gotta bail," Peko said. "Text Shantí and tell her to meet us at de lighthouse in Swope Park." In her mirror she could see the police car coming toward them at full speed.

Peko made a sharp left turn onto the park's grass. She drove on the bumpy surface until she reached the concrete path. A quick left turn and she was headed back in the other direction.

"Hurry up, gurl!" Peko shouted. "Me just bought us some time."

Tiki flipped up her phone and started to text Shantí.

Cody saw the car turn into the park. He smiled to himself thinking that they had made a mistake. Cutting out his lights, he turned onto the grass, then drove full speed ahead toward the concrete path. She was about two hundred yards away from the lighthouse, when out of nowhere, the police car crashed into the Magnum, spinning it around. The impact made Peko hit her head up against her door window and Tiki's gun fell out of her hand.

Cody hit his head up against the dashboard so hard that he was temporarily knocked out. By the time he came to, Peko and Tiki had recovered and were out of their demolished car. Tiki, thinking that she was back home in Jamaica, fired three rounds into the police car before they took off for the lighthouse.

When they arrived, they didn't see Shantí's black Chrysler 300C anywhere. Police sirens could be heard nearby. Breathing hard, they ducked inside of the building for cover.

They hadn't been inside a good minute when they heard sirens right outside. Rushing to the window, they saw two police cars speed by on their way to the wrecked squad car. Peko looked down and saw the gun in Tiki's hand.

"Gurl, get rid of dat before yu get us killed."

Tiki wiped the gun clean using the sleeve of her shirt. Glancing around, the only place that she found to hide the gun was inside a heater vent. A flash of excitement came across Peko's face when she saw the grill of Shantí's 300C pulling into the entrance.

"Let's go, Tiki. Shantí just pulled up."

They ran outside waving their hands in the air, trying to flag her down. Shantí giggled at the pair looking like fools waving their hands as they ran up to her car. She stopped to let them in.

"What are y'all doi—"

"Gurl, just go, shit!" Tiki yelled, interrupting her. "Before da police see us."

Chapter 2

Tukey could hear the phone ringing in her sleep, but she didn't want to get up to answer it. She pulled the covers over her head, hopping to muffle the loud sound of the ringing.

The ringing stopped. As soon as she began to drift back to sleep, the bling tone of her cell phone started playing. Tukey grunted as she tossed the covers back. She got up and walked buck naked over to the dresser where the phone was.

"Hello," she answered sleepily.

"Tukey, this is Shantí. Peko and Tiki done fucked up again. You need to get over here."

Tukey let out a breath of hot air. "Where's here?"

"At the club. We'll be in your office."

Tukey hung up the phone and ran her fingers through her dreads. She peered across the room at the sexy young tender that was asleep in her bed. Even balled up in the fetal position, Tukey could still make out the curvy shape of her body.

After a quick shower, she started to get dressed. "Teka!" she called out. "Teka, get up! Me got sum't'ing dat me got ta go take care of."

Lateka sat up in bed, forcing herself to wake up. The chilly air that blew through the open window made her nipples harden. Running her fingers through her sandy, curly hair, she asked, "What time is it?"

Tukey picked up her iced-out pink Jacob watch off the dresser. It was a little after midnight, but she didn't bother informing Lateka. Lateka crawled out of the bed then moped to the bathroom.

Tukey squeezed into a pair of faded Rocawear jeans, a pink and white Baby Phat jersey and a pair of pink and white Air Force 1's. She clipped her phone on her hip then was ready to go.

"Teka!" she yelled impatiently. "Gurl, hurry ya ass up!"

Lateka came back into the room. "I had to pee," she said, bending over to pick up her clothes.

* * * * *

After she dropped Lateka off, Tukey drove out to her club on 82nd and Troost. Club No Draws was Kansas City's hot spot and had been since it opened six months ago. It was a newly built modern club that catered to the young crowd, particularly the young ballers who didn't know what to do with their money besides kick it.

The club was two buildings inside of one. On one side was the dance floor, two bars, a kitchen that served only fried chicken wings, fish and fries, four red felt pool tables and a stage for local artists to perform. If you possessed a pink laminated card with two skeleton keys on it, you could order Ecstasy pills along with your drink. All you had to do was show your card, then ask for a pop-n-shot, which meant a pill to pop and a shot of liquor to wash it down with. Out of the club alone, Tukey sold about forty-five hundred single pills between Friday and Sunday.

The other side of the club was called The Ho'ling Alley. It had a long runway stage with a pole, twenty lap dance booths and another small stage with a shower nozzle coming out of the wall. Instead of water it spit out milk, chocolate and whipped cream. The set rate for a shower dance was fifty dollars and the stripper could be naked, but the customer had to remain in his or her underwear.

Pussy could be bought at the strippers' discretion. Tukey didn't mind as long as she received her thirty percent. At a near-by motel, they kept six rooms on reserve for the weekends at the strippers' expense.

Tukey pulled her pink Hummer, sitting on twenty-six inch pink and chrome spinners, up to the valet. Reaching into her console, she took out her platinum chain with two diamond skeleton keys dangling from it. She slipped it on and then checked her face in the mirror. Smiling, she got a look at her two platinum and diamond crowns that covered her side teeth. One was on the top row and the other was directly underneath it. When she was high off Ecstasy she would grind them together.

Rhyme Tyme, the valet, opened up the door for her. "Hey, boss lady," he said pleasantly.

"Hey, Rhyme," she said as she exited her truck. She named him "Rhyme Tyme" because every time she saw him, he would rap for her. "What rap yu got for me tonight, mon?"

He cleared his throat before he said, "The party's poppin'. The bitches flockin'. The night is long and the drinks are strong. And I'm gon' kick it 'till they all go home."

Tukey smiled as she handed him a twenty dollar bill. "Dat was tight. Yu keep on and me gonna take yu tu da studio."

He responded by nodding his head. He knew that she was only bullshitting, but it was nice to hear.

She stepped inside her club and heard Lil Flip's "*Game Over*" blaring through the sound system. On the dance floor, the girls were getting low while the guys danced stiffly, trying not to wrinkle their creased pants. The big shots were buying up the bar while the pool sharks ran the tables.

After a few hugs and handshakes, she finally made her way over to bar #1. The heavyset bartender immediately stopped smiling in some chick's face and rushed to tend to her.

"What can I get for you, boss lady?"

"A pop-n-shot of RémyRed," she ordered. A tall, handsome young dude at the bar had his eyes on her. She winked at him then focused her attention back to Big Corn, the bartender.

He brought her the drink and the pill wrapped in a napkin. She popped it then took a huge swallow of her drink. "Put it on me tab," she joked, then walked away.

Through the two-way mirror that was behind the bar, Shantí watched Tukey down her drink and walk away. She took a seat at the long wooden conference table next to Peko, waiting for the boss to come in.

"Mon, me hope she doan come in here trip—"

Tukey walked through the front door. Her two younger cousins were sitting at the table looking nervous. Casually, she sat her drink down then took a seat in her wing-back, pink leather chair that sat at the head of the table. For a few minutes she didn't speak. The silence would make her two cousins very uneasy.

Tukey regarded Shantí's face. She couldn't believe how good she still looked after having AIDS for three years now. The medicine was expensive, but it seemed to be prolonging her life. For those types of results, Tukey would continue to shell out top dollar to help save her friend.

Nobody outside of their crew knew that Shantí had AIDS. Sometimes Tukey would order her to sleep with the enemy. A slow death was the worst kind. She loved knowing when somebody was going to die before that somebody did.

Every once in a while, she would feel bad and regret being the evil woman that she had become. But the feelings never lasted long after she thought about what happened in her past that brought her to this point in her life.

The Ecstasy pill was beginning to take effect, putting an instant smile on her pretty chocolate face. The gleaming pink diamonds inside her mouth sparkled brightly in the dimly lit room.

"So," Tukey finally said, "tell me what happened."

Peko chose to be the one to explain the situation to her. When she finished, Tiki sat there waiting to get chewed out for shooting at the police.

"Did yu report me car stolen?" Tukey asked Shantí.

"Yes. Anitra went down to the police station to fill out a report," Shantí explained. "You know she's hot, right?"

"Yu did not tell her where me was, did ya?"

"Come on now, you know me better than that. I told her that you went by your mom's to check on Mi'kelle."

"Good!" Tukey stood up. "Now me about ta go get me dance on." The Ecstasy had her feeling too good to continue to trip on them.

Twenty minutes later, Tukey was on the floor dancing to Chingy's *"Balla Baby."* There was a dude dancing in front of her and one in back of her. She shook it real fast, then stopped. Then shook it again, and dropped. There was a line of guys waiting to dance with the new queen pin of Kansas City.

Outside, a platinum-colored BMW 745 pulled up to the valet. Chris a.k.a. Fuzzy and his cousin, Black, stepped out of it. Fuzzy handed Rhyme a twenty, then they both entered the club. They were VIP so they didn't have to pay the twenty-dollar cover charge.

Fuzzy was short – about five feet eight with brown skin, a fade and an evil glare in his eyes. Black was tall, thin and black as a pair of polished boots. He and Fuzzy both had a mouth full of gold and diamond teeth. While Fuzzy never displayed his, Black couldn't keep his mouth closed.

They strolled over to The Ho'ling Alley and ordered orange juice and a couple of pills, then found a table. Alcoholic beverages were not served inside the strip club. A stripper named Naughty was naked on stage making her booty clap while perverted men threw money on the stage by her feet. At first sight of Fuzzy and Black, the money hungry strippers rushed over to their table, offering their services.

Sweating lightly and nearly out of breath, Tukey walked over to bar #2. She was dehydrated and in desperate need of a drink.

DJ Bigga Figga started the club mix. "All the ladies!" he yelled. "All the ladies in the house that suck dick say, 'Yeah.'"

"Yeah!" the women all shouted in unison.

"All the hoes in the house say, 'Woop! Woop!'"

"Woop! Woop!" the freaks shouted, throwing their hands in the air.

"To the windoooow, to the wall," DJ Bigga Figga sang. "'Till all you females crawl. Everybody say, 'There's some hoes in dis house.'"

"There's some hoes in dis house," the crowd repeated.

"What can I get for you, boss lady?" Tina, the bartender at bar #2, asked.

"RémyRed," Tukey shouted over the loud crowd. She leaned up against the bar and eyed her establishment.

The club looked like it was filled to its 850-person capacity. As usual she was very happy with the turnout.

"You can do it put ya' back into it," Ice Cube rapped.

"Heeeey!" the women hollered as they bent over, putting their backs into it.

Tukey's club business was doing great, but as the days rolled by, she was taking more and more losses. Stick up men were always trying to rob a member of her all-female crew. Not only that, but the police were constantly hassling them as well. She was beginning to think that somebody had put the word out for the police to pull over every young black female driving a nice car. Something had to give soon or she would be out of business.

Though she probably had more bread than most of the hustlers in the city that didn't speak Spanish, she still wasn't satisfied. She was in it to win it until they put her corpse up under the map. Jail was not an option. She'd been there once and had no plans to go back. And she definitely wasn't going to go out like her baby daddy did over a piece of ass. Every time she thought about him, she got sick to the stomach. They could've had the world together, but he gave his life up after he caught a bad case of tender dick.

Tukey sipped on her drink. From way across the club she could see that slick-ass bright smile of Black's. She took off in his direction.

A sexy, chocolate, curvy young tender was sitting on Fuzzy's lap, grinding on him. Black was busy stuffing money in everything in a G-string that crossed his path.

Tukey snuck up behind Fuzzy. "Yu see sum't'ing ya like?" she whispered into his ear.

He didn't have to turn around to know whose mouth those words had come from. "I see some ladies in here who should be having my baby," he said drunkenly.

A short, stacked, cocoa-complexioned stripper named Mocha Cream was on stage lying on her back with her legs behind her head, exposing her huge pussy hole. She pushed her finger in and out to the beat of Christina Milian's "*Dip It Low*." Tukey walked over to the stage, grabbed Mocha's hand and then slowly sucked the juice off her fingers.

"Mmm," she moaned on her way back over to Fuzzy. "You ought ta try some of dat."

Black almost came in his pants. The mere presence of Tukey aroused his hormones. Her smooth chocolate skin and her healthy five foot, ten inch frame was hard not to crave.

"Maybe later," Fuzzy said. "Right now, let's go talk business."

"Follow me tu me office."

Anitra had returned and was sitting at the conference table inside Tukey's office when she walked in. She could tell by the angry glare in Anitra's eyes that she was pissed.

"Where you been all night?" Anitra bellowed. She stood up wearing a snug-fitting Baby Phat denim jumpsuit. Her hair was cut short with a texturizer in it.

"Me went by mummy's tu see—"

"Stop lying, Tukey!" Anitra hollered. "I called over there. I know you were with that bitch Lateka. I'm not no damn fool."

"Ca'an we talk about dis later? Fuzzy and Black is coming in here." Anitra bit down on her bottom lip, tapping her fingernail on the table. "T'ank yu."

Black knocked on the door.

"Come in," Shantí said. She had been standing by the door observing the whole scene.

They took seats across from Anitra. Her poked out lips made it very clear that she was upset about something.

Black took out a pack of Newports. "Everything all right in here?" he inquired. He knew that Tukey was fucking around behind Anitra's back.

"Everyt'ing's cool," Tukey stated as she took her seat at the head of the table. "Now, what's up?"

Fuzzy spoke up. "We trying to get twenty units."

Tukey faced Anitra. "Ca'an we do it?"

Anitra opened up her folder and looked over some paperwork. She was the accountant for both their legal and illegal business. She kept track of all profits and washed their money through the club. All of it was too much to wash, but she cleaned enough for them to spend freely.

"Yes," Anitra said. "But we're getting low, so it'll cost more."

"What!?" Black scowled. "You bitches always trying to get over. We gon' pay the regular price or nothing at all."

"Den get de fuck out," Tukey said nonchalantly. "We doan even deal wit' caine. We sell pills. Me just da middle woman, but me gots ta get mine off de top."

Her nonchalant attitude was one of the reasons why Fuzzy

couldn't stand her. The other reason was because she was a woman who was getting more money than he was. But she was their plug, so he had to deal with it for the time being.

He leaned toward Tukey and said, "Come on, cut us some slack. You know I'm trying to get shit right before Q gets home." Q was his older brother who was doing time in the feds.

Tukey said, "Q doan put food on me table. Matter of fact, Q cyaah put food on his own table from where him at." Shantí laughed.

Black knew there was no use trying to talk her arrogant ass down, so he wouldn't waste any more time trying to. When he looked at Tukey's face he saw a mask like she was hiding something. And he would bet that it had something to do with the unexpected death of her baby's daddy.

The man was getting money real tough in the city. Then one day he just up and killed himself inside a hotel room. That never made any sense to Black or anyone else who knew Keith. But it didn't surprise him when Tukey suddenly became a major player in the game almost overnight. Word on the streets was that Keith was worth a few million when he died, so it was no secret where her bankroll came from.

"So how much y'all talking about?" Fuzzy quizzed.

"Eighteen a cake," Anitra replied.

"If yu doan have enough money, we ca'an front yu de rest," Tukey added to insult them.

Black said, "The money ain't a thing. It's y'all's prices that jump up and down every time we cop."

Anitra shrugged. "This ain't a debate. Take it or leave it."

"What choice do we have?" Fuzzy said as he stood. "We'll take it."

"Good," Tukey said. "Yu ca'an tek Mocha Cream and Hpnotiq over to de motel and me will send Peko and Tiki over wit' ya stuff in de mornin' before check out time."

"They on the house?" Black inquired. "That's the least you

can do."

Tukey sucked her teeth. "Sure, why not. Just have me money ready."

"It's all good."

Fuzzy and Black shook hands with the two ladies, then left the room. Tukey was high and anxious to go back out and kick it some more, but she knew Anitra had other plans for her. She leaned back in her chair, preparing for another heated argument.

Chapter 3

Sergeant Cody Brown walked out of the hospital emergency room with a slight concussion and a bandage on his forehead. A patrol car, driven by his partner, Dulow, was waiting out front. Dulow was a big, young cop who stood about six foot six, had dark skin, braided hair and a quick temper.

Cody was young, too. He was dark brown with curly hair and stood about two inches shorter than Dulow. At the age of twenty-seven, he had more citations than most of the senior officers in his precinct. He and Dulow played on the same football team in high school, and both had plans of going to the NFL, but life didn't turn out like they had planned.

Staying in school and making good grades only got them a guaranteed sixteen bucks an hour working on the police force. While they moonlighted to make ends meet, the guys who dropped out of school to sell dope lived like kings. They drove around in fifty-thousand dollar cars while Cody and Dulow made payments on cars that they shared with their spouses. Life was a bitch for the hard workers.

Secretly, both officers wished that they were on the other side living a risky life and getting money in the process. They were tired of being envious. They wanted to be envied for a change.

"How's your head?" Dulow asked as they drove up Troost.

"It's cool." He laid his head back against the headrest.

Dulow chuckled. "That's what your ass get for not calling for backup. I told you about that solo shit."

Cody glanced out of his window, tuning Dulow out. He dreaded going home to his nagging-ass wife, Tiera. If she wasn't complaining about money, she was complaining about sex. If not that, she was complaining about the weather. She was never satisfied. Sometimes he wished he could just up and walk out on her and their three kids.

"What's up man?" Dulow said, noticing that Cody was in deep thought. "Don't worry. We gon' catch up with them bitches who shot at you."

"That's the last thing on my mind," Cody said in a low voice. "Something's got to change in my life, and I mean fast, before I fuck around and wind up in the nuthouse."

"I'm with you there," Dulow agreed. "My life ain't the best right now, either." Dulow peered over at his partner. "From partner to partner, I'm down for whatever. Fuck this job. I don't know how in the hell we ended up being cops anyway. We was raised in the fucking hood."

"Shit, your guess is as good as mine."

A half a block ahead they saw a pink Hummer pull out of the club parking lot. It came to a slow halt at the red light. Dulow crept up next to it, stopping as well. He couldn't help but stare at the big chrome wheels that continued to spin even though the truck had stopped moving.

Usher's *"Burn"* could be heard pounding out of the Hummer while the beautiful driver bobbed her dreads to the beat. Feeling she was being watched, Tukey looked over at the car. She continued to lip sync as she returned their stares. Dulow threw his hands up like he was trying to holla.

After cutting the music down, she lowered her window. "Wha' sup?"

Dulow let down the window on Cody's side of the car. "Pull over so I can talk to you," he commanded.

Tukey frowned. "Please! Me doan talk tu police."

"So if I wasn't a cop, I'd have a chance?"

"Me way out of ya league, mon," she replied. "Ya gotta be street tu get some of me." When the light turned green, she waved and hit the gas.

Dulow's feelings were hurt. "I knew I shouldn't have joined the academy with your ass," he said angrily as he pulled off.

Cody was laughing. "Be cool, man. It's gonna get better later."

*   *   *   *   *

Tiera was standing over the stove boiling Ramen noodles when she heard Cody opening the front door. Their house wasn't large, but it was clean and nicely furnished. Even though they shared it, they had a new Suburban parked in the driveway.

Dressed in an oversized T-shirt and shorts, she walked barefoot to the living room to greet the king of their castle.

"Hey, hubby," she said with her arms extended. They embraced. "What happened to your head?"

He touched the bandage. "Fender bender. Wasn't nothing." He walked past her to the kitchen. "What're you cooking this time of morning?"

"Nothing for you," she replied smartly. "For some reason I woke up craving some Ramen noodles and eggs." Picking up the fork, she started stirring the noodles. "You should've grabbed you something on your way home. You don't bring enough money in this muthafucka for me to cater to you."

He glared at her in disbelief. "Look who's talking shit! If you would get up off your ass and get a job, we wouldn't be in half the debt that we're in."

She turned around, looking up at his handsome face.

"You wasn't saying that shit when I was lying on my back letting you pump all them babies up in me, were you?"

Not bothering to answer, he turned and walked off, shaking his head.

"That's right," she yelled at his back. "Walk your broke ass off like you always do. I knew that you wasn't gonna be shit when we were in school." She turned back to the noodles. "Mama told me that I should've stayed with Kenny." She said that a little louder than she intended to.

"What!?" Cody hollered as he walked toward her. She jumped back away from the stove. His eyes were narrow slits. "What you say?" He picked up the pot of noodles, then slung them across the kitchen. "Tell Kenny to feed your ass then, bitch!" He stormed out of the kitchen.

"I hate you!" she screamed.

* * * * *

Upstairs, Cody stopped to peek inside Codesha's room. She lay in bed, coughing from a cold that she was coming down with. He picked her up and began patting her back. After a while, her cough started to die down. Glancing around her room, he noticed that she owned every toy that a child could want. What she didn't have was a college fund or anything that would ensure her a good education. They didn't even own the house they lived in.

"It's OK, baby," he said softly. "Daddy's gonna take care of everything. Just be patient." He lay down on her bed with her on his chest and drifted off to sleep.

* * * * *

The next morning, Cody dropped his two healthy kids off at school and then drove to the station. When he got inside, he found Dulow sitting at his desk with his feet up, reading the newspaper.

"Get your feet off my damn desk," Cody ordered. He waited for Dulow to get up, then he sat down. Dulow sat in one of the chairs in front of the desk.

"So what's the word around here this morning?" Cody asked

before sipping his coffee.

Dulow folded the newspaper, sitting it on top of the desk. "Well, everybody's laughing at you about last night."

Cody took a deep breath. "I almost forgot about last night." He grunted. "Which reminds me that I have to make a report." He removed a manila folder out of the bottom desk drawer. "You know we found three thousand Ecstasy pills in the car."

Dulow whistled. "That's a lot of money somebody lost."

"You're telling me. What was interesting was a short while later, some woman walks into the police station and reports the car stolen. That a coincidence or what?"

"Not likely." Dulow shifted in his chair. "With the world the way it is, you can't blame them for trying to get paid."

Cody eyed his partner suspiciously. "You know, the more I talk to you, the more I get the feeling that you want to be one of them."

"And you don't?" Dulow quizzed. "I'm standing on what I said last night. Fuck this job!" He glanced around the room to see if anyone was eavesdropping on their conversation. When he saw that no one was paying them any attention, he turned back to Cody. "You could've been killed last night, and for what? A fuckin' sixteen-dollar-an-hour check. We risk our lives for crumbs."

"Brown," a fat white officer said.

"What do you want, Getzschman?" Cody asked.

"Captain wants to have a word with you in her office."

"Wait here," Cody said, standing up. "Be back in a sec."

Captain Twila Kirby was a tall, muscular but beautiful redhead with pale skin. Grateful to be a woman in her position, she did not abuse her power or look down on the officers who worked under her.

She sat erect behind her cluttered desk twirling her thumbs, waiting on Cody to walk through the door. Cody knocked once, then entered.

"You wanted to see me, Cap?" he asked, noticing that she had her game face on.

"Have a seat, Sergeant Brown," she said, motioning to one of the chairs in front of her desk.

Cody took a seat without taking his eyes off of her face. He tried hard to keep them from traveling down to her breasts. She sensed resistance and suppressed a flattering smile.

After taking a sip of her black coffee, she said, "I wanted to go over last night's little ordeal with you." She sat back in her chair. "So brief me on what happened."

Shrugging, he said, "It's simple. They were driving too fast. I attempted to pull them over, but they fled. So I used my academy training and tried to stop their vehicle using mine, instead of risking them running over an innocent bystander. Then they got away."

He sat erect while her blue eyes probed his body suspiciously. Rumor around the station was that the Captain was a lesbian. But it was something about the way that she looked at him that made him think otherwise. In fact, Cody was sure that she was attracted to him.

"So that's it, huh?"

"Yes, ma'am," he confirmed. "Aw, yeah, they did find three thousand Ecstasy pills in the car." He smiled triumphantly. "So as it turns out it was a felony stop."

"Well ... I guess congratulations are in order," she said as she stood up. They shook hands. "Thanks to you, the streets will be much safer, Sergeant."

* * * * *

Tiera Brown sat with her legs crossed in front of the TV watching *"All My Children."* Nervously, her foot bounced up and down inside of her flip-flop. Every ten minutes she would peer over at the cordless phone that sat on the glass coffee table. She was tempted to make the call that might add some spice to her dull life. Earlier that day, she had called her old friend,

Kenya, who was Kenny's sister, and asked for his phone number. As fate would have it, Kenny had been inquiring about her also.

She looked over at the phone one last time before she leaned over and picked it up. Before she dialed any numbers she paused to weigh her options. On one hand, she had an attractive husband who did his best to put food on the table. They had three beautiful daughters and a nice home. The only problem they had was money, and that was because they didn't possess much of it.

On the other hand, there was Kenny, which would be a gamble. He was tall, sexy and financially stable. At least that was how it appeared on the surface. But best of all, he still had feelings for her. She wondered if her three babies would be included in his feelings for her. A nigga would tell a woman anything to get some pussy. Infidelity was strong grounds for divorce. That would mean no alimony checks if she were to get busted.

To add some excitement to her life, she was willing to take the chance. Finally, she dialed Kenny's number then sat back as she waited on an answer.

Chapter 4

On Sunday evenings, most of the money gettas in the city gathered at Paper Boy's crap house to try to break one another. Ten thousand dollars was the minimum amount of money that could be cashed in for chips. That was a tactic that Paper Boy used to keep all the wanna-bes out. In there, you had to be willing to lose as much as you could win.

The crap house opened on Sunday and wouldn't shut down until the following Monday. At one time it was open all weekend, but after Club No Draws opened up, most of the players chose to kick it rather than gamble. So he figured that the best thing to do would be to open it up on Sunday. That way, everybody would get a chance to win the paper back that they spent kicking it on Friday and Saturday.

Six crap tables were up and running at one time. In the back room standing around a large, round, felt table were seven of KC's finest. They had about two hundred thousand in chips stacked around the table.

Herm was fading Tukey on a ten thousand dollar bet. Fuzzy and Black were side betting on her while Kenny, Dewey and Slic Vic were fondling their chips as they waited for the dice. Tukey, standing at the table in a blue KC Royals jersey and a fitted ball cap cocked to the right, winked her eye at Shantí before she rolled the dice. They landed on four and one.

"Bet another five," she challenged him. "Den another five, me nine or five."

"You ain't said nothin'," Herm said in his loud, high-pitched voice. If anybody in the house came close to her status, it was Herm. He was plugged with some Cubans from Miami who were dumping bricks on him by the truckload.

Fuzzy called a two thousand dollar side bet that Tukey would hit her point. Kenny accepted.

"Jump five," Tukey shouted as she threw the dice. She rolled double threes. She shook and rolled them again. "Feva in da furk house." This time she hit.

Herm cursed under his breath and his facial expression showed contempt.

Tukey laughed as she raked in her chips. "Paper Boy," she called out over the noisy crowd. "Get us another round of drinks over here, rude bwoy."

"Bet back," Herm demanded. "That ain't shit." He tossed another five grand in chips on the table.

"Unt unh, Herm," Slic Vic protested. "My fade."

Herm shot the smaller man a threatening look. "Fuck dat!" he said hotly. "Bitch just hit me for fifteen grand. I want some get back." He turned back to Tukey. "Shoot dice."

She smiled at Slic Vic, showing her gleaming pink diamonds. "Don't worry, Vic, me got plenty money tu go around," she assured him.

"Yeah, OK," Herm spat back. "You ain't like that."

"Sheeit, mon, me come in dis game worth seven figures," she boasted. "Bwoy, ca'an ya top dat?"

"Just roll the damn dice," Herm ordered. "I ain't trying to hear all that bullshit."

Dewey frowned. "Herm's right. Bitch, you ain't shit," he stated, hating because she was a woman.

"Yu cyaah put dat on shit," Tukey said before she threw the

dice. "Me gon' break yu chumps and be back at me club in time for da concert tonight."

* * * * *

Nine o'clock rolled around. Tukey was in Fuzzy's pocket for eighteen grand and had big Herm down thirty-one. She continued to buy rounds because she knew that the drunker they got, the easier they would be to trim. She hadn't succeeded with her plan to break them, but it was time for her to leave. Killa Tay was performing at her club tonight and she wanted to be there.

Herm had a furious look on his beefy face. If Tukey ran out on him now, he would more than likely become violent. Men got like that when things weren't going their way. He was a huge dude with a quick temper. Scared she wasn't, but she didn't have time to get into any bullshit.

Tukey motioned for Shantí to come to her, then whispered something into her ear. Shantí nodded and walked away. While the players continued to gamble, Tukey snuck away to the money booth to cash in her winnings.

Paper Boy counted it out to her, minus his cut, and then placed the money inside a blue cloth bag.

"Make sure you return next week," he said coolly. He wanted to fuck Tukey, but never could bring himself to pursue it. He assumed that she was too far gone on pussy to want his dick.

"PB," she said in a soft voice. "Why yu always lookin' at me like yu wanna fuck, mon?"

He was at a loss for words. The frank question had taken him by surprise. Before he had a chance to speak, Shantí had returned. She motioned for Tukey to come over.

Tukey nodded at her. "Well, me guess me will have to find out later, Paper Boy." She smiled, then walked away.

Herm saw Tukey trying to creep away out of the corner of his eye. "Wha'sup, Tukey?" he yelled in a loud, angry voice. "I know you ain't gon' just leave with my money!" Everybody looked in her direction.

"Me got business tu tend tu, mon," she informed him. "Me have ta catch yu again next week."

"Bullshit!" he said harshly. He walked around the table in her direction. Shantí stuck her hand inside her Coach bag, fingering her .38. Tukey was the reason why she was alive and she would do anything to protect her.

Knowing that Shantí was strapped, Tukey held her ground. "Mon, me outta here. Fuck what yu talkin' about."

Herm scowled. "Bitch, you better watch—"

Shantí drew her gun. Tukey raised her brows and smiled.

"Like me said, me got business tu tend tu." They began inching backward toward the door. "Anytime y'all wanna try tu win ya bread back, yu ca'an find me in me club."

She could sense Herm's piercing eyes on her back as she walked out to Shantí's car. There was no reason for her to be alarmed because she knew that Shantí wouldn't hesitate to pop his ass if he got out of line. Her days on this earth were numbered, so what did she have to lose?

Just when Tukey felt that she was gaining respect as a hustler, some hater would do something to make her feel otherwise. To them she was just a bitch, no, a dyke bitch with money. The way she saw it was that she had two choices. One was to cash out and get her cut of the game while she was still ahead; or two, say fuck them niggas and deal with the funk as it came her way. She would choose the latter. She was gonna earn her respect no matter what she had to do to get it.

Tukey stopped by her crib to shower and change clothes. Killa Tay's limo was parked out front when she and Shantí pulled up to the valet. They didn't have time to kick game with Rhyme, so they tipped him and kept on going.

Killa Tay was on stage wearing a white wifebeater and a platinum chain around his neck. Two hype men wearing blue Rocawear sweatsuits were up there with him.

Tukey fell right in with the crowd, singing along to his old song, *"Mr. Mafioso."* When he spotted her, he winked his eye and kept on rapping. The girl next to Tukey took off her bra, then tossed it up on the stage.

"I wanna fuck you!" she shouted.

The Crips were C-walking while the Bloods threw up the B. They didn't particularly like dancing to Crip music, but it was all good for the night. All they wanted to do was kick it and hopefully take some of the young freaks home.

Niggas popped their collars and held their arms up, flossing their diamond watches. The ladies didn't hold back; they were half dressed, fully drunk and thizzed out. They were paving the way for tonight's fucking and tomorrow's hangover.

Cody, Dulow and another officer named Dickie pulled their patrol car up into the crowded parking lot of Club No Draws. The line of people waiting to get in was still stretched around the corner. A group of people in a van saw the police car patrolling the lot and kept driving.

Cody parked beside the Hot 103.3 radio station van. They were hoping that some shit would pop off so they could crack some heads. Dulow was waiting on the chance to use his new police Taser. Dickie was also a big, young black cop. He spoke in a low, deep voice. He rode along with them because his partner, Casey, had wrecked their patrol car the night before.

Cars and trucks on big shiny rims kept loading into the parking lot. They could only imagine the money that the owner would be making tonight. Dickie's perverted ass was wondering how much pussy was up in there.

"We need to snatch these corny-ass uniforms off and step up in there one day," Dulow said. "They up in there kicking it while we're sitting out here hoping that a fight breaks out." He shook his head in disgust.

Cody didn't disagree because he was feeling the same way. To tell the truth, he was really there to get another look at the woman they saw driving the Hummer the other night. He had been thinking about her ever since. Those dreads and her smooth, chocolate skin tone, *umph*. He could just imagine how her naked flesh would feel up against his.

"What do y'all say we go up in there next week?" Dulow asked seriously. "We can go shopping that evening, then hit the club that night. You know what I'm saying? Let's dump the wedding rings for one night."

"Can't," Cody said regretfully. "I'm working next week."

"And I'm working overtime," Dickie added.

"Overtime?" Dulow snorted. "What a crock of shit."

* * * * *

Club No Draws closed an hour ago. The strippers were turning in Tukey's percentage while the bartenders and the doorman turned in the night's take.

Tukey and Shantí sat next to each other at the conference table counting money while Anitra did the books. A money counter was sitting on the table to assist them. Mocha Cream turned in Tukey's percentage five hundred dollars short. She stood next to the table, tapping her foot impatiently, waiting on Anitra to mention it.

After Anitra counted the money, she referred to her notes. Thinking that she had made a mistake, she repeated the same process over. Same result.

She frowned. "Mocha?" Anitra said without looking up. "I don't think I have to tell you that you're five hundred dollars short."

"You sho' right," she replied smartly. "You don't have to tell me."

Tukey stopped counting money and glanced up at Mocha. She was standing with one hand on her hip, looking like there was no need to explain herself.

"May I ask why?" Anitra quizzed. She looked up at Mocha for the first time.

"Because," she nodded toward Tukey, "she never reimbursed me for fucking Fuzzy the other night. Hpnotiq either."

"Speak for yourself," Hpnotiq said sassily as she stood in line.

Tukey cleared her throat and said, "Mocha, doan mek me get up and put me hands on yu."

Even though Tukey never raised her voice, Mocha knew that she wasn't joking. And she didn't want to get beat down in front of everybody in the room. Reluctantly, she reached into her bra, pulled out a wad of money, counted out five hundred and sat it on the table. Without another word, she walked out of the office.

Tukey stood to address the room. "Anybody else in here feel like me owe yu sum't'ing ... tek it all and doan come back." She glanced around the room at all the silent faces, then sat back down.

"Next," Anitra called out.

* * * * *

Anitra and Tukey were on Interstate 435 headed to their new home in Overland Park, Kansas. Tukey sat low in the passenger's seat smoking on some dro that she copped from her weed man, Fat Sack. Lil Jon, Usher and Ludacris came on the radio singing "*Lovers and Friends.*"

Tukey passed the blunt to Anitra and turned up the volume. Tukey sang along with Ludacris' verse. Placing her hand on Anitra's thigh, she began to rub it seductively.

"Girl, you gon' start something," Anitra warned.

Grooving to the beat, she unfastened the belt on Anitra's black slacks, then unzipped them. She lifted her hips so Tukey could pull her pants down to her thighs.

"What you doing, baby?" Anitra whispered.

"Me about tu give yu some highway head," Tukey said.

She positioned her body and lowered her head as she planted a tender kiss on Anitra's pelvis. "Ummmm ..." she moaned as she began to suck on her clitoris. Anitra's legs twitched from the sensational feeling between her thighs. Grabbing Tukey's dreads, she encouraged her to proceed. A truck full of teenagers who were riding next to them were astonished.

"Y'all see what I see?" the driver asked his passengers.

"Man," the one next to him said. "I wish I was the bitch who's driving right now."

Anitra relaxed in her soft leather seat with one hand on the wheel and her attention on the road ahead. Like a boss player was how she was feeling. She had plenty of money, a big house and a bad-ass down bitch to go with it. What more could she ask for?

Chapter 5

Peko and Tiki were at the mall buying some new outfits. Tiki was trying on her tenth pair of boots when her cell phone started vibrating on her hip. She flipped it up.

"Tiki speaking," she answered.

"Tiki, this is Kiria. I'm having a little get together later and trying to get some double stacks."

"How many yu want?"

"'Bout a hundred of 'em. You gon' give me a deal or what?"

Tiki admired the way the boot looked on her foot in the mirror before she said, "Me will hook yu up. Are yu giving dis shit away or are yu sellin' it?"

"Selling it, girl. What you think?"

"Me was just wondering. Give me a minute." She closed her phone, then went to find Peko.

Peko, trying to find the right scent to go on her carmel-colored skin, was getting on the sales clerk's nerves. She kept her running back and forth to the back room where the stock was.

"Us gotta roll," Tiki said as she lugged a bunch of shopping bags from various clothing stores. "Business is callin'."

"In a minute, gurl. Ya like da way dis smells?" Peko put the perfume bottle up to Tiki's nose.

"Mm hm, gurl. Get me one, too."

The two girls finally forced themselves out of the mall. After they served Kiria and a few others, they were left with nothing to do. They had already eaten at the mall, gotten their nails and feet done and still had a whole day ahead of them. No Draws was open for happy hour, but Peko didn't want to see Tukey until she was out of pills. She still had plenty left, so it would be no time soon.

Tiki pulled her candy-green '87 Chevy Caprice, sitting on all-gold bead lace Daytons, into Good-to-Go to get some gas. The short clerk who stood behind the counter saw her fine ass waltz in and damn near forgot to breathe. Her thick hips and plump booty were bulging out of her faded Apple Bottoms. Out of the cooler she grabbed a six-pack of wine coolers and a six-pack of beer.

At the counter, she took a thick roll of money out of her front pocket. After flinging her long micro braids back out of her face, she peeled off two twenty-dollar bills.

"Me will tek dis and twenty on pump four, please," she said, ignoring his lustful stare. The way he was looking at her, one would swear that she was standing there naked.

"What's that accent you're speaking with?" he inquired.

"Me Jamaican, mon," Tiki said evenly.

He glanced out the window at her clean Chevy squatting on big rims. The Louis Vuitton top and matching guts really set it off.

"That your car?" he asked, being nosy.

"Yep," she replied. "How would yu like tu drive me?"

He opened his mouth, but no words came out. The question took him by surprise.

"If yu a real rider, den yu should be able tu answer me question, right?" She licked her glossy lips. "Den me will give yu a test drive."

"What's the question?"

"Seh me is an automobile, and me gears shift one down and

five up." She held up five fingers when she said five up. "What am me?"

He pondered the question for a second. "A four wheeler?"

She picked up her sack. "No! A Ducati Triple Nine R." He looked at her confusingly. "It's a motorcycle." He watched as she swayed out the door.

While Peko was pumping the gas, two dudes in a candy-apple red Chevy Caprice on Daytons drove up and parked at pump #3. Up close she could see ghost patterns of naked bitches in his paint. That gave her the idea to get naked men painted on hers.

The pretty-ass driver stepped his muscular frame out of the car and approached her. "How you doing?" he asked, looking her body up and down.

"Me would seh fine, but me doan wanna hear yu say, 'Yu sure are.' So me just gonna seh good. And you?" Her brown eyes went with her blond micro braids.

"I'm good," he replied coolly.

Peko's eyes probed his body from his freshly braided hair down to his Perry Ellis boots.

"Yu lookin' good tu, mon," Tiki complemented as she came up behind him.

Peko said, "Gurl, tek ya hot ass over dere and holla at his frien' on de passenger side, mon."

"Y'all would make a good match up," Tiki said. "Being dat y'all are both passengers." She chuckled at her own humor, displaying a small attractive gap between her two front teeth.

"What the hell country are y'all from?" the guy asked after hearing their broken English. The accent that they spoke with made them even more attractive.

The guy who was sitting on the passenger's side of the red Chevy cranked the beat up. Fat Joe's *"Lean Back"* was vibrating the ground and windows of both cars.

Tiki took that as a challenge. "No him didn't." She opened

up her door and sat down in the driver's seat with her feet hanging out the car. Flipping through her CD case, she didn't stop until she found what she was looking for. After popping it in, she cranked up the volume.

"Move! Get out the way! Get out the way! Get out the way! Move!" Ludacris sang, then the bass kicked in.

Tiki reached under the dashboard and turned up the Epic Center, making the bass even deeper. The dude in the red Chevy turned his music off in defeat. His two fifteen-inch Lanzars were no match for Tiki's four fifteen-inch Strokers.

The dude who was talking to Peko said, "Why don't y'all come over to our apartment in Friendship Village? We can kick it over there."

Peko peered at the dude who was sitting in the car. He was busy eye-fucking Tiki's body. They both seemed safe enough. Plus, she knew that Tiki wouldn't go anywhere unless she was strapped.

"OK," Peko agreed. "Us will follow y'all." She placed a manicured finger on his chest. "But us not ... fuckin'."

"I'm cool wit' that. We just wanna kick it with you two fine honeys. I know y'all got some of them Jamaican trees to smoke on." He also figured that once he got them high and drunk, they would become eager to get freaked. His cozy apartment made ladies feel comfortable to be naked in.

* * * * *

About a block away from the apartment complex, the driver of the red Chevy started mobbin' from side to side, showing off his gold Daytons. Tiki felt compelled to do the same. She spun the wheel from left to right. Peko had a beer in her hand that got shaken up after Tiki started driving crazy. Quickly, she let the window down then stuck the bottle out before the overflowing suds got on the leather seats.

"Gurl, ya shook up me damn beer," Peko said angrily.

It was just their bad luck that Cody was working as a security guard at the complex for extra money. He was patrolling the area when the two Chevys pulled into the gates. From where he sat, he could see two long-haired girls inside the green car. One of them had an open bottle of beer hanging out the window.

Cody put the old white Chrysler Plymouth security vehicle in drive. Both cars were rounding the bend. Patiently, he waited for the red Chevy to pass, then pulled out in front of Tiki. She brought the car to a screeching halt. Before they knew what was going on, Cody was out of his car, rushing toward them. Another security patrolman saw what was going on and went to back him up. Through the rearview mirror, Tiki saw the other car pull up behind her to prevent her from escaping.

Her heartbeat sped up. She knew that it was the end of the line for them. There was a gun under the seat, plus she had over two hundred Ecstasy pills stashed inside the horn of her wooden Nardi steering wheel.

The driver of the red Chevy saw the security guards jump down on the girls and wanted no part of whatever was going on. Continuing on around the path, he drove all the way to the other side of the complex and out the back way.

Cody knocked on Tiki's window. It was a little chilly outside, but warm for it to be the beginning of December. She let the window down.

"Would you two ladies step out of the car please," he ordered. After they got out, he ordered them to step over to his car and place their hands on the hood.

He knew that he couldn't give them a thorough search because he was a male officer, so he radioed the police and requested the assistance of a female officer. The other security guard kept an eye on them while Cody searched their car. Cold steel was the first thing he felt when he searched under Tiki's seat.

Out of the corner of her eye, Tiki saw Cody walking toward her. She kept her face pointing straight ahead to avoid eye contact.

Cody held up the gun. "Either one of you care to tell me who this belongs to?" He was speaking to both women, but his eyes never left the side of Tiki's head.

Neither said a word.

"All right," he said, putting the gun inside his coat pocket. He stepped back to the car to continue the search. Using past information that he learned from his informants, he popped the horn cover off of the steering wheel. Bingo. A plastic bag full of blue pills was stashed inside the neck of the wheel.

A blue police cruiser followed by a paddy wagon pulled up at the scene. A medium-sized, manly-looking woman with a box-style haircut emerged from the police car. Out of the wagon stepped a pretty young black female police officer who was putting on a pair of rubber gloves.

Cody was getting out of the Chevy when the butch cop walked up.

"What do we have?" she asked, eyeing the plastic bag inside of Cody's hand.

"Drinking and driving, carrying a concealed weapon and possession of a controlled substance," he stated proudly.

Peko's chin fell to her chest and Tiki's jaw dropped. They no longer felt like hardcore gangsta drug dealers. Instead, they felt like two little girls who wanted their mother. But neither would ever admit her fright to the other.

* * * * *

Anitra was nearing her third mile on the treadmill that was stationed on the sun porch. Her iPod was turned up too high for her to hear the phone ringing. She was already breathing heavily, but still had another two miles before it would be over.

She was lost in the music when she felt their Puerto Rican maid's hand touch her arm. She gladly hit the emergency stop button, bringing the belt to a halt.

"What is it, Rose?" she asked, panting. Anitra picked a

towel up off the guardrail.

Rose handed her the cordless phone. She put it up to her ear.

"Hello," she answered, trying to regain control of her breathing. There was silence. "Hello."

"Anitra, dis Peko." Anitra didn't miss the alarm in her voice. "Me and Tiki got stopped and dey claimed tu have found a gun and some Ecstasy pills."

Anitra stepped down off the treadmill as her mind sought the right questions to ask.

"Did you tell 'em anything?" Anitra asked nervously.

"No! All us said was dat us want a lawyer." Anitra knew there was a "but" coming. "But, dey found Tukey's name in me phone."

"And?"

"And, dey asked me a lot of questions about her. Dey wanted tu know a lot of t'ings about her. Like if her got her club from dealin' wit' drugs or sum't'ing. Stuff like dat."

"That's silly," Anitra said, knowing that the call was probably being monitored. "Did you tell them that y'all were her little cousins?"

"Nah. Me ain't got not'ing tu say." Peko paused for a moment. "So what do us do now?"

"Just be cool and keep your mouths closed. After I take a shower, I'ma call our lawyer. You're not felons, so you should be cool. How's Tiki holding up?"

"Playing hard, but she'll be fine. Just do what ya ca'an for us, please Anitra."

"I'ma get right on it."

"T'anks." Anitra was about to hang up until she heard Peko say, "Anitra."

"Yes."

"Doan worry, us ca'an hold our own," Peko assured her. In other words, their mouths were closed.

Anitra hung up the phone and hurried to the shower. When she finished, she searched the rolodex for the number of their lawyer, Brad W. Simon. It was too late for him to be in his office, but for a new case he accepted house calls. Brad was hungrier for money than any street hustler she knew.

Chapter 6

Cody got up out of his bed an hour before midnight. He was working the graveyard shift and had to be at work by twelve. First he showered and shaved, then put on his uniform. During a final check in the mirror, he discovered that his goatee was a little crooked. Other than that, he didn't look a day over twenty-two.

Tiera had sent the kids over to her mother's for the weekend. She claimed that she needed a break so that she could have some time for herself. Sounded like an excuse to her mother, but she didn't question her youngest child. She was getting old and wanted to maintain a healthy relationship with her kids until her time was up on this earth.

Cody came down the stairs and saw his beautiful wife lying across the couch, reading a novel. She looked so sweet and innocent with her little reading glasses on. Her smooth, pale skin was glowing from where he stood. *How could something so beautiful cause so much stress?* he wondered.

"I'm headed to work," he informed her. He picked his keys up off the table.

"Gimme kiss," she said without looking up from her book.

He gave her a quick peck on the cheek. "See you in the morning."

Closing up the book, she stood up. "What time will you be back?"

He shrugged. "A little after eight. Depends on if I stop and get me some breakfast or not."

"Well, I'll be here waiting on you."

He was putting on his coat when he read the title of the novel that she was reading. "*A Project Chick*, huh?" he said, referring to the book. He laughed. "Who decided to write your life story?"

Fuck you, square ass pig, she thought. *I'd rather be a project chick than a fucking sell out.*

* * * * *

Tiera waited a good thirty minutes after Cody left before she called Kenny. She had to give him enough time to put some distance between him and home. After a thirty-minute drive, he would be too far away to turn around in case he'd forgotten something. If Cody ever busted Kenny up in his house, it wasn't a question as to what he would do to him.

Kenny was sitting inside a nearby Burger King, eating a Whopper, when he heard his bling tone start playing "*Born to Mack.*"

"He gone yet?" Kenny asked, answering his phone.

"You on your way yet?" she replied seductively. He hung up.

About six minutes later, he was ringing her doorbell. Tiera removed her shirt and threw it on the couch. When she opened the front door, Kenny saw her like he had never seen her before. Naked.

"You bring your gloves, champ?" she asked from the doorway. He pulled two single condoms out of his pocket and held them up for her to see.

"Round one," she said eagerly, then jumped into his arms. "Ding, ding."

"I'ma give you some ding ding all right."

* * * * *

Lateka was thizzin and her hormones were on fire. Lying in her bed, she had her hand inside her panties, fondling herself. She moaned softly as she fingered herself into an orgasm. After a few minutes her pussy became soaking wet and she wanted to be penetrated. Reaching for the phone, she picked it up off the bed and called Tukey.

"Hello," Tukey yelled over the loud music.

"Hey, baaaby, it's me."

Tukey smiled at the sound of her voice. "Yu sound horny."

"Mm, I am," Lateka said seductively. She was squirming on her bed. "Why don't you shake your bitch and come satisfy me with your king-sized snicker."

"Me cyaah just—"

"I promise you'll be back before the club closes."

Tukey felt moisture inside her lace panties. There was something about Lateka that she couldn't resist.

"Ya t'izzin, baby?"

"Thizzin and sizzlin. Now get yo' thick, sexy, chocolate ass over here and put out my fire."

Anitra was gliding through the crowd headed for the DJ booth where Tukey was standing.

"Me will be over in a minute," Tukey said quickly.

"Don't forget to bring the ten inch tidy with you." Tukey closed the phone just as Anitra reached her.

"Where you been, boo? I've been looking all over for you," Anitra said.

"Over here checkin' de DJ about playing de same damn songs over and over again." She put her hand on Anitra's shoulder. "Baby, me have tu go mek a run."

"OK. I'll hold things down until you return."

She kissed Anitra, tasting the Long Island Iced Tea on her tongue.

On her way to the bar, Tukey realized for the first time that she was a little drunk. She staggered a little, but quickly regained her balance.

"Let me get a bottle of Grey Goose and a couple cans of Red Bull," she ordered Big Corn.

"Comin' right up, boss lady."

It took a moment for Tukey to realize that she was standing in front of a two-way mirror and Anitra was sure to be on the other side, looking through it.

She leaned over the bar. "Corn. Why doan ya just bring de bottle out to me truck."

"I can't leave the bar unattended, boss lady."

"Den pull Dacari's ass off dat stage and have her bring it out to me."

* * * * *

Cody had just finished writing a young lady a ticket for driving with one license plate. He got back into his vehicle, backed up in the middle of 75th Street, made an illegal U-turn, then headed in the opposite direction.

He was sitting at a red light facing Troost Avenue. All of a sudden, a silver Camaro on big rims made a quick turn onto Troost, spinning its wheels in the process. Running the red light, Cody took off after the speeding car. The driver must have spotted the police car coming up behind him because he slowed down and started driving like he had some sense.

Cody didn't want to hit the lights and pull him over right away. His mere presence would make the driver sweat bullets. Then the driver would become nervous and make a stupid move, like try to elude him. This time he would call for backup instead of trying to be a hero.

The traffic began to thicken as they neared 82nd Street. Cars were pulling in and out of Club No Draws like it was a dope spot. The driver of the Camaro tried to blend in with the other cars by turning into the club's parking lot.

Cody was about to hit his lights until he saw the valet pull Tukey's pink Hummer up to the front. *She has on too much ice for her to just be in the club business,* he thought. She had on a tight pair of jeans with blue suede patches on them, blue suede boots and jacket to match. He couldn't get over how sexy she was.

He hadn't gotten a real good look at her face, but he was quite sure that it matched that Serena Williams body of hers. Before he knew it, the driver of the Camaro had parked and gotten out. Smiling triumphantly, he waved at Cody, then stood in line with the rest of the crowd.

Tukey got into the driver's seat. Thirty seconds later, a girl dressed in a leather G-string, matching halter top and exotic stilettos came out carrying a bottle of liquor and two cans. Cody backed into an area of the parking lot that wasn't lit up. She took the stuff from Dacari, sitting it in the seat next to her. Tukey sat there holding up traffic until she found the right CD. Deciding on R. Kelly's Greatest Hits, she slid it into the deck and put it on "*Bump N' Grind.*"

She drove right past the patrol car without noticing that Cody was sitting there. Grooving to the beat, she hit her signal, then turned out into traffic. Cody pulled out behind her.

Sitting low in her seat, she cruised down the busy street. All eyes were on her. She couldn't even stop at the light without some nigga blowing his horn or flicking his lights at her. Like always, she put up a peace sign and kept on rolling.

"*Sex Me*" came on. Tukey cut up the volume. Her mirrors vibrated so hard that she couldn't see the police car behind her. When she got close to Lateka's house, she decided that it was time to pop a couple pills. Opening up the vodka, she popped the pills, then took a swig. The straight alcohol burned as it went down her throat. Her face balled up from the bitter taste. She made a right turn on 64th Street. She accidentally ran over the curb, spilling some of the drink on her lap.

"Damn it!" she cursed.

Yelp! Yelp!

Cody hit his sirens behind her.

"Fuck!" she cursed again. The last thing she needed was to get pulled over reeking of alcohol. Plus, she had a bag of pills in her glove compartment and an ounce of K-town in her console. Since the weed was closest to her, she took it out and stuffed it in the crotch of her jeans.

Yelp! Yelp!

She hit the mute button so she could see out of her mirror. The officer in the car appeared to be black. *Good!* she thought. Maybe she could con her way out of going to jail.

Tukey pulled over inside the Landing Mall's parking lot. Taking out her license and insurance card, she waited patiently for fate to take its course.

Cody glanced at the breathalyzer sitting on his passenger seat, then decided that he wouldn't need it. He had no intentions on arresting her. He just wanted to put her in a submissive position. Put the little rich broad in her place. But if he found drugs in the truck other than weed, then that would be another story.

Her phone beeped, signaling her that she had a text message. She flipped up her phone. The message was from Lateka. "Where are you?" the message read. She texted her back, telling her to hold on.

Cody grabbed his ticket book and exited the car. Casually, he walked up to her window. She let it down with a big smile on her face. The first thing he noticed were the pretty pink diamonds that were gleaming inside her mouth. He flinched at the sight of her up close. Something was very familiar about her face. Those sneaky brown eyes and high arched eyebrows. There was a small scar above her eye, but it didn't hurt her features any.

"Your license, please," he stated in a professional tone. "And your insurance card." She handed them over willingly. He placed them inside his coat pocket. "Now step out of the car, please."

She sighed deeply as she reached into the backseat for her

Kangol skull cap. After she placed it over her head, she got out.

"Step back to my car," he said, motioning in the direction of the patrol car.

She tried to walk as straight as possible, but even a child could tell that she was intoxicated. Subconsciously, she started gritting her teeth.

"Hands on the hood," he instructed her.

"Yu gonna frisk me, mon?" she said flirtatiously. "Go 'head. Yu doan need tu call a female officer."

He smirked. "OK." Starting with her shoulders, he ran his hands down over her big breasts.

"Get a good feel," she said as she pushed her butt back into his crotch.

Cody didn't move away. Instead, he pushed back and continued to search her voluptuous body. He moved his large hands down between her legs.

"Yu feel anyt'ing out of de ordinary?"

He discontinued the search and took out his cuffs. Carefully, he put her arms behind her back, securing them.

Feeling her body tense up, he said, "Relax. This is just for precaution. Now hold tight while I search your vehicle."

Tukey knew that as long as he didn't call for backup, she had a chance of getting out of the situation, even if she had to give him some pussy. Assuming that he found the dope.

Through the back window she could see him going through her stuff with a flashlight. All of a sudden he stopped and held a plastic bag up in the air. She cursed herself for being caught slipping so easily. Tukey wondered if her charm would work or if he was one of those "white niggers." Fine as he was, she hoped that he wasn't an Uncle Tom.

He exited the car and slowly approached her. She gave him a flirtatious look. He held up the bag.

"Me tek dem tu have a good time," she informed him. "Yu ever tried one?"

"I don't use drugs." He put his radio up to his lips.

"Wait! Cyaah us handle dis wit'out callin' it in?" she pleaded. "Isn't dere sum't'ing dat me ca'an do?"

His eyes roamed her body. "You ahh ... you attempting to bribe me?"

"Me just attempting tu offer yu sum't'ing tu receive sum't'ing," she replied. "If dat's a bribe, den yes, me am."

He took out her driver's license and read her name. Seeing the name Tukey Tosh printed on the license jump-started his memory.

"Tukey Tosh? You didn't happen to go to Metro Tech when you were in high school, did you?"

She began to relax. "Yes," she replied. "How yu know?"

For the first time, he cracked a smile. "I can't believe you don't remember me."

She got a thorough look at him but still didn't have a clue as to who he was. And the look on her face said so.

"Cody. Cody Brown," he said, reminding her. "You remember showing me them titties behind the stairwell when we were freshmen?"

A light popped on inside her head. "Cody?"

"Yeah."

"Bwoy, yu gotten huge since den. Yu didn't use ta be so tall."

"That's because I wasn't through growing," he said. "I wondered what happened to you. I saw the story about Keith in '*The Call*' a few years back. I couldn't believe that he killed himself."

Tukey pretended to be sad about it. "Yeah, none of us could. But what's done is done. What's up wit' yu?"

His eyes shifted down toward his badge.

Giggling, she said, "A police officer, huh? Me cyaah believe dat. Yu was on de varsity team wit' Keith."

After biting down on his bottom lip, he replied, "Yeah, well as I remember it, Keith was the reason why I couldn't have you."

"Life doan always turn out as planned, mon." She shrugged.

"Look at me ... me about ta go tu jail and shit."

Cody sighed heavily. There was no way in hell that he was going to arrest her now. He didn't care if he did find the pills. It wouldn't serve him any purpose to lock her up. Besides, he was hoping that they would remain in contact after this.

"Let me take off those cuffs." She turned around so he could release her hands. "I guess I can give an old friend a break."

She couldn't believe her luck. "T'anks, Cody," she said, relieved. "If yu ever need anyt'ing, doan hesitate tu call, mon." She produced a business card from her coat pocket.

"So you're a club owner now?" he said, reading the card. "Maybe you can give me some work some time. I bounce from time to time for extra cash." He produced his card also.

"Off-ic-er Brown," she said, pronouncing every syllable in his name. Giggling, she said, "Me never would have t'ought."

He blushed with embarrassment, ashamed that he walked a beat for a living. And here she was a club owner. "Me either," he replied.

Tukey sensed his resentment after she referred to his occupation. But she saw him in a different way, now that she knew who he was. She admired his dark skin, his good grade of curly hair, full lips and his dark brown eyes. His face looked like Michelangelo took a chisel and carved it out of a piece of dark chocolate. He had to have been at least six foot four, and she could only imagine the size of his love muscle. He noticed the lustful look in her glassy, red eyes. For a minute he said nothing, letting her get a good gander at what he had to offer.

"You liking what you see?" he quizzed. The old high school Cody was starting to show.

"Maybe. How about yu? Yu likin' what yu see?" She turned around as if she were modeling. "Is dat enough for yu tu decide? Or do yu need ta see me naked, mon?"

His lips wanted to say yes, but his mouth wouldn't open. Despite how he felt about Tiera, he was still married to her. But it felt good to be hit on by such a beautiful woman.

Holding up his left hand, he exposed his wedding ring. She nodded in acknowledgement.

"It still doan hurt ta look, Cody," she said softly. "But if yu touch it ... yu might forget about wifey."

"So, how about you?" he asked, leaning back up against the hood of his car. "You ever move on after Keith ... you know?"

She nodded her head. "Me engaged to ano'er woman," she informed him. She watched his reaction to her last statement.

A shocked look appeared on his face. "Damn! I guess people really do change with the times."

"Me guess so. Just remember me told yu dis. Yu doan have tu have a king ... tu be a queen, Cody."

For a moment they watched each other in silence.

"Well," Cody finally spoke, "here's your identification back." He handed it to her. "Remember what I said about the bouncing gig."

"Me sure me will be able tu find sum't'ing for yu ta do." She hopped into the driver's seat of her Hummer. "Yu should come by me club one night. Me promise tu show yu a good time."

"I don't think so," he said, smiling. "I'm a policeman now and that ain't my thing." He closed the door for her. "Unless I get the job as a bouncer."

Tukey began to feel pity for him. Here he was, risking his life for the state to be a better place to live, but still he had to work odd jobs to feed his family. No wonder Keith chose the dope game over a nine to five.

"Bye, Cody."

"All right now. Take care of yourself, Tukey."

Tukey watched him march back to his car. "Umph," she said to herself. "Me bet he could mek dis wildcat sprung off dick again."

It had been years since she had some real beef up inside her. Seeing Cody tonight reminded her of how much she missed having a man in her life and the taste of a real dick inside her mouth.

Tukey placed a DVD of all music videos into her TV-DVD player. Six screens came to life at once. Chingy popped up on the screen. She cut the beat up loud enough for Cody to hear.

Chingy sang, "You could ... roll wit ... meeee ... if you was my babyyy."

He caught the message, then chuckled to himself as he got in his car. She drove away slowly with her head out the window and one hand on the steering wheel. Throwing up a peace sign, she smashed back out into traffic.

Inside the car, Cody fondled the bag of pills. He was tempted to throw them out the window. Instead, he put them inside his pocket. They could come in handy later.

Chapter 7

Sitting in front of the city jail, parked in a no parking zone, were Anitra and Tukey. They impatiently waited for the bail bondsman to bring Peko and Tiki out. Luckily, their lawyer made a deal with the DA to keep the case in the state court instead of handing it over to the feds.

Tukey was vexed by her two younger cousins' carelessness. Twice within the last couple weeks they had run-ins with the law, losing over three thousand Ecstasy pills in the process. Biting down on her bottom lip, she peered at the front entrance at the various people that were coming and going.

Twenty minutes later, the bondsman walked out with the two wild-looking females in tow. Tukey exited the car. Looking shitfaced, the two stopped in front of their older cousin. Without hesitation, Tukey reached back and slapped Peko across her face, then back handed Tiki. The violent act took both girls by surprise.

"Whoa!" the bondsman hollered and stepped between the three. "Not out here, Tukey. This time you'll be the one I'm bonding out."

Breathing rapidly, she glared at Tiki furiously, figuring that it was probably her fault. Peko was usually the smarter of the pair.

"Get ya asses in de car!" she ordered in a motherly tone of voice. She waited until they were inside before she spoke to Johnny, the bondsman. "Good lookin' out, mon." After they shook hands she got back in the car.

Anitra pulled her red Dodge Magnum from the curb out into traffic. For the first few miles they rode in total silence. Occasionally, Peko would look at the back of Tukey's head and attempt to speak, but nothing would ever come out. So she decided to let either Tiki or Tukey break the silence. She didn't want to be lashed out at again. Tukey was too strong to try and whoop.

"Tukey," Tiki finally said. "Me just—"

"Shut de fuck up!" Tukey yelled harshly. "Me doan want ta hear not'ing out yu damn mouth, Tiki."

Tiki frowned. They had kept their mouths closed and Tukey was still treating them like shit. She sucked her teeth. Tukey was thicker, but Tiki was nobody's punk. She already regretted letting Tukey get away with smacking her. Anybody else would have been stabbed, shot or beat the fuck up.

Tiki tried speaking again. "Damn! Bitch, yu act like—"

"Pull dis car over, Anitra," Tukey commanded. She began taking off her watch and earrings.

"What're you about to do?" Anitra asked curiously.

"Me about tu beat dis bitch down," she said hotly.

Tiki said, "Me not scared of not'ing or nobody."

Anitra said, "I am not about to pull over so y'all two cousins can fight in the middle of the damn street."

Tiki scowled. "Me doan need yu protection, Anitra," she said smartly.

Anitra was offended. She shot daggers at Tiki through the rearview mirror. "OK, smart ass," she said, pulling over on a dead end street.

Tukey was the first out of the car. Peko grabbed Tiki's arm, but she snatched away. Anitra was prepared to break it up if it got too far out of hand.

Tiki was just as tall, but not as thick as Tukey. She was probably the quicker of the two, but Tukey worked out and was much stronger.

The two squared off in the middle of the street. Tukey held up her fists in a boxer's stance. Coincidentally, Tiki held hers the exact same way.

Tukey tried to rush in but Tiki backed up. Tukey swung, this time instead of backing up, Tiki swung also. They collided, both throwing and landing wild blows. After a few hits were exchanged, they started to tussle. Somehow, Tiki made the terrible mistake of letting Tukey pull her shirt over her eyes, making it impossible for her to see. Taking advantage of the situation, Tukey struck her repeatedly in the head with good solid hits while holding on to her shirt.

Thinking quickly, Tiki slipped out of the shirt, exposing her bare breasts. Though she was dazed, she continued trying to attack Tukey. A quick left and a right sent her down to the pavement, face first.

Anitra stepped in. "That's enough, y'all." Tiki got up, still ready to battle. "I said that's enough!" Anitra shouted. "Peko, get your sister."

Peko tried to grab Tiki, but she yanked away. "Get ya fuckin' hands off me," she said angrily.

Tukey wasn't satisfied with the outcome. "Yu want some more, bitch?"

"Yu ain't did not'ing," Tiki said, picking up her torn shirt.

Anitra pressed her hands firmly up against Tukey's chest. "It's over, y'all. Get both ya asses back in the car."

Tukey shook her head disapprovingly. "Dat bitch not sitting behind me." She ran her fingers through her locks. "She better start walkin'."

"Me doan care," Tiki said defensively. Her hair was out of place and her shirt was ripped in the front. She looked at her shaking hands and saw bleeding scratches on them. "Scratching-ass bitch!"

"Yu should've kept ya head up," Tukey said. "Better yet, let's go again."

"Bullshit!" Anitra yelled as Tukey lunged forward. She started pushing Tukey toward the car. "Get your ass in."

Tiki started to walk away, leaving Peko standing there looking lost. She wasn't sure if she should go with her sister or get in the car. Baby girl was stuck between a Magnum and a long way home.

Seeing Peko standing in the middle of the street debating on what she should do, Tukey made up her mind for her.

"Pull off, Anitra," Tukey commanded. Looking out the window at Tiki walking up the street, she started to feel bad. "Her doan need tu walk by herself," Tukey said. Though she was angry, Tiki was still her blood. "But her need tu learn a lesson."

She wasn't mad because they got busted. Hell, she would've been busted herself if it weren't for Cody. What pissed her off was the fact that every other week they would get themselves involved in some kind of bullshit. Being that she was responsible for them, she wanted to do everything that she could to protect them.

Peko heard the Dodge start up. Neither looked at her as Anitra backed onto Pasco, then sped away. Not believing what just happened, Peko threw her hands up and ran to catch up with her sister.

* * * * *

Mi'kelle was sitting at the kitchen table playing with the food on her plate. Her grandmother, Arie, was too busy yapping on the phone to pay her any attention. Sneakily, Mi'kelle got up and walked her plate over to the trash can. She glanced at Arie to make sure that she wasn't watching. Arie was busy cleaning the kitchen counter. Hurriedly, she dumped the remainder of her food into the trash. By the time she turned around, Mi'kelle was back at the table, smirking deviously.

"Yu finished already?" Arie asked in disbelief. Mi'kelle nodded her head. "Yu a greedy likkle gurl."

Mi'kelle's smirk turned into a frown. She hated it when her grandma talked to her like she was a baby.

"Grandma, must I keep reminding you that I'm eleven and a half years old?"

Arie didn't hear her, because once again, she was gossiping into the phone about someone else's business. The doorbell rang. Mi'kelle instantly jumped up, running to go answer it. A big grin appeared on her chocolate face after she saw who it was.

"Hey, mummy's gurl," Tukey said excitedly as she reached out for her.

"Hi, mama. Did you bring me something?" Mi'kelle inquired. She knew that every time her mother came around she had something for her.

About a year ago, Arie insisted that Mi'kelle stay with her so that she wouldn't be exposed to the immorality that went on inside Tukey's home. Arie did like Anitra as a person, but she was not at all happy about the lesbian relationship that she was having with her daughter.

To ensure Mi'kelle's well-being, Tukey bought Arie a big house in the suburbs of Kansas and furnished it nicely so her daughter could live comfortably. She also invested money into bank CDs and a college fund to secure Mi'kelle's future in case something ever happened to her.

Occasionally, Mi'kelle would ask about her father. She just couldn't understand why God would want her daddy up in heaven with him and not at home with her. When those questions came up, Tukey couldn't supply the answers. Guilt would consume her heart and she would just walk away.

Every time she looked at Mi'kelle's face, she would see Keith's face. That was one of the reasons she didn't come around often. Sometimes she would ask herself why she did what she did. She liked to think that she did it because he killed her uncle. But the real reason was because of the hurt she felt after she found out that Keith had married Selina while she was doing a bid for him. How could he do her like that? Especially since she had his child. And not once did proposing to her cross his mind. She didn't really want him to die. The last thing she thought was that he would actually kill himself, but she did want to put his dick on lockdown. Permanently.

Financially, Tukey was there for Mi'kelle, but it was Arie who raised her and taught her how to become a woman. Tukey would no longer want to live if Mi'kelle ever found out that she was the one who deprived her of having a father. All of her friends at school had one, so what gave Tukey the right to take hers?

Physically, she didn't pull the trigger that killed him. She just put him in a position in which he was faced with two options. One was to live out the rest of his life suffering both physically and mentally. The second option was for him to take the gun that she supplied him with and end it before it ever got started. He chose the latter.

Tukey dug into her pocket and came out with a small gray box and handed it to Mi'kelle. It was obvious that it was a ring. Still, Mi'kelle couldn't wait to see what it looked like.

Her face lit up like the sky after she saw what was inside. "Thank you, mama!" It was a white gold ring with a quarter-carat princess-cut diamond setting. Tukey saved the matching chain to give to her on Christmas.

"Yu should've gotten her a damn cell phone," Arie commented as she watched the two hug. "Me tired of dem nappy-headed bwoys callin' here all night."

Tukey broke the embrace. "What bwoys? Ya got bwoys calling yu now?" she asked in disbelief.

"Since last year," Mi'kelle said matter-of-factly.

Arie put her hands up. "Before us get into all dat, Anitra, get ya skinny butt in here and shut me door. It's cold outside."

"I smell food," Anitra said, sniffing the air.

"Go on back to de kitchen. Me will mek yu some plates."

With her arm around Mi'kelle's shoulder, Tukey walked toward the back of the house. "After us eat, us gonna talk about dem bwoys dat yu got calling."

"Where is Aunt Shantí?" Mi'kelle asked, changing the subject.

"Me doan know," Tukey replied slowly. Now that Mi'kelle had mentioned it, Shantí had seemed a little distant lately.

* * * * *

Across the state line, inside a comfortable suite in the Marriott Hotel, Shantí was bent over doggy style getting some much-needed dick from a guy named Derrius. With her face buried in the sheets, she took the big dick, enjoying every stroke.

They had been at it all night. Slept until two the next afternoon, then went at it again. It had been a while since either of them had some sex, so they wanted to enjoy it while it lasted.

It wasn't until eight o'clock when the two finally forced themselves apart. With big smiles of satisfaction on their faces, they began to get dressed.

While Derrius slipped on his jeans, she eyed him closely. He was medium height, had sexy gray eyes and a nice body. By the way he stroked her last night, it wasn't a mystery as to why he came in contact with the AIDS virus. She could just about imagine how many women that he used to have lined up, waiting to feel his powerful thrust. His only mistake was that he wasn't a fan of condoms. A mistake that would soon cost him his life.

While Shantí pulled her panties over her freckled pelvis, Derrius watched her attentively. The night before, he stopped at a Mexican restaurant where he would not be seen by anyone he knew. His plan was to drink himself until he was damn near comatose, then hopefully he would get killed in a car crash on his way home.

He was sitting at the bar finishing up his third drink when a cute freckle-faced woman walked through the door. He could look in her red swollen eyes and tell that she was on the same mission as he. The fancy clothes and bling that she wore could only fool the naked eye. But another human being that shared her same despair could see right through the flash.

After he watched her down her first drink, he decided to make his move. He went and sat next to her at the end of the bar where he ordered another round. Shantí didn't really care for any company, but it felt nice to be hit on.

As the night went on, their conversation got deeper. Then they got drunker, and their hormones started to heat up. For the rest of the night, both temporarily forgot the sorrows that brought them there in the first place.

Even though he wasn't, she assumed that he was about to ask her to leave with him. He was too nice of a guy for her to put at risk by not wearing a condom, so she voluntarily told him about her illness.

Derrius learned that she used to be a fast, hot pants freak in her past life. Then eventually she came in contact with the AIDS virus after having sex with her live-in boyfriend, who she later found out was an undercover homosexual. That's when Derrius felt compelled to share his tragic experience with her as well.

Before they knew it, they were in bed together working off some of the stress, though it would only last temporarily. After they finished dressing, Derrius grabbed hold of her waist, pulling her toward him.

"Am I gonna see you again?" he inquired.

Feeling attractive again, she shrugged as if she were playing hard to get. "Maybe." She flashed her still pretty smile.

Derrius frowned after he saw her mouth bleeding for no apparent reason.

"What's wrong?" she asked, noticing the peculiar look on his face. He rushed to the bathroom to get a towel.

Suddenly, she began to taste her own blood inside her mouth. Embarrassed, she cupped her mouth and turned away. A minute later he returned with a washcloth in his hand.

"Here," Derrius said as he handed it to her.

Reaching back, she took the washcloth without facing him. "Thanks."

Not wanting to embarrass her any further, Derrius walked over to the door and opened it. "I'll be in the lobby when you're ready," he informed her. Then he left.

* * * * *

The parking lot at the bar where they met the night before was empty except for Derrius' beat up old Buick Regal. Shantí pulled her 300C up next to it.

Derrius looked shamefully at his old bucket. He felt funny being that she was driving such a luxurious one. Shantí was looking straight ahead when he turned to her. She was too embarrassed by the earlier incident to look him in the face.

"You OK?" Derrius asked sincerely.

"Yes," Shantí replied bashfully.

He sighed as he contemplated what to do next. Finally, he said, "Will you call me?"

For the first time since she had been in the car, she turned to face him. Shantí eyed his handsome face. Derrius had no insecurities about his looks so he didn't blush, nor did he turn away. Instead, he leaned forward and planted a kiss on her lips. It wasn't that he was horny, he just wanted her to know that she had nothing to be ashamed of. He was infected as well and had no reason to look down on her for what happened.

After the kiss ended, Derrius opened up the door. "You've got my number ... use it." Then he got out.

Derrius was fumbling with his keys when her heard her window lowering. He turned around.

"Thank you," Shantí said with teary eyes. "And don't worry, I will call you."

Derrius just smiled and nodded his head.

On her way down Truman Road she popped in her favorite CD, "*The Diary of Alicia Keys.*" Her mellow mood was abruptly interrupted when "*Drop It Like It's Hot*" came on, alerting her that she had a call. Tukey's number appeared in the caller ID of her cell phone.

"What, mother?" Shantí said, answering it.

"Gurl, where have yu been?" Tukey yelled at her. "Me been lookin' all over for yu."

"Minding my own," Shantí quipped.

"Yu all dat now, huh?" Tukey replied jokingly. "Seriously, tell me what's goin' on?"

"Gurl, you not gonna believe it when I tell you."

Chapter 8

Tiera woke up alone. She wiped the sleep from her eyes. After a quick glance at the clock on the dresser, she learned that it was eight thirty in the morning. She thought how Cody should be sitting behind his desk enjoying a hot cup of java, and now that he had switched back to days and the kids were in school, she and Kenny could do things outside of late night creeps. Like meet each other at a nice restaurant for lunch.

Picking up the phone off the nightstand, she dialed Kenny's number.

"Wha'sup, love?" he answered in a sleepy voice.

"You dream about me last night?" *Damn, I sound like a desperate housewife*, she thought to herself.

"Mm hmm," he lied.

"Boy, you—" Hearing the toilet flush inside the bathroom adjacent to her room interrupted her. "Call you right back," she whispered quickly before hanging up.

When she looked up, she saw Cody standing in the doorway with his arms folded across his chest.

"You've been a bad girl," Cody stated in a calm voice. His eyes peered at her accusingly.

Feeling shameful, Tiera put her head down.

"Baby, let me explain," she said timidly. "I be lonely—"

"What the hell does lonely have to do with you cleaning up the damn bathroom?" he said in a loud voice. "I work hard all day to pay the bills. The least you could do is keep my fucking house clean." He turned and stormed away.

After a while she heard the front door slam. She sighed with relief, glad that he didn't allow her the opportunity to expose herself.

"Man, that was close," she said to herself out loud. Getting out of the bed, she hurried over to the window to peep out.

Cody's blue Crown Victoria was pulling away. It was under twenty degrees outside, finally feeling like December. He closed the crack in his window and cut the heat up.

"Damn, it's cold," he said as he reached for his coffee. He tasted the bland liquid. "Needs sugar." He reached into his pocket for a couple of packs of Sweet'N Low. In the midst of the contents was Tukey's business card.

With a puzzled look on his face he held up the card. He had almost forgotten about that night.

"Umph," he grunted, then put it back inside his pocket.

Headed in the opposite direction was a candy-green Chevy Caprice. It had tow lot numbers written across the windshield. He knew that it was the same one that he had pulled over at the apartment complex. As the Chevy passed him, he and Tiki made eye contact.

"Back out already," he said to himself. He shook his head unbelieving of how much of a joke the American justice system was.

* * * * *

Rhyme Tyme was getting warm in the unlit booth when he saw Tukey's H2 pull up. He ran out to get her door.

"Afternoon, boss lady," he said, flashing his gold-toothed smile. "Or should I say good night? Yo' club is outta sight. The fishes, they gon' bite. I thinkin' 'bout quitin' ... syke."

They high fived. "Bwoy, yu on ya way." She chuckled. "But

doan keep playin' about quitin' on me. Yu hear?"

While the doorman, Guru, paved a way for Tukey, she politely waved and shook hands with the small crowd of people.

* * * * *

Later on that night, Herm pulled up to the valet in his new Yukon Denali, followed by five other new whips. There were two things that he never went to the club without – one was his entourage, and the other was his sawed-off double-barreled shotgun. Rhyme Tyme knew that Herm was a big tipper, so he hurried over to the truck before Alf, the other valet, could get to him.

"Wha'sup, Herm?" Rhyme said, smiling as usual. "I know shits goin' great. But the niggas still gon' hate. I—"

"I ain't trying to hear that bullshit tonight, Rhyme," Herm interrupted in his loud, high-pitched voice. "I'm not in the mood. You gon' fuck around and get yo' whole fuckin' grill knocked out."

"Fuck you," Rhyme said to himself as Herm walked away.

Herm angrily spun around after he heard Rhyme smash out, burning up his brand new rubber. He promised himself that he was gonna slap Rhyme for such a disrespectful act.

At the door he was pat-searched and asked to produce his VIP card. Irritated, he flashed it and marched past Guru before he was forced to cause a scene.

Herm didn't really want to come to Tukey's club to kick it. He hated her for reasons that he probably didn't know himself, not to mention that the last time he saw her, she was walking away with thirty-one thousand dollars of his. But Club No Draws was the hot spot for the moment, so since he loved to be where the hoes were, he didn't have any other choice.

He and eleven of his dogs bum-rushed the VIP taking up three tables. A skinny waitress wearing a leather thong outfit and thigh-high leather boots came to take their orders.

"Bring us six bottles of Mo," Herm ordered. "Run a tab 'cause we're gonna be here for a while."

* * * * *

Tukey was sitting on the edge of the conference table inside her office, topless, while Anitra sat in the chair in front of her, sucking her titties. She stopped briefly to take a sip of Dom, then went back to work. They didn't stop when the waitress who served them barged in unannounced.

"What is it?" Tukey asked, looking down at Anitra while she bit on her nipples.

The waitress didn't flinch. It wasn't the first and it surely wouldn't be the last time she would walk in on them while they were going at it.

"Herm and his crew just walked into the VIP."

"Tell ... mmm," she moaned. "Tell security tu be ... mmm ... tu keep ... ta be on alert."

Picking up the bottle, Tukey took a long swig, held it inside her jaws, then bent over and kissed Anitra in the mouth. The bubbly flowed through their locked lips and down their chins.

The waitress shook her head. She never understood how two women could be attracted to one another. Turning to leave, she gently closed the door behind her.

Drunk and ready to freak something, Herm made his way over to the strip club to see some booty. After viewing several dancers strip on stage, he finally set in on a stripper named Coffee Brown. He asked her to join him in the booth for a lap dance.

She waited for the DJ to start the next song. When she heard Juvenile's *"Slow Motion"* come on, she immediately went to work. She grinded her booty on his lap while her titties jiggled in his face. Unable to control himself, he reached down between her legs and tried to cop a feel.

"Unt unh. Don't touch," Coffee warned. "It's against the rules."

"Sellin' pussy is, too, but that ain't never stopped you," he reminded her.

His narrow, bloodshot eyes warned her that he was drunk. Her first mind told her to end the dance and return his money, but the song was halfway over and her son still had to eat. So she continued to tease him.

She grabbed the back of his fat head, putting his face into her breasts, hoping to pacify him until the song ended. The tactic only enticed him even more. Before she knew it, she felt his finger slide under her G-string into the crack of her ass.

Reflexively, she smacked him. "You've gone way too far now," she hollered hotly.

He responded by pushing her off of his lap and onto the floor. "Fuck off me then, bitch!" he growled.

Security saw the altercation and rushed over to her aid.

"What's the problem?" the security guard asked her.

Coffee got up off the floor. "He's the problem," she said, pointing at Herm. "He's drunk and can't keep his hands to himself."

The security guard faced Herm, who was standing and looking him eye to eye. "Straighten up," he stated, "or I'ma throw your big ass out of here."

"Say what you want," Herm said. "Just don't make the mistake of putting your hands on me."

"Hopefully it won't come to that."

Through discussing it, Herm stomped past him back to his table.

* * * * *

The DJ announced last call, ready to bring the party to a close. Tailing closely behind his crew to the front door, Herm had two white girls on each side of him. One toyed with his chain while the other held his hand. He had some kinky sex acts planned for the two Ex junkies to perform.

Dino, the smallest member of their crew, was thizzed out,

drunk and ready to start some funk. Paper Boy was in the parking lot, leaning back up against his Cadillac STS, macking on a big booty light-skinned freak. He was tipsy and trying to find something to fuck tonight.

Dino pointed in Paper Boy's direction. "Ain't that the nigga who let that bitch sneak out the crap house with Herm's money?" he asked Lil John.

Lil John squinted his eyes as he tried to get a good look.

"Yeah, that's him. Herm ain't trippin' on that shit no more."

Dino wouldn't leave well enough alone. "If he ain't, I am. I don't like that nigga no way. Always on somebody else's bitch and shit."

Lil John looked down at his short, egghead friend. "Wanna whoop 'em?"

"Hell yeah. Let's go, cuz."

Paper Boy happened to glance up as they were walking toward him. The hard mug on their faces said that it would not be a friendly visit. He stood his six foot, two inch frame straight up with his fist balled, prepared to swing if it came to that.

Dino stepped ahead of Lil John, looking as if he were about to rush Paper Boy. Trained to go at will, Paper Boy swung, hitting Dino hard above his left eye. The girl who he was talking to hurriedly got out of their way. Instead of following up, Paper Boy stepped back with his guards up, waiting for Lil John to make his move.

"Run up, nigga!" Paper Boy challenged. "I don't know what you niggas tripping on, but I ain't ducking nothing."

By the time the rest of their crew knew what as going on, Paper Boy and Lil John were slugging it out while Dino went looking for something to pick up. A huge crowd gathered around the fighters, trying to see somebody get hurt.

Lil John's left foot slipped out from underneath him, causing him to stumble. Paper Boy hit him with a double punch that sent him down to the concrete, then started kicking him. Before long, Paper Boy had nine more niggas to deal with. They jumped in kicking and hitting him in the head and face.

Rhyme had pulled Herm's Denali around to where the commotion was. Herm quickly reached in and grabbed his shotgun from beneath the seat. From a distance, he watched while his guys went to work on Paper Boy.

Ashanti's *"Only U"* was playing out of the wall stereo inside Tukey's office. Anitra was sprawled on the floor naked with a two-seater dildo stuck in her. It was L-shaped. She had the small one in her, while Tukey sat atop of the big one. She was humping herself into an orgasm when the security guard barged in.

"Boss lady!?" he shouted. He stopped to consider if he was seeing what he thought he was seeing.

"What!?" Tukey yelled, irritated by his sudden interruption. She was almost there until that cocksucker came in and ruined it.

"We got trouble out in the parking lot," he said, staring at the two naked women.

Tukey sighed heavily. "Me on me way. Try ta gain control before de police show up."

He took one last photographic look before he left. If he had a choice, he would rather jump between them instead of the group of drunk niggas.

Herm saw all twenty of the security guards rush out the door with clubs in their hands. He and the two girls who he was with hopped into his truck. Sticking the sawed-off out the window, he fired two shots in the air.

Boom! Boom!

The crowd quickly began to disperse. Everybody was running for the safety of their cars. Security sprayed mace into the air. Women were breaking their heels off their pumps as they tried to run for cover. Satisfied with what he had done, Herm tossed the shotgun onto the floor, then sped off.

About a block away from the club, Kenny turned up the beat in his Infiniti. He had hopes of catching some hoes as they were leaving the club. Even after it closed, it usually took about an hour for the parking lot to clear out. Dudes hung outside the club by their whips so that the girls who they were in the club spitting at could see what they were driving. The girls would prance around in low-cut shirts with their thongs showing, hoping to get chosen.

People were scattering to their cars. The ones who were already in their cars were pulling out of the lot in a hurry. Kenny drove up wondering what the hell was going on. His first thought was that some fool had shot up the club. He was about to join the exiting traffic until he saw the security guards helping his partner, Paper Boy, into his STS.

A big black security guard stood blocking the road. He had his arms extended and his palms up. His intention was to stop the Infiniti coming their way. Kenny stopped the car, got out and jogged over to the scene.

"Hold it right there," the guard ordered.

"That's my cousin," Kenny informed him. The man allowed Kenny to pass.

Paper Boy looked up after he heard Kenny's familiar voice. His eye was swelling fast, his lip was busted and a bump was growing on the back of his head. Other than that, he was all right.

"Who you get into it with?" Kenny inquired as he got a good look at his face.

"Dino and Herm."

Kenny became enraged. "Man, let's go get them niggas. They couldn't have gotten too far in all this traffic."

"I ain't got my thumper."

"Sheeit, I got mine." Three police cars pulled into the parking lot. "Let's get outta here. We can meet up at the Amoco."

Paper Boy nodded his head.

Tukey walked out of the club followed by Anitra. At first sight of the police, she ducked back inside, leaving Anitra out there to answer their questions.

* * * * *

Dino, Lil John and several others were lingering in Amoco's parking lot. Several blunts were being passed around while they discussed and laughed about what they had done. Two young women, one light and one brown-skinned with blue contacts, approached Dino and Lil John. They wore tight, short skirts that were split up the sides.

"Sup, LJ?" the light-skinned one said.

He peered down at her, smiling from ear to ear. "Hey, Tina."

"Tanya," she quickly corrected him.

"Right, right. I didn't recognize you with the blond hair." Tanya looked at Dino who was eyeing her friend lustfully.

"Who's your friend?" Tanya asked.

"I'm Dino," he cut in. "I don't need nobody to speak for me." He adjusted the blue ball cap on his head.

"Well, Dino," she pointed to her friend, "this is my girl Erica." They shook hands.

Erica asked, "So what y'all got up for tonight?" She was hoping that they would be able to kick it with them.

* * * * *

It took a while to get through all the traffic. Finally, Paper Boy made his way to the Amoco. As he approached the entrance, he spotted Lil John rubbing on Tanya's booty. He did a quick scan of the crowd. Everyone was there except for Herm, Chris and a few other don't knows.

Paper Boy continued on down Troost while he tried to call Kenny on his cell phone. He was hoping that they wouldn't see him driving by.

"I'm almost there," Kenny said, answering the phone.

"Hurry up! These niggas down here slipping. I'ma park my car behind the bank on 60th."

"I'm right behind you."

"Come on, nigga!" He hung up then reached inside his glove compartment for his burners.

Kenny showed up two minutes later. Paper Boy jumped in on the passenger's side. The car sped off before he could close the door good.

"Where yo' thang at?"

From underneath his seat Kenny produced a black Mac-11, then handed it to him.

Lil John saw the Infiniti pull into the gas station as he continued to talk to Tanya. He caught a glimpse of the driver, but didn't bother looking at the passenger. Dino didn't see anything. He was too busy trying to run his hand up Erica's skirt.

Paper Boy cocked the Mac, then lowered his window. Dino finally decided to look up. His eyes nearly popped out of his head after he saw the gun pointed in their direction. In a desperate attempt to save his own life, he pushed Erica toward the Infiniti and broke.

Then gunshots rang out.

Although five of the men were strapped, they were too busy trying to escape to remember that they were. Everybody scattered in different directions. Tanya made the fatal mistake of trailing behind Lil John, who was one of the targets.

Two slugs from the Mac-11 went through the back of her neck and came out of her face. Erica screamed after she saw her friend's lifeless body hit the ground.

Kenny spotted Dino running down the street trying to get away. Hurriedly, he drove out of the Amoco lot. Dino heard a car coming up behind him, then instinctively turned around. He heard the first shot that tore through his chin. The second cut his lights out before he could feel the pain from the first.

Herm, Chris and the two white girls watched the whole

scene in horror. They were stuck in the drive-thru at the Wendy's across the street. Angrily, Herm ordered the girls out of the truck. Shaken up from all of the gunfire, the two suburban girls happily obliged.

Chris was in the driver's seat. Tired of doing nothing, he cut the wheel and drove over the curb and through some shrubbery. When he reached the pavement, he bolted away in pursuit of the fleeing Infiniti. Herm loaded his shotgun and pulled the hammers back on both barrels.

"Gon' fuck dese niggas up," Herm said angrily.

They sped down 64th Street, passing Dino's body that lay dead on the side of the road. It would do them no good to pull over and find out what they already knew.

Kenny saw the headlights of the Denali about a half block behind them but he had no idea that they were after him. He drove quickly back to the bank where Paper Boy had left his car. Thinking they had gotten away, they shook hands and promised to meet up the following day.

"Hold up, Chris," Herm said as they turned the corner. They could see Paper Boy getting in his Cadillac.

"Wha'sup?" Chris asked impatiently, not understanding why Herm suddenly wanted to stop.

"I only got two shots in my gun. If I try to shoot both of 'em, one of 'em might get a shot off." Paper Boy sped away.

Chris yelled, "Man, they getting away."

"Chill. We gon' follow Kenny's ass home. Then I'ma blast his ass."

When Kenny pulled up at his house, he grabbed the empty Mac and got out. He was nearing his porch when the Denali stopped in front of his house.

"Shit!" Kenny hollered as he ran up on his porch.

Herm stuck the gun out the window. Kenny was diving behind the stone walls on his porch when he heard the blast. A burning pain shot through his arm where the buckshots entered him.

Chris stayed there for a minute to make sure that Kenny didn't get back up.

"Let's roll," Herm said.

Chapter 9

Tiki sat with her legs folded on her leather recliner inside her plush apartment. She was playing a racing game on her Xbox while Destiny's Child sang "*Soldier*" through her Pioneer stereo system. Bobbing her head to the music, she steered the car on the screen through various courses.

Someone knocked on the door.

Tiki didn't bother getting up. She would wait for Peko to answer it. Peko finally appeared after the sixth knock.

"Yu didn't hear somebody knocking on de damn door?" she yelled, walking past her.

Tiki looked at her, frowned, then focused her attention back on the TV. Shaking her head in disgust, Peko opened the door.

"Hey cousin," Peko said, greeting Tukey. Shantí was standing behind her.

"Wha'sup?" Tukey said as she walked past her into the apartment.

Shantí wrinkled her nose. "It smells like weed every time I come over here." She faked a cough.

"Ya know how us do it, rude gurl," Peko said with a smile. "Us Jamaicans got ta stay high. A blunt of sticky tu get de day goin' and one tu end it."

"Roll one up," Tukey said as she took off her coat. She

plopped down on the love seat.

Tiki shot her a disapproving look. After rolling her eyes, she continued to play the game.

"Me gotta go get de blunts," Peko said.

"I gotta use the bathroom," Shantí said on her way to the back.

Tukey stared at the side of her cousin's face. Tiki reminded her of herself. Pretty, tough and hot-headed. It had been days since she had seen Tiki and she missed her dearly. Feeling a pair of eyes on her, Tiki turned in her direction. Instead of a frown, Tukey had a pleasant smile on her face.

"What?" Tiki asked, trying to play hard. In truth, she missed Tukey, too. In fact, the night before, she drove out to Tukey's house to apologize. She had made it all the way to her block when she changed her mind and turned back around. If Tukey wanted to make up, she knew where to find her.

Tukey sat up. "Yu still mad at me?"

Tiki went back to playing the game. She took her sweet time answering her. "Maybe," she replied.

Tukey started playing with her nails. "Well ummm ... me just wanted tu say dat me sorry." She looked at Tiki with pleading eyes.

"Well me doan accept," Tiki replied stubbornly.

Tukey stood up. "All right." She started to walk away.

"Because me de one who should be sorry," Tiki said to her back.

Tukey stopped and turned around. "Awee," she said, holding her arms out in front of her. Dropping the controller, Tiki jumped up to hug her cousin.

"'Bout damn time," Peko said, walking into the room.

Tukey motioned for her to join them. Shantí saw the three of them standing in the middle of the room hugging.

"Don't leave me out," she said, running over to them.

"Come on, gurl," Tiki welcomed her. "Yu know dat yu family, tu."

They were all hugging when Shantí's bling tone started playing, interrupting them. She broke the embrace. Derrius' number showed up on the caller ID.

"Umph, this my baby," she boasted as she smiled from ear to ear. "Wait 'till you see him."

"Whaaaat?" Peko said confusingly.

"Doan ask," Tukey said, already knowing what they were thinking.

* * * * *

Niecy's restaurant was crowded as usual. Out of all the places to get a good breakfast in the city, Niecy's was chosen by most young blacks. It wasn't a fancy place. It was just a small kitchen that served good food and was located on the most popular street in Missouri—Prospect.

"Steak and eggs to go, please!" a waitress yelled to the cook.

A middle-aged couple and their two children were exiting the joint at the same time Tukey and her crew were entering. They waited patiently for the family to exit before they walked in.

"Party of four?" the owner asked when they walked through the door.

Shantí nodded.

"Hold tight. A table will be ready in a moment." Tukey grabbed "*The Call*" off the counter to read while they waited.

* * * * *

Traffic was moving slowly because of an accident that happened a block away. Cody grew tired of waiting. He turned on his siren, clearing traffic so he could drive through. He paid no attention to the angry glares from the civilians who were stuck having to wait.

Dulow nodded his head. "One of the benefits of being the law," he said sarcastically.

Cody stared at him in disbelief. "Would you please stop

complaining all the damn time? Be grateful for what you have."

"You be grateful," Dulow replied. They rode for a few blocks in complete silence. From a distance he could see the sign outside Niecy's restaurant. It read, "Steak-N-Egg Special." Instantly he became hungry. "Stop up ahead so we can get something to eat."

* * * * *

"Ain't not'ing wrong wit' getting hit in de butt," Tiki defended.

Every girl at the table a had sour look on her face, except for Tukey.

"Dat is so nasty," Peko said. "Me is a freak, but dat is taking it a bit tu far." She drank some of her orange juice.

Tukey chewed and swallowed a piece of toast. "Me let Keith get de butt once or twice," she admitted. "It takes some gettin' used tu."

"Y'all crazy," Shantí said, laughing.

"Not all of us," Peko corrected her. "Us doan all like de same t'ings."

Shantí couldn't help but ask, "How many dudes have you fucked, Tiki?"

"Mmm," she murmured, "about forty or so."

"Dat's a lot of dick," Peko commented.

"What about yu?" Tiki asked Peko. "Yu cyaah be tu far behind me."

"Yes me am," Peko defended. "Me probably had sex wit' 'bout ... unmm ... t'irty-five guys."

"Wow! Five less dan me," Tiki retorted.

"So! Yu only twenty-one years old, Tiki."

"And yu only twenty-two, so what's de difference?"

Tukey said, "Both yu whores shut up."

Cody and Dulow entered the restaurant. Tiki immediately recognized Cody as the security guard who arrested her. Only now he was in a policeman's uniform.

Tiki whispered in Tukey's ear, "Dat's de cop who busted us."
Tukey looked up and saw Cody's fine ass standing there.
"Who? Him?"

"Yes," she said in a low voice, as if he could hear her.

Hmpf? Tukey thought. Since Cody had let her off the hook
when he had busted her, maybe he could be persuaded into letting her cousins go as well.

When Peko glanced around and saw Cody, she almost
screamed.

"Tu—"

"Shhhh!" Tukey said. "Me know. Us have tu play dis by ear."
She faced Tiki. "Follow me lead."

"Me not about tu flirt wit' no pigs," Tiki stated firmly.

"If yu want ta get out of dis yu are tu." Tukey wiped her
mouth, then applied some gloss to her lips. "Start flirting wit'
his friend."

Dulow saw the table full of pretty ladies staring at him.
Shantí was the only one who didn't have a clue as to what was
going on.

Tiki waved at him. He waved back.

"Hi sexy," she said out loud.

The customers inside the restaurant stopped what they were
doing and peered at Dulow. He blushed as he glanced around
the room at all the staring faces. Embarrassed, he faced the
counter hoping that they would all resume what they were
doing.

The owner directed them to a booth by the window. While
Dulow was ordering, Cody saw Tukey eyeing him savagely. She
blew him a kiss, then winked at him. He smiled as he looked
away. Dulow was saying something that Cody didn't hear. He
was too busy being entertained by Tukey. She was swallowing a
long strip of bacon like it was a greasy dick going down her
throat.

Shantí saw Tukey flirting with the policeman. "Girl, what

are you doing?" she asked curiously.

"Teasin' him," she replied, barely moving her lips.

"Maybe you should fuck 'em," Shantí suggested. "You *are* overdue for some dick, Tukey."

They didn't know that was Tukey's plan from jump. She had been wanting to fuck Cody since back in the day. Now she had a good reason to. Hopefully, she would please him enough for him to let her cousins off the hook. And if it went that far, there was no telling how far across the line he would go. Who could stop her with the police in her pocket?

Tukey promised herself that it would just be a business fuck. She wouldn't get sprung off the dick, but she did hope that he slung a mean one.

Tukey applied another coat of gloss on her lips. "Let's do dis."

Dulow was in the middle of a cop story when Cody saw them coming their way. He sneakily kicked Dulow's foot under the table, then nodded in their direction. By the time Cody looked back, Tukey was sliding into the booth next to him. Tiki sat next to Dulow.

"Yu want some cream in ya coffee?" Tukey asked in a seductive tone.

"Only if it comes outta you," Cody retorted, trying to sound cool. Back when he was in school, he was as cool as a kid could be. He hadn't lost it. He just sat it on the shelf the day that he said, "I do."

"When yu gonna let me give yu some of dis Jamaican funk, Cody?"

His little soldier was trying to salute in his trousers. Cody laughed, not knowing how to respond to such a blunt question. Dulow felt Tiki's hand creeping up his thigh. His body tensed up. She had a smile on her sneaky chocolate face.

"How about yu, Mister?" Tiki asked Dulow. "Yu want a taste of dis Crown and Coke?"

"Last time I drank some Crown I passed the fuck out," Dulow said. "Right after I fucked the shit outta my wife."

Tiki stood up, showing off her curves. "Ya wife look like dis from de back?" She bent over as if she were tying her shoe.

Shanti's mouth fell open. "Do you see this?" she asked Peko.

"Umm hm," she mumbled. "Me gurl's sum't'ing else."

Cody recognized Tiki but didn't mention it. He followed their lead because he knew damn well Tiki knew who he was. It was obvious that Tukey had informed her about what he did for her that night. She was probably hoping to receive the same favor. But he wondered how far they would go to get it.

Tired of procrastinating, Tukey said, "Why doan us all meet up after ya shift is over? Den us ca'an pick up where us left off behind de school stairs."

That confused Dulow and Tiki.

"Y'all know each other?" Dulow inquired.

"We have a past," Cody answered, still looking at her. "She went to school with us. You don't remember Keith's girlfriend?"

"Vaguely."

"So what's up?" Tiki asked. "Yu gonna give us some of dat RoboCop dick or what, mon?"

Dulow looked to Cody for an answer. Cody cleared his throat as he contemplated his next move. He hadn't cheated on Tiera since they exchanged vows. But they hadn't made love in weeks, and she hadn't sucked his dick since the second year of their marriage. Tukey was an unaccomplished mission, so why not at least get the notch under his belt? It would only be a one-time thing anyway.

Cody finally said, "I've got your card. Let me straighten things out at home, then I'll ... we'll call y'all." He felt like they were kids planning a skipping party with two horny girls.

"Do dat," Tukey said, getting up from the table. She took out her bankroll and tossed a twenty on the table. "Breakfast is on me."

Long legs and bouncing booty cheeks were all they saw as they watched them sway back over to their table. Cody wiped his mouth and tossed the napkin on his empty plate.

Peko and Shantí were all smiles when the two girls returned.

"Y'all handle it?" Peko inquired.

"Yep," Tiki answered. "Me doan even t'ink he recognizes me."

Shantí said, "Would somebody please tell me what that was all about?"

Tukey shot her a devious look. "Us is about to get in cahoots wit' de blue suits."

* * * * *

Tiera called Kenny's phone for the tenth time that day. Frustrated, she slammed the phone down after he didn't answer. She couldn't figure out what was going on. Had he gotten all he wanted from her and disappeared? Or did he find a new woman to occupy his time? Whatever it was, she would find out.

She walked to the bottom of the staircase.

"Codesha, Tera and Coera!" she yelled up the stairs. "Get y'all's damn rooms cleaned up. Now!" She took her anger and frustration out on them, and was storming toward the kitchen when the phone rang.

"Hello!" she said hotly.

"Can I speak to Tiera?" a female's voice said.

"Who's calling?"

"Sonya," she replied in a stressful tone.

"This is her." Tiera went into defense mode. She hoped it wasn't one of Kenny's other bitches calling her house. That she couldn't have. It would create nothing but havoc inside her home. For a moment she regretted giving Kenny her home number.

"Hold on a minute," Sonya said. Tiera could hear her passing the phone to someone.

"Hey," Kenny mumbled in a low voice.

"Kenny!" she hollered, sensing that something was wrong.

"Yeah. I ... I got shot last night."

"Shot? By who? Are you all right?"

"Yeah. I'm just glad that they were buckshots. Otherwise I'd be dead."

Tiera heard a car pull up in the driveway and rushed to the window to peep out. Cody was taking off his vest to put in his trunk.

Quickly, she asked, "What hospital are you in? I'm coming up there."

"Truman."

"OK. I gotta go, baby." She hung up the phone, then dashed up the stairs. The fact that he called her from the hospital made her feel special.

Cody walked in and tossed his keys on top of the fireplace. He hadn't been able to keep his mind off of Tukey since he left the restaurant. What kind of excuse was he going to use to get out of the house tonight? The thought of sneaking around on his beloved wife had him filled with excitement.

Picking up the remote, he turned to the Channel Nine news. Then he took a pack of Newports out of his shirt pocket and pulled out a cigarette. After firing it up, he dropped down on the sofa. Feet could be heard moving about on the second floor. Looking up at the ceiling, he wondered what they were up there doing. He took a long drag, then placed the cigarette inside the ashtray.

Sitting back on the couch, he squirmed and shifted until he made himself comfortable. Soon he dozed off. Minutes later, his eyes fluttered open after he heard Tiera and the kids trampling down the steps. One child was begging for McDonald's, one wanted to take a nap and the baby, while being held by her mother, was just happy to be living.

"Where y'all headed?" Cody quizzed, seeing that the kids

had on their coats.

"They're out of school for the holidays and my sister wants to keep them until Christmas Eve." She picked her purse up off the table. "She's having a little get-together for women and children, so I probably won't be back tonight."

After standing to stretch, Cody gave her a quick peck on her cheek. He bent over to kiss his baby as well. Then the other two curly-headed girls.

"Bye, daddy," they said.

"Bye. And button up your coat, Coera."

Soon he found himself all alone. Hurriedly, he ran upstairs to prepare for the night. He needed to shave and run through the shower. Tonight he would kick it like a player, not like the square that he had become over the years. Whatever Tukey wanted to do tonight, he was down for. Even if it was something illegal.

* * * * *

"I'm not cool with this," Anitra said as she watched Tukey pack an overnight bag.

Tukey zipped it up. She walked over to Anitra, put her hand on her cheek and began stroking it gently.

"Me promise dat me know what me doing," Tukey assured her. "It's gonna work out good for business."

Anitra moved away and took a seat on the leather massage chair next to their bed.

"Speaking of business, don't you think that we should pull out now?" she said seriously. "I mean ... we're worth a couple of million. Why risk our lives just so we can spend crazy and feel important? That doesn't make any sense."

Tukey sighed. "Us already been dere, remember? In two years us almost went t'rough a million dollars, Anitra."

"That was before we built the club."

"Yu right. And yu know how much it cost tu build dat damn club, tu. Us bought dis house. Me dawta's house. All dem damn cars. Jewelry. Shopping. Trips. Bills. Shit, de list goes on and on. And me only know one way tu tek care of all dat stuff."

Anitra shook her head. "What kind of a monster have you turned into, Tukey? You not no damn man," Anitra yelled.

Tukey looked at her as if to say, *don't you got a lot of room to talk.*

"So why don't you leave this drug shit to the niggas out there on the street?"

Tukey shrugged. "Me guess dis is de way me am. Livin' dangerously wit' Keith for all dat time did sum't'ing to me." She stood over Anitra. "Now either yu gonna be wit' me on dis 'till de end ... or yu ca'an walk away now," she said seriously.

"Oh, I'm with you," Anitra said calmly. "I just hope what you're doing doesn't cost us in the long run."

Chapter 10

Cody gave himself one last look in the mirror. His curly hair had grown a little but so had his goatee. He was dressed in a pair of black slacks, Stacy Adams shoes and a snug fitting crew neck shirt that flossed his muscular build.

Dulow pulled up in his two-year-old Bravada, honking the loud horn. Cody slapped on some cologne, grabbed his leather jacket and hit the door.

"Let's go, man!" he could hear Dulow yelling through the open passenger window.

Cody got into the passenger seat. "Hold your goddamn horses. You act like you ain't never done this before. Remember JoJo and Janae?"

"Yep," he said as he drove away. "I also remember JoJo saying that you raped her when we got to school the next day." They both laughed.

"Yeah, that bitch got me with that one, didn't she?" He peered at Dulow. "You bring some condoms?"

"Nope! I'm going raw dog tonight. Just like the old days."

"I hear ya. I told myself that I was gonna be down for whatever she's trying to do tonight. Fuck all of this square shit."

* * * * *

On the way to the hotel, Tukey told Tiki to stop by Fat

Sack's house to pick up a sack of Indo. Then they picked up a couple bottles of Hennessy Privilège from the liquor store. In her purse she packed four Red Dragon Ecstasy pills to help get the two stuck-up cops going.

Tukey wanted to get fucked in a crazy way and what better way to get fucked than on Ex? She could tell by the bulge in Cody's pants that he was either packing a big dick or a backup gun.

Sex wasn't her only mission. Tukey Tosh was a clever girl who had a plan for Sergeant Brown. Fucking him real good was just the first stage of her plan. The next was to wine and dine him to show him how the other side did it on a regular. By the time Tiki and Peko were ready to go to court, they would be able to make him take the stand and say whatever they wanted him to say, kind of like he was a dummy and Tukey had her hand up his ass, making him speak.

Growing up playing chess with her father not only taught her strategy but patience as well. The last time she had to put a plan into effect, she managed to cause the demise of her baby's daddy and his whole crew.

"So what do yu t'ink?" Tukey asked. "Should us get two rooms or a double?"

"Ya feeling kinda mannish tonight, huh rude gurl?"

"Right, right." Tukey giggled. "Dis is gon' be de greatest challenge of me life."

Tiki smiled. "Me cyaah believe us trying ta get in cahoots, as yu call it, wit' de police."

Tukey took out some Blueberry Royal Blunt papers and rolled one up. She looked around to make sure that there weren't any police in sight before she set fire to it.

"Us only got one life tu live, Tiki," Tukey explained. "Why not live it tu de fullest? Ya know what me sayin'?"

"Right or wrong, me wit' ya 'till de end, rude gurl." They gave each other dap.

Tukey lit the blunt, then sat back in her seat, puffing on it. Her bling tone started playing.

"Hello," Tukey answered.

"Where y'all want us to meet you?" It was Cody.

"Us will meet ya at de Marriott. As soon as us check into de double room, me call ya."

Cody hung up the phone, grinning.

"What they say?" Dulow asked anxiously.

"They said that they're getting a double room at the Marriott."

"A double? Man, we about to kick it."

* * * * *

As soon as they received the call from Tukey, the two impatient cops flew down to the hotel. Inside, they took the elevator to the fourth floor. They walked slowly until they found the room that they were looking for.

They could hear Nelly and Jaheim singing *"My Place"* through the door. Cody knocked twice.

"Come in!" Tiki yelled over the music.

Once inside, Cody saw something that instantly set his hormones aflame. He had to look at Dulow to see if he really saw what he was seeing. They could smell incense burning. The lights were dim, but their chocolate, naked bodies could still be seen sprawled across the beds. They both held gold pimp glasses full of Hennessy.

The girls motioned for the men to join them. *"My Place"* went off, then New Edition's *"Hot 2nite"* came on. Tukey stood up on her knees and began to undress Cody. Tiki did the same to Dulow. Once they were undressed, the girls admired the tall, chiseled black studs. Cody's organ appeared to hang down to the middle of his thigh.

Tukey licked her lips hungrily as she began to caress it. "What ya workin' wit' over dere, gurl?" she inquired to see if Dulow measured up to Cody.

Tiki held his heavy dick inside her hand. "Me doan know how long, but it's about three inches t'ick," she said enthusiastically.

Both guys were ordered to lie on the beds. The pimp glasses were then placed inside their hands and they were told to drink up.

Tukey lay down beside Cody with one hand on his chest and one leg over his. While he drank, she ran her tongue over his upper torso. Cody looked to Dulow who was receiving the exact same treatment. He smiled, then closed his eyes, enjoying her tender lips on his body.

The feel of his hard flesh made Tukey cream between her legs. She sucked his nipples savagely while rubbing her pelvis up and down his leg. The small hairs on his thigh stimulated her clitoris, causing her to rub harder. She ran her tongue up his neck and all the way to his ear.

"Ya want to slip away into a world of Ecstasy?" she whispered.

"Yesss," he said in a low voice.

She picked up two red pills that were on the table between the two beds. After swallowing one of them, Tukey placed the other inside Cody's mouth. She took the glass from him and filled her jaws with the cognac. Then she pressed her lips up against his, spitting the fluid into his mouth. Cody swallowed without thinking twice about it.

The mixed CD switched to Beyonce's *"Naughty Girl."* Tukey stood up on the bed. Raising her hands high above her head, she began swaying her thick hips from side to side. Cody lay there mesmerized by the pretty woman with the perfect body dancing over him.

Feeling the music, Tukey slipped away into her own little world as she waited for the pill to take effect. Tiki and Dulow were in the 69 position, but they weren't performing oral sex. Dulow's eyes were closed while she licked his inner thighs and kneecaps. Gently, he massaged her butt cheeks with his huge hands.

Three songs later, Tukey peered down and saw beads of sweat on Cody's forehead. Smiling devilishly, she knew that the pill was taking effect. His body would be so sensitive now that a simple touch would make him squirm like a snake. Spreading his legs with her feet, she lay down between them. Reaching down beside the bed, Tukey picked up the Hennessy bottle and took a swallow to wet her dry throat. She gently began to stroke his hard dick. His face changed expressions multiple times. Soon, Cody felt her tongue and warm saliva on his balls.

"Shiiit!" he moaned with pleasure. That encouraged her to proceed.

Tukey licked him from his balls to the very tip of his dick, then started licking precum out of the hole. Before he knew it, half of his swipe was jammed down her throat. It took her several tries before she forced the tasty head of his dick down into her esophagus.

The intense feeling caused him to grab hold of her dreads. Removing his hand, Tukey continued to suck it viciously. The taste of that sweet dark meat made her cum on herself.

"Oooh shit, baby!" he moaned. "I love you." Yep, the pill was definitely working.

Tukey rubbed his big, juicy dick under her chin and across her face. Just the feel of it made her want to cut it off and sew it on Anitra. Seriously, she hoped that she didn't get sprung on his d.i.c.k.

* * * * *

An hour had passed. Cody had Tukey doggy style, facing Tiki's direction. Dulow had Tiki in the same position only she was facing Tukey's direction. Subconsciously, they both gritted their teeth while they pounded hard dick into the two girls vigorously.

"Ah! Ah! Ah! Ahhh!" they all grunted and moaned with

each powerful stroke. The potent narcotic had both of the horny girls cumming back to back while the men went long and strong.

Tukey could see the pleasureful and painful expression that Tiki's face was making and vice versa. She pushed back on Cody meeting him pound for pound.

"Ooh, I ... lo ... lo ... ve ... yu ... Off ... icer," Tiki stuttered as her eyes rolled into the back of her head. She propped her left leg up on the headboard so he could drive even deeper. Moaning, groaning and naked flesh slapping together could be heard all out in the hallway.

* * * * *

Ten minutes later, the cops had both girls side by side on the same bed. They had their feet over their shoulders while they ran dick in and out of them. All four of their backs and asses were dripping with perspiration. And they all gritted their teeth while saying, "I love you," through tight lips. Gritting, sweating and repeatedly saying, "I love you," were just three of the side effects of using Ecstasy.

Tukey held Cody's ass, guiding him to her G-spot, while she raced for her fifth orgasm.

"Please doan cum," Tukey pleaded, knowing full well that it didn't make a difference if he did or not. The pills would provide him with enough stamina to go all night.

Not one time while they were popping pills and having sex did either of the cops think about their wives or their occupations.

Chapter 11

Arie and three of her friends sat around the table laughing, playing cards and drinking rum. Unopened presents, torn up gift wrapping paper and toy parts were all over the floor and under the Christmas tree. Mi'kelle, six of her cousins and two of her friends were in her bedroom trying on their new clothes. They couldn't wait to wear them to school after the break.

Every once in a while the kids would start arguing over something petty, then Arie would storm in cussing and yelling until they stopped. Every time she came in, she would threaten them by saying, "If me have tu come back, me promise dat yu woan like it." Mi'kelle estimated that she had made that same threat five times already and nothing had happened.

Tukey and Anitra were standing on the back deck sipping Dom out of champagne glasses. They held one another, enjoying the unbelievably warm weather. Tukey gazed into Anitra's green eyes.

"Merry Christmas, baby," she said happily.

"It wouldn't be without you," Anitra said, then she raised her glass for a toast. "Here's to you, Tukey. You've sacrificed so much so we could live like queens. And you're doing all you can to save the life of a friend, no matter what the cost." Her eyes began to water. "I love you. Cheers to you, baby."

"Here, here," a voice said behind them.

They turned around and were shocked to see Shantí standing there, teary eyed. She walked over to them and the three embraced in a group hug.

"Thank you so much, Tukey," Shantí cried.

"Doan ... mention it," Tukey replied weakly. "Us going tu be together till God do us part." She kissed Shantí on the forehead, then broke the embrace. "Come on y'all. Let's go eat some curry goat."

* * * * *

The doorbell rang.

Tukey was too busy talking to her daughter to answer it. Anitra strolled barefoot over to get the door while picking a piece of goat off of her plate. She opened the door without peeping out first.

"Yes?" she said, staring at the well-dressed, handsome man. He had a wrapped gift inside his hand.

"Is Shantí here?"

"Yes. Come in," she said, motioning with her free hand. "You must be Derrius."

"Yep." He smiled. "And you must be Anitra?"

"Mm hm." She focused her attention on the gift. "Who's that for?"

"Aw," he said, looking down at the box as if he had forgotten about it. "This is for her niece, Mi'kelle. I've heard so much about her from Shantí that I feel like she's my niece, too."

"I'll take it. You can go over there," she pointed to the bar on the north side of the living room, "and fix yourself a drink while I go get Shantí."

Derrius regarded the lavish house in awe. It was big with high arched ceilings and stained hardwood floors. A huge chandelier hung from the ceiling just above the long mahogany dining room table. Four middle-aged women laughed drunkenly while attempting to finish a card game. He didn't see the men who were in the TV room, watching a basketball game and telling lies.

*   *   *   *   *

The alcohol that Shantí consumed earlier that night came traveling back up through her mouth, violently. Every day was becoming a struggle for her stomach to hold down various drinks. When she finished, she moved over to the sink and cut the water on. Her eyes were sunken and dark circles were forming around them. Now looking in the mirror, she did not recognize the woman she saw. Her skin was blotched and her cheeks were hollowed.

Quietly she began to sob, knowing that her time on this earth was nearing the end. She refused to let Tukey and Anitra know how badly she had been feeling lately. It was her problem; she had already burdened them enough.

Anitra knocked on the door. "Shantí? You in there?"

"Yes," she said, trying to disguise the stress in her voice.

"Well hurry up! Somebody's here to see you."

"In a minute." She rinsed her mouth out with some Scope that was in the medicine cabinet. After she fixed her makeup, she exited the bathroom.

Tukey and her Uncle Dave were standing in the hallway talking when Shantí flew past them with her head down. Tukey sensed that she was trying to avoid her, but she didn't say anything about it.

Dave stood in front of Tukey, motioning with the glass in his hand while he talked to her. He was jet black with a low haircut. Six platinum chains were draped around his neck and he sported a diamond ring on eight of his ten fingers. Four solid platinum teeth filled the bottom row of his mouth.

"So, rude gurl," he was saying, "how yu like it now dat yu doing ya own t'ing?"

Tukey shrugged. "It has its ups and downs, but me like de excitement."

"Right. Ya know if yu have any trouble, me will send me bumba claude posse down here in a hurry."

"Trouble is minor. Not'ing me cyaah handle."

Slowly he nodded his head up and down.

"Did yu bring de pills?"

"Me did," he confirmed. "Me brought brown ones, red ones and green ones. Me got it all, mon." He sipped his drink. "Dat shit really sells down here."

"Mon, me club is poppin'. Two t'irds of de crowd be white people who are tryin' tu get t'izzed out. Me mek so much money off Ex on de weekends dat me doan have tu sell blow."

Pointing a slim, jeweled finger at her chest, Dave said, "Never settle in dis business, Tukey. Sell it all and get it all while ya ca'an ... and give nuttin' back. Yu hearin' me?"

She nodded.

"Good." He took another sip. "Me never told ya how grateful me am for ya taking out Keith. Him killed me brot'er, den yu killed him no matter what bond ya had. Dat's loyalty tu de family. T'anks." He stuck out his hand.

"Ya welcome," she said, shaking it. Dave didn't know that wasn't the only reason she did what she did. Keith had hurt her in more ways than one.

Dave said, "De only problem dat me have now is transportin' de shit. Me lose a shipment every t'ree trips. Ya lucky dat me got de pills here safely dis time." He sniffled, then pinched his wide nose. A habit that he'd developed since he started using cocaine years ago.

Derrius stood in the living room between Tiki and Peko while they lusted over him. He shifted his gaze from girl to girl as they both drilled him with questions. Who was he? Did he have a woman? Did he think they were cute? Did he know how to eat pussy? Was he gay, etc.

Finally Shantí showed up and rescued him. His gray eyes lit up at the sight of her.

"He's with me," she said, taking him by the hand. "Come on, baby."

"I guess I'll see you two later," he said, following Shantí.

The two sisters' hearts skipped beats. They had just realized what they had almost gotten themselves into. Derrius was the guy who Tukey had told them about. The one with AIDS who Shantí had met at the bar. All it would've taken was a couple Ex pills and a few drinks and Derrius could've had his way with either of them. And they both knew it.

As they both turned, headed in different directions, they thought of how easily they could've ended up victims of the AIDS virus, had they met him in another place. From that moment on they would be more cautious about who they gave it up to. And they would definitely start using condoms.

Shantí led Derrius upstairs to the guest room. While she secured the door, he took a seat on the comfortable bed. She turned around and stared at his cute face and broad shoulders. He motioned for her to come here.

She took her time walking to him. Reaching up, he pulled her down on top of him. Knowing that not long ago she was bent over the toilet, throwing up, Shantí avoided kissing Derrius in the mouth. Instead, she gave him her cheek and neck to caress with his lips.

His tender touch made her want to cry. Usually when a good thing came into her life, it would leave just as quickly as it came. That's how she knew that her life would be over soon. Shantí held him tight, savoring the moment while there was still time.

He rolled over on top of her. A frown appeared on his face after he saw the tears in her eyes.

"What's wrong?" he asked softly.

Sniffling, she murmured, "I love you. But I know that

what we have will soon be over."

Understanding her meaning, he said, "I love you, too." He wiped the tears from her cheeks. "Let's just enjoy each other while we can."

Chapter 12

The 63rd Street Police Station was crowded this New Year's Eve. It was still early and already civilians were being brought in for DWIs and DUIs. This year they put more cops on patrol, hoping to be able to stop the violence before it started.

Young officers, black and white, were amped with anticipation, knowing that before the clock struck twelve, something major was gonna jump off. Strapped with tasers, guns, handcuffs, mace and whatever else they needed to assist them, they jumped into their assigned patrol cars and took to the streets.

It was cold outside, unlike the week before, but the weather didn't stop people from being out and about and preparing for whatever New Year's party they would be attending.

Cody sat at his desk typing up a report for a CCW arrest that he had made earlier. Without asking to be seated, Captain Kirby sat down in one of the two chairs in front of his desk.

"Your wife called while you were out patrolling," she said, watching him closely.

"Yeah?" he said without looking up. "What she say?"

She picked up a sheet of paper off his desk and looked at it. "She won't be home when you get there. Said something about going to the gym."

Cody snatched the paper out of her hand and placed it back

on the desk.

"Attitude this morning?" she inquired.

Momentarily he stopped typing and gave her his full attention. "No. Is there something that I can do for you, Captain?"

"No. I'm just bored, so I dropped by your desk to fuck with you." She stood up. "But since you're in a cranky mo—"

"I'm sorry," he said, interrupting her. "I've had a lot on my mind lately."

"I understand. I'll leave you alone to your thoughts." Slowly, she began to walk away. She stopped suddenly. "Coffee later?" she said over her shoulder.

"You buying?"

"Yep."

"Then it's a date." He admired her thin legs and flat behind as she walked away.

* * * * *

A little while later, Cody was parked outside a convenience store waiting on Dulow's slow ass to come out. Reaching inside his coat pocket for a cigarette lighter, he felt something peculiar. He pulled it out to see what it was. It was the bag of pills that he took from Tukey the night he pulled her over.

Too busy examining the bag of pills, Cody didn't see Dulow come out of the store. Before he knew anything the door was opening and Dulow was sliding in next to him.

"What the hell is that?" Dulow inquired, sitting a brown paper bag down on the seat next to him.

"What do you think it is?" Cody said smartly. "You popped one the other night. It's Ecstasy."

"Man, is that what they had us on that night? I swear I was up for three days."

"Yeah, me too." Cody put them back inside his pocket. "But the high did feel good, I have to admit." He couldn't believe what he was confessing out loud.

Dulow whistled agreeingly. "It had me feeling too damn

good." He paused for a moment in thought. "I've been thinking about that night ever since. Even while I was having Christmas dinner with my family."

They both laughed.

"It reminded me of the first time I ever smoked a joint." He shook his head. "I've been thinking about Tukey, too. I better ... no, *we* better stop fucking with them before we end up losing our families."

"Let's just play it by ear," Dulow suggested. He wasn't ready to leave the two freaks alone just yet. "If they call, we gon' kick it with them. If they don't, cool. It was fun while it lasted."

Cody was deep in thought as they cruised up Prospect Avenue. Dulow looked out his window. Crackheads were loitering on corners, trying to solicit clientele for the hustlers that stood on post. At first sight of the police car they all began to scatter.

Two young black dudes in a Benz were driving on the side of them. Dulow gave them a friendly wave. The driver nodded. The first intersection that they came to, the driver of the Benz turned off, not wanting to be anywhere near them.

That could've been me, thought Cody. *I would have been as good of a hustler as any of them dudes.*

* * * * *

Anitra finished running her daily miles on the treadmill. When the belt slowed to a stop, she grabbed her towel off the guardrail and stepped off. She called for the maid to clean up her mess as she walked through the house, toweling herself dry.

Halfway up the circular staircase, Anitra heard the shower running in the bathroom. In her room she removed her clothes then strolled to the bathroom. Through the glass doors she could see Tukey sponging her naked body.

Tukey flinched when she heard the door open. Relived to see Anitra standing there holding a sponge, she stepped back, letting her in. The sweat beads dripping from Anitra's chin to her nipples made Tukey's nipples stiffen. She couldn't believe how her body reacted sexually to both men and women. She could remember a time when the thought of two women sleeping together would turn her stomach.

Tukey helpfully took the sponge from Anitra and applied some body wash to it. Anitra stood straight up while Tukey soaped her body.

"So how are things going with your cop friend?" Anitra inquired.

Tukey bent over, washing between Anitra's legs. "Me have not called him yet. Lift up ya foot." She squeezed the sponge over Anitra's toes, letting the soap run between them.

Anitra stared down at the top of Tukey's head. Tukey glanced up in time to catch her staring.

"What?"

Anitra hesitantly said, "Was it good?"

"Has sex ever been bad while ya on Ex? Get under de water so yu can rinse off. Hater!" she joked.

She let the water run into her mouth, then spat it out. She faced Tukey. "I'm not comfortable with you giving away my goodies like that."

Tukey seized her waist, pulling her up close.

"Me promise dat it's gonna pay off in de end," Tukey assured her. "Just be patient wit' me." She planted a kiss on her lips.

"Just be patient," Anitra repeated. "If you say so."

* * * * *

A little while later, Anitra sat in front of the computer inside the den typing up programs for the New Year's party. Frustrated with her uncreativeness, she snatched off her glasses and rubbed her eyes.

"Shit!" she yelled out in frustration.

Tonight was going to be off the chain and she wanted everything to be perfect. It was a pink party affair. Several contests would be taking place for various cash prizes. The best thong set, the tip drill and the cat-fighting contest were just a few events that would be taking place for the New Year.

Tukey strolled in carrying the cordless phone in her hand. She plopped down on the sofa that sat in front of a shelf stacked with books by various black authors. Anitra glared at her.

"Who you calling?"

The phone had already started ringing. Tukey put her index finger up to her lips, signaling her to be quiet. Anitra put her glasses back on and faced the computer.

Cody was tailing a blue Toyota while running a check on its license plates when his phone rang. Still in pursuit, he answered it.

"Hello."

"Do ya miss ya likkle Jamaican cuisine?" After she said it, she realized that "Jamaican cuisine" was what Keith called her. In the future she would not use it again.

"Why wouldn't I?" he responded.

Anitra overheard the sexy tone in which Tukey spoke and couldn't help but eavesdrop.

"Well, yu have not called me. Me was gettin' de feelin' dat y'all did not enjoy me and Tiki's company."

"That's not it. As a matter of fact, I was just talking to my partner about that."

Dulow regarded him curiously. "Who's that?"

Cody ignored him. "So what have y'all been up to?"

"Not'ing. Me been t'inking about dat good dick yu put in me dat night, mon."

Fed up with the disrespect that she was receiving from Tukey by talking freaky to Cody, Anitra got up and stormed out of the room. Tukey rolled her eyes at her.

"Speaking of the other night," Cody said, "I think we should—"

Dulow hit him on the shoulder. "Don't do it," he mouthed.

"Ask her can we do it again."

"Cody," she called.

"Yeah, I'm here." The Toyota that he was tailing had turned off.

"Me having a New Year's party at me club tonight. Why doan yu come by and have a few drinks? Me promise ya wifey woan be dere."

"I don't know, Tukey."

"What?" Dulow quizzed.

Cody covered the phone with his hand. "She wants us to come to her club tonight," he explained.

"I'll be there if he won't," Dulow yelled loud enough for her to hear.

"What doan ya know?" Tukey inquired. "Me pussy not hot enough for ya tu come back for seconds?"

"Don't go there with me. You could tell by how loud I was moaning that I loved it."

"Den it's all good. Me will be waiting, Officer Brown," she said, then hung up before he could object.

Chapter 13

By ten o'clock that night, Club No Draws was filled beyond its capacity and still had a line around the corner. Red and white strobe lights flashed around the room while white fog-like smoke rose from the floor. "*Dick Clark's New Year's Rockin' Eve*" was being shown on the huge projection TV that hung from the ceiling behind the stage.

Security was tight. Two people had already been arrested for trying to sneak in weapons. Big Corn and Tina were busy running up and down the bar, filling orders. They were selling four different types of Ex pills for the fiends who wanted to get thizzed out. So far, they had sold at least one pill to every person who bought a drink.

Local rappers Skatterman & Snug Brim were on stage performing their hit single, "*Lap Dance*." Tonight the girls were informed that anything goes. Tukey hired a film crew to tape the party. Tapes would be made available for a price at a later date, so if the girls wished, they could display their private parts. The strip club was having a mature night for males and females.

Chicken wings, fried fish and French fries were displayed on a long table. No one would have to drink on an empty stomach. Tukey had to give something away for free for all the money that she was going to make tonight.

Every so often, Tukey would survey the room to see if Cody was among the crowd of thizzers. Anitra was too busy playing host and enjoying the show to pay any attention to Tukey.

Several girls were turned around at the door for not having on pink drawers. Flashlight in hand, Guru searched every girl who came through.

After being warned by security to not cause any trouble, Herm and his crew bum-rushed the VIP. They ran their usual tab and instructed the waitress to keep the bottles coming.

Fuzzy and Black were over by the pool tables ordering round after round for themselves and the flock of hoes around them. Black was one of the judges for the best thong contest, so the contestants were trying to suck up to him, hoping to score some premature points.

Outside, Cody and Dulow pulled up to the valet in Cody's Suburban. Alf ran over to the big truck and opened the door for him. Cody stepped out dressed in a polo shirt, starched jeans and a pair of Birdman boots. Dulow sported a tan blazer, jeans and Perry Ellis boots.

Alf frowned at the five dollar bill that Cody handed him. It was no wonder Rhyme didn't rush to serve him. If the car or truck wasn't rimmed up, Rhyme wasn't interested in serving them. Tips were a big part of his take-home and he wanted the most for his services.

Cody eyed the long line unbelievingly. People would wait in line for an hour just to kick it. Tiki had just collected a bag of money from Guru when she saw Cody and Dulow out in the parking lot. She rushed outside to catch them before they reached the end of the long line.

"Cody!" she yelled. "Dulow!"

They turned and saw Tiki standing in the doorway. Her curves fit nicely into the Baby Phat jeans that she had on.

As they walked her way, she noticed how much better they looked in street clothes. They walked like two robots but they were still cute. *Umpf*, she thought.

Smiling warmly, Tiki embraced them when they reached her. She let them know that they didn't have to wait in line and that there was a table available for them in the VIP.

Their eyes sparkled with amazement at all the fine honeys prancing around, and just the club itself. Seeing all the jewels and iced-out grills made Cody feel out of place. He even saw a few people who he had arrested before.

A bottle of Cristal was chilling in an ice bucket next to their table. Tiki instructed the waitress to bring two champagne glasses and a couple of party hats. Then she apologized for having to leave them, but promised to return after she turned in the moneybag.

Cody bobbed his head to the beat of the music. While he eyed the room, he focused in on a short, stacked light-skinned girl wearing a blue sheer and lace thong outfit with money sticking out of her stockings. She didn't seem to be the least bit shy walking around with her ass out.

Mocha saw Cody staring a hole through her. She made a mental note to get at him before he left.

Tukey stepped up to the bar and was about to yell for Corn when she saw Cody in the mirror. He was sitting directly across from the stage. She couldn't hold back a smile, happy that he had chosen to spend his New Year's with her instead of his wife. After she checked her makeup, she went to join them.

Cody was laughing at something that Dulow was saying when he saw her coming. Her curves hugged a tight pink leather pantsuit. Her jacket only had one button fastened and she was braless. She swayed voluptuously over to their table.

Standing to give her a hug, Cody wrapped his arms around her, making her feel secure. Tukey broke the embrace, then motioned for the waitress. After she ordered another champagne glass, they all sat and engaged in a little small talk. Soon Tiki returned and joined their little party.

The four of them flicked up in the picture booth. They took one with both girls in the middle. Another with the cops grabbing their asses. Then they switched up. Tukey was grabbing Dulow's ass while Cody held one of Tiki's titties. The last picture was of all four of them making a toast.

Sweating and out of breath, Herm left the dance floor and sat at the bar for a breather. He saw Tukey and two unknowns giggling and playing touchy-feely in the VIP.

Herm thought Tukey was a bad bitch. If he didn't hate her so much he would probably try to get some of that Jamaican coochie. Just for some excitement, he thought about starting some shit with the new faces, but security had already warned him about causing trouble.

After a drink, Herm scanned the floor for a new dancing partner. He looked past eleven girls before he spotted what he was looking for. Peko, dressed in a pair of low-cut jeans that showed off her pink thong, was dancing between two guys. One palmed her booty while the other danced so close that his dick was poking her in the stomach.

Herm wondered if he could get her to leave with him. Peko was definitely worth shooting at. He broke out his pink card and ordered a couple Ex pills, then made his way over to the dance floor.

Tukey and Tiki talked the cops into hitting the dance floor. It was packed but they managed to squeeze their way into the crowd. Cody started out stiff, but after the alcohol took effect, he loosened up and stayed on beat.

The Game and 50 Cent's *"How We Do"* came thumping out of the loud sound system. Tukey backed her thang up while Cody pushed up on it. A dirty grin appeared on her face when she felt the hard lump in his pants. She bent over and touched the floor.

Cody held her waist, making sure that she didn't get away from him. The pleasant smell of her Burberry perfume filled his nostrils. From that moment on, his life would never be the same. Soon he would be spoiled on clubs, money and the broads that came along with it all.

* * * * *

Eight songs later, Tukey took a break and let Cody mingle with the crowd. She spotted Peko leaning over the pool table preparing for a shot while Herm helped her out from the rear. Slowly, she crept up on them to see what was going on. By the time she made it over there, Peko was sitting on the edge of the table getting her breasts fondled.

"Me see yu and me cousin are getting tu know each other well, mon," Tukey said to his back.

Herm turned around with a drunken smirk on his face. "Hey, Tukey," he said loudly. Sweat was pouring down his beefy face. The wild look in their eyes said that they both were thizzin. So he was probably in love with everyone that he came in contact with.

"Wha'sup, Herm?" She decided to use the moment to gain his friendship. "Tell de waitress dat ya next bottle is on me."

Peko adjusted her strapless shirt so that her nipple wouldn't be showing. She was ashamed that Tukey had caught her like that. Especially with Herm of all people.

"Hi," Peko said bashfully.

Peko noticed that there wasn't a trace of anger on Tukey's face. But being that she was high on Ex, she really wasn't sure of what she was seeing.

"Tukey, I'm in love with your cousin," Herm said excitedly. "I love you, too."

"Den why doan us start gettin' along?" Tukey stuck out her hand.

Instead of shaking it, he threw his arms around her, hugging her tight. Even though Herm was fucked up, he was perfectly aware of how her chest felt up against his.

"Don't worry 'bout nothin'," he said drunkenly. "From now

on, you and me cool."

"Me gonna hold yu tu dat." Tukey fixed her gaze on Peko. "Mek sure ya show him a good time, huh."

Peko smiled weakly. "Me will."

"OK," Tukey said, still eyeing her. She gave Peko one last look before she walked away. She stopped at bar #2 and told Tina to send a couple of Naked Bitches over to Cody's table. A "Naked Bitch" was a type of Ecstasy pill.

Tiki was sitting between the two cops at their table. They were watching the tip drill contest take place on stage. A brown-skinned, semi-attractive waitress came over with a folded napkin in her hand and placed it on the table.

"Boss lady says for y'all to drink up," she said. Picking up the Cristal bottle, she refilled their glasses. Dulow unfolded the napkin and saw the blue pills.

"Hurry up and pop 'em," Tiki encouraged them. "Me know ya remember how good it felt de last time." She placed her hand on Dulow's leg.

Dulow looked at Cody, shrugged, then swallowed the pill, washing it down with champagne. Cody hesitated as he thought about the oath that he took as a cop. Dulow didn't seem to mind, so why should he? Finally, he swallowed it.

Tiki found them amusing. "Who in dis whole club would t'ink yu guys were pigs, mon?"

Dulow refilled his glass. "Baby, the way I feel right now," he said, "I could care less about being a cop. Fuck the police!"

Cody laughed so hard that he spat out his drink.

"Ya feel like a real man now, huh mon?" Tiki said. She threw her arm around him.

"Sho ... in the fuck do," he stuttered drunkenly.

She snickered as she watched him down glass after glass of Cristal. Soon after the pill took effect, he would become thirsty enough to drink her pee pee. Feeling kinky, Tiki unbuttoned her pants, then pulled them down to the middle of her thigh.

"Hand me dat bottle," Tiki told Dulow.

Eager to see what she had planned, he quickly obliged. Carefully, she tipped the bottle, pouring the champagne into her panties. She quivered as the cool liquid ran down her warm flesh.

"Suck it outta me panties, baby." She held her panties open revealing her soaking wet kinky bush. He glanced around bashfully. Impatiently, she grabbed the back of his head, pushing his face down between her legs.

A shocked expression appeared on Cody's face after he saw how freely they did their thang out in open view. Little did he know that the club catered to an Ex crowd. And where there was Ex, there was sho' nuff gonna be sex. What Dulow was doing under the table was just one of the many sex acts that went down under the roof of Club No Draws.

Anitra announced that the cat-fighting contest was about to start. All the contestants needed to take the stage. Cody grabbed the champagne bottle and walked up to the stage. He wanted to get a closer look at the freak show.

He grimaced at some of the freaky shit that went on up there. It was pathetic how a woman would degrade herself for a measly thousand-dollar cash prize.

Mocha Cream snuck up behind him and squeezed his ass. He turned around expecting to find Tukey standing there. Instead, he saw the girl from earlier gazing up at him with a grin on her face.

"Wha'sup, sexy?" she said in her childlike voice. "I ain't never seen you up in here before."

Mocha helped him by wiping the sweat off of his forehead. His eyes wandered down to her breasts that came within inches of touching him.

"See something you want?" she asked, inching closer.

He licked his lips. "As a matter of fact I do," he said flirtatiously. "Why something as fine as you walking around in a thong and high heels?"

She nodded toward the strip club. "I'm working. I've got a show coming up in a few minutes."

"Aw yeah? Maybe I'll come watch. What's your name?"

"Mocha Cream," she replied, extending her hand.

"Cody." He shook it.

"Nice to meet you, Cody." Looking over toward the stage, Mocha saw that the white girl, Vanilla Split, was almost through performing. "Let Mocha give you a lap dance, baby. Mocha will make you cream in your pants."

"Maybe later." Sweat was dripping from his head and he found himself talking through a closed mouth.

"You thizzin, huh?" she asked, recognizing the symptoms.

"If that's what you call it, yeah," he replied.

"Wanna see something?" Reaching down, she pulled the front of her thong to the side so he could get a glimpse of her shaved pussy.

Cody stepped back so he could get a good look at the tattoo on her pelvis. It was a tipped over mug that spilled liquid down toward her hole. The words "Take a sip" were tatted across her flat stomach.

"I like that," he said, smiling.

Taking him by the hand, Mocha began pulling him toward the strip club. "Ya know this kitty can be bought," she said. "For the right price, I can be your toy for the night.

"I love you, Mocha," he said slowly.

"Yeah. Mocha loves you too, baby."

They had come within a few feet of the strip club when Mocha felt Cody being pulled away from her. Curiously, she looked back and saw Tukey pulling him in the other direction.

"Him taken," Tukey said over her shoulder.

"Damn, Tukey, why can't I have 'em?" Mocha could feel the money slipping away from her.

"Sell dat shit tu somebody else."

"Hatin' ass bitch!" Mocha said under her breath.

Tukey was furious that Cody had let Mocha take him that far. She had to do something to regain his attention. When they got to her office door, she began kissing him roughly. Without looking, she reached back and twisted the doorknob.

"What're we doing?" he inquired.

"Me want a quickie," she murmured.

* * * * *

At five minutes to midnight, the waitresses began passing out free glasses of champagne. Everyone was about to toast the New Year. Tukey had showered in the strippers' locker room, and now she was on stage with Anitra, Shantí, Peko and Tiki. All of them had one arm around the neck of the other while they held their glass inside their free hands.

Everybody had their party poppers, whistles and hats on while they waited for the big moment to arrive. On the projection TV, they watched as the huge ball began to lower on Times Square.

Cody and Dulow had become sick and were helped by security to a hotel room. Part of Tukey's plan was to break up their happy homes, especially Cody's. A married man staying out all night was a sure fire way for him to fall out with his spouse. Tukey would be there to listen to his problems when he needed a friend. She was setting the stage for a partnership between them and the law. She couldn't lose.

Tukey gazed at the thizzed out crowd of mostly white girls through glassy red eyes. Fuzzy and Black were smiling as usual. Herm was barely standing. Tukey grinned thinking about how she could use Peko's pussy to her benefit. Maybe she would offer her to Herm as a peace offering to seal the gap in their friendship.

Anitra started the ten second countdown and the crowd joined in.

"Ten, nine, eight, seven, six, five, four, three, two, one ...

Happy New Year!" They all shouted. Everyone clinked their glasses with the person next to them.

Anitra and Tukey shared their first kiss for 2005. They kissed for what seemed like an hour as fireworks popped outside, but it wasn't even a minute.

Chapter 14

Kenny, still banged up but up and running, dropped Tiera off at about two o'clock in the morning. After a long kiss goodbye, she dashed into the house to get cleaned up before Cody got home. Since he was supposed to be working New Year's Eve night, she crept off with Kenny to a party at his friend's house. Ever since he had gotten shot, he became more cautious about the places where he hung out.

When the clock struck twelve, Tiera had her legs wrapped around Kenny while they brought in the New Year with multiple orgasms.

After a long, hot shower, she brushed the taste of Kenny's dick out of her mouth. She would never go as far as kissing Cody with Kenny's cum fresh on her breath. Tiera slipped on her pajamas, then hopped into bed. She desperately wanted to fall asleep before he returned home. Finally, after about ten minutes of lying in the dark, she dozed off.

Beep! Beep! Beep!

Smacking her lips, Tiera rolled over, ducking her head under the covers. The alarm clock continued to beep. Finally, she gave in. Getting up out of the bed, she groggily stepped over to the dresser and shut off the alarm.

After falling back on the bed, she rolled her body up in the covers and shut her eyes. Something was wrong. Her eyes popped open, then she turned to the left. Cody wasn't there. Tiera didn't have to look at the clock to find out that it was ten o'clock in the morning. Cody should've been home hours ago.

"Cody!" Tiera yelled toward the open bedroom door. She angrily jumped up to search the house for him. "Cody!" she yelled again on her way down the stairs.

There was no sign of him. The house looked the same as it did eight hours ago. She snatched up the phone, dialing his cell number. She impatiently listened as it rang and rang until the voicemail picked up.

"Where the fuck have you been all damn night!?" Tiera yelled into the phone. "Call your wife. Better yet, bring yo' ass home." She slammed the phone down on its base.

A little over an hour later, Tiera was standing in the window smoking a cigarette, awaiting his return. She couldn't believe that he had the audacity to stay out all night, lying like he had to work overtime. As if she hadn't been in the arms of another man just hours before. She was just upset because he was coming in later than she did.

Hopefully, Cody won't check his voicemail and learn that I'm already home, Tiera thought. She remembered telling him that she would be at her sister's getting drunk. Now she could bust him before he could wash the bitch's smell off him.

By the time their Suburban pulled into the driveway, Tiera was on her fifth cigarette. She crushed it out in the ashtray, ready to check his ass the minute he walked inside the door.

Cody stepped out of the truck, letting the cold air blow on his face. His stomach was feeling queasy and his head was pounding. He prayed that Tiera had spent the night at her sister's house. If she caught him coming home this late and out of uniform, there would definitely be a fight.

Tiera was standing there with her arms crossed, tapping

her foot when he came in. Her nose wrinkled up after she smelled the stark reek of alcohol coming out of his pores. And the clothes he had on were not a part of the uniform that he left in yesterday.

Cody peered at her angry face, dumbfounded. The queasy feeling in the pit of his stomach was no longer just from the alcohol, but also from fear. He was afraid of what was about to happen next.

"You know ... it's funny," Tiera began in an even tone, "I don't remember you leaving the house dressed like that." Cody stood silently while his brain searched for a good lie to tell.

"Who is she?"

"Who is who? Look, don't start that shit with me!" Cody stepped past her. "I'm tired and I want to lie down."

"Don't start what shit?" Tiera hollered, walking after him. Cody stopped at the bottom of the staircase and faced her. "If I done something like that, you would be bashing my head into the fucking wall right now."

His icy stare caused her to flinch. "If it was you? Who in the hell do you think you're fooling? You know, I'm glad this came up. Every night for about a month now you've been leaving the house in a hurry, talking about hanging out with your sister. When I know damn well that y'all don't get along."

"What are you saying, Cody?" she asked curiously. "That because you think I'm cheating on you, you went out and cheated on me?" Tiera's eyes were watery.

"I'm saying that ... you ain't the angel that you pretend to be." With that, he turned and jogged upstairs.

Tiera ran after him. Catching up with him at their bedroom door, she grabbed his arm, spinning him around. Cody snatched away from her.

"Bitch, don't ever touch me like that again!" Cody yelled harshly. His hard words forced her to take a step back.

Tears were streaming down her cheeks. "So ... have you

been seeing someone?"

Looking down at Tiera's heaving chest, Cody started to feel pity for her. She was pretty, but lazy, nerve-wracking and slick as an oil spill. For years he had learned to live with her fucked up ways. Now that Tukey was in the picture, his family felt like baggage that was holding him back from life. A life that he had been deprived of for far too long. Tukey had given him a taste of a baller's life and that's how he wanted to live.

His silence answered her question. Tiera brushed up against him on her way into the room and slammed the door. Sitting on the edge of the bed, she placed her face inside her palms and sobbed uncontrollably.

Through the door Cody could hear Tiera's cries. He let out a gust of hot air, then slowly opened the door. Her small elfish body looked helpless sitting there crying like a child.

Cody sat next to her and cradled her in his arms. Tiera gazed up at him helplessly. Purposely he ignored her stare. Reaching around the back of his head, she pulled her face up to his. At first he tried to resist, but eventually he gave in and kissed her.

Tiera stopped and peered up at him. "I promise I've never cheated on you," she said convincingly. "You and our three kids mean too much to me to do anything that stupid. I love you."

Suddenly, Cody began to feel guilty about where he was last night. He couldn't believe what he had come so close to doing to his innocent wife. A couple nights of passion had him ready to turn his back on his family like Richie in the movie "*Harlem Nights*." Reality hit him in the face. He was a father with a nice home and a pretty wife. Why walk out on them just to be in the streets?

Cody laid Tiera on the bed and rolled over on top of her. She stared up at him lustfully. They began to kiss passionately. She raised her arms high above her head so he could easily pull off her shirt. Her small breasts were exposed. While she anxiously waited for him to seize them with his mouth, she noticed a strange look on his face.

"What's wrong, baby?" she asked, panting.

At first sight, Cody thought that they were small bruises on her chest. After further examination, he could very easily tell that they were marks of passion, put there by the lips of another man.

"You funky-ass bitch!" he shouted. Cody peered down at her lying face with both hate and hurt in his eyes.

"Why are you calling me names, Cody?"

Squeezing Tiera's neck, he lifted her off the bed. "What ... is wr ... ong ... with you?" she said as she struggled to get free.

After Cody got her inside the bathroom, he made her face the mirror, then pointed to the marks.

"What the fuck are those?" he inquired hotly. "Lie and I swear to God I'ma push your head through that goddamn mirror."

Breathing rapidly, Tiera stared in the mirror at the marks that covered her right titty. She was too busy rushing last night to notice them. Her mind flashed back to her sprawled out over Kenny's bed while he bit her nipples, causing her to let out a painful but pleasurable scream.

Her head being pushed violently into the mirror brought her back to reality. Screaming, Tiera placed her hands over her bleeding forehead. Unsympathetically, Cody pushed her out the door onto the floor. She was temporarily dazed.

"I promise I would never cheat on you," he mocked. "You and our three kids mean too much to me."

Tiera was crying like a child. Cody stepped back when she reached out for his leg.

"Keep your filthy hands off me. Now who is he?" he demanded. She cried even harder. "Who you been fucking while I'm at work?"

Sniffling, Tiera looked up at him. "While you're at work?" She chuckled. "I don't recall ever seeing you go to work like that. Not in those clothes. And you smell like liquor." She looked at the blood on her hands, then back to him. "So don't go casting stones when you've been just as sinful as me."

"I'ma show you sinful." He walked into the bedroom. Soon she heard drawers being snatched out of the dresser and onto the floor. Still woozy, Tiera got on her feet and went to see what he was doing. Cody had a suitcase open on the bed and was tossing clothes into it.

"Cody, what are you doing?"

"Fuck it look like I'm doing?" he said without stopping. "I refuse to let your trifling ass stay in my house another night."

Rushing toward him, Tiera grabbed Cody's arm trying to stop him. His defensive reflexes caused him to smack her across her face. She stumbled back onto the bed.

"Cody, please don't do this!" she pleaded, holding the side of her face. "Go ahead and whoop me. If I can forgive you, I know you can forgive me."

Cody stopped and glared at her. "Men do fucked up shit," he explained. "But when his wife gives herself to another man," he paused, "ain't no forgiving that shit."

"Don't try to justify the shit you done," she hollered, pointing her finger in his face. "The only reason why you're so eager to put me out is because you want to be with your whore. Whoever the bitch is. You can't just put your kids out in the streets."

"I'm no longer sure that they're mine. They might be that nigga who you've been creeping with kids."

Tiera's face balled up with rage. Suddenly she attacked him kicking and screaming. "You ... puuussy!" she yelled while she clawed at his face.

Grabbing her small wrist, Cody twisted her arm behind her back, then shoved her onto the bed. She landed on her face and quickly whirled around.

"Why are you trying to hurt me, Kenny?" She looked up at him with her hair hanging wildly into her face, not realizing what she had called him.

Cody dropped the handful of clothes inside the suitcase. His eyes narrowed as he said, "What you call me?"

"Co ... dy," she stuttered.

"The hell you did," he said angrily. "You called me Kenny." He nodded his head knowingly. "So that's where that bullshit came from a few weeks ago."

Tiera eased back up against the wall after seeing the enraged look on his face.

Their white neighbor, Mrs. Mathis, was jogging in place on her walkway, warming up for her morning run. Her long blond ponytail bounced up and down while she admired her impressive set of bouncing knockers. She stalled for a minute, hoping that Cody's handsome self would come out with the trash. She knew that he lusted after her muscular legs and tight ass when she jogged past him.

Her blue eyes bulged with excitement after she heard his front door opening. To her surprise, out flew two suitcases that crashed on the ground, followed by Tiera being shoved out with it. The door slammed behind her. Mrs. Mathis watched in astonishment as Tiera picked herself up off the ground. Blood trickled down the side of her head.

"Oh my God!" Mrs. Mathis exclaimed, then ran to her aid.

From the living room window, Cody could see Mrs. Mathis helping Tiera next door to her truck. Every few steps Tiera would look around to see if Cody was coming. Mrs. Mathis had never known Cody to do such a thing before.

Mrs. Mathis had pulled her 4Runner out of her driveway when Cody bolted out of the front door, running up to her SUV.

"Pull off! Pull off!" Tiera shouted. "He's crazy."

"You call the police on me and I'll divorce you for infidelity and you won't get nothing!" Cody yelled into the open window of the moving vehicle. He stood in the middle of the road breathing hard, watching as the taillights disappeared down the road.

Chapter 15

A week later, Tukey drove her Hummer out of the nail salon's parking lot. As she neared the intersection of 39th and Rainbow, a police car drove by, headed in the opposite direction. She thought about Cody. Even though he was just supposed to be a pawn in her plan, she found herself thinking about him a lot.

She thought that whoever Cody's wife was, she should consider herself lucky for being able to lock down that sweet meat. Although Tukey loved Anitra, she wouldn't mind sharing her home, and bed, with a real man like Cody on a more permanent basis. But Anitra would never go for it. They would be fighting over the coochie like two dogs. She smiled at the thought of it.

Tukey unclipped her phone off of her hip. "Cody," she said into the phone, then it automatically dialed his number.

"Hello," he answered in a gruff voice.

"Yu sleepin' dis time of day?"

Cody sat up on the sofa wiping sleep from his eyes. "That's what I usually do on my days off." He picked his Newports up off the table. "How about you? Don't you ever get tired of clubbing all night?" The unlit cigarette dangled from his lips as he spoke.

Tukey made a right turn onto Ward Parkway, keeping her

eye on the police car two cars behind her. "Me didn't club last night." She giggled. "Is dat all yu t'ink me do?"

"Really Tukey, I don't know what to think of you." He lit the cigarette. "Why don't you tell me about Ms. Tosh?"

"Have yu ever had jerk chicken?"

"I don't think so."

"Me know dis great Jamaican restaurant on ... ya know what, on second t'ought, me have a yen for some ribs. Meet me at KC Masterpiece on de Plaza and me will tell ya sum t'ings about me. OK?"

"I'ma need a couple of hours. I got to make a run by the department to submit a urine sample. In other words, a drug test. Then I'll be there."

"Doan worry yaself about da Ex pills. It only takes a couple days for it tu get out of ya system."

"All right, I'll see you in a lil bit."

"Cody, next time brush your teeth when you wake up, before ya start smoking."

He laughed. "You're a funny girl."

* * * * *

Two hours later, Tukey sat inside the parking garage watching *"Friday After Next"* on the many TV screens inside her truck. Through her windshield she could see Cody's Suburban pull into the garage. She could tell it was Cody by his correct posture. He sat erect like a rookie cop fresh out of the academy. She couldn't believe how square he had become over the years.

Cody didn't see her when he walked by her truck. Tukey honked the horn. When their eyes met she motioned for him to get in.

"Hey."

"How you doing?"

"Fine," she said, staring at him. If she wouldn't have been on her period, she would've fucked him right there in the garage. Tukey visualized him wearing a red fitted ball cap with a jersey to match and a platinum ... no, rose gold chain around his neck. *Man, he would look so fine*, she thought.

Cody admired the interior of the truck. The walnut wood grain, the TVs inside the visors, the MP3 player and the platinum ring with the huge princess cut diamond on her finger. The girl was doing too much.

Tukey fired up a Blueberry Royal Blunt. After she hit it a couple times, she tried to pass it to him.

"Nah, I'll pass."

"Come on, mon," she pleaded with smoke flowing out of her nostrils. "Yu took ya piss test already. Dis will mek yu hungry before us eat." She waved it in his face.

Cody wondered why it was so easy for her to persuade him to do wrong. Knowing that he shouldn't, he took the blunt anyway. Cody inhaled too deeply and immediately started choking. He almost dropped the blunt on the leather upholstery.

Tukey hurriedly snatched the blunt before it fell.

"Green-ass nigga," she said jokingly.

"You think that's funny, huh?"

"Very funny," she admitted. "Doan worry, baby." She put her hand on his head, caressing his soft hair. "Me gonna tek good care of yu."

* * * * *

After they finished filling their bellies, Cody followed Tukey to the ATM to grab some cash. They stopped at every store on the plaza, spending big money in all of them. She bought him shoes, jeans, shirts, cologne and had him fitted for five suits.

When night fell, they got high again and caught a comedy show at the theater. Tiera had called his phone so many times that he was forced to cut it off. The cold night air blew on their faces as they walked around the plaza. Cody tried not to think about his wife and the kids. He had found a new love.

Not only was Tukey a freak, she was paid and pretty. At the

end of the night, they stood in the garage putting Cody's bags inside his truck. After a long hot kiss, they parted ways.

Cody couldn't believe that they didn't end the night wallowing under some crisp bed sheets. Tukey didn't tell him that it was that time of the month. She wanted him to believe that it was by her own will power that she resisted her sexual urges to take him home with her.

* * * * *

Cody got up early the next morning, took a brief hot shower, then clothed and fed himself. It felt good waking up alone. He now had the freedom to do whatever.

On the sofa, he picked up the remote turned the channel to BET. R. Kelly and Jay-Z's video, *"Big Chips,"* was playing. He observed the clothes they wore and their moves.

Half-naked freaks surrounded them. Cody's mind began to drift. He had taken Jay-Z's place in the video. In his dream he was throwing hundred-dollar bills in the air. He desperately wanted that life to become his reality.

* * * * *

Tukey watched the tsunami disaster on TV while she hurriedly dressed for church. She walked down the hall to the bedroom where Mi'kelle stayed when she spent the night. She tapped on the door.

"Mi'kelle, hurry up!" Tukey yelled through the door.

Tukey's family practiced the Voodoo religion of the Loas & Gods. But when Keith was alive, Tukey and Mi'kelle used to attend Paradise Missionary Baptist Church with his mother. She didn't believe in it but out of respect for her man, Tukey switched her religion to Baptist.

Anitra had caught a cold and was too sick to attend. Tukey kissed her goodbye then joined Mi'kelle downstairs.

"Mama, let's go!" she yelled impatiently.

Once they were inside Anitra's car, Tukey had a thought. She should see if Cody wanted to come. It would be refreshing for her to show up with a handsome man. The undercover hoes that sat in the front pew wouldn't be able to keep their composure.

* * * * *

Cody gathered his dirty clothes and carried them to the basement. He hated having to separate and wash his own laundry.

Hearing his cell phone ringing all the way upstairs only added to his frustration. After dropping the soiled clothing on the floor, Cody ran to answer it. He was ninety percent sure that it was Tiera calling with another one of her meaningless threats.

"Hello."

"Mornin'," Tukey said. "How is me baby today?" Mi'kelle regarded her curiously.

"Terrible. I'm doing my own laundry," he complained.

"Awww, ya poor man. Next time me will send dem tu de cleaners for yu." He headed back down into the basement. "Come tu t'ink of it, doan yu have a woman for dem t'ings?"

Smiling weakly, Cody turned the washing machine on.

"Had a woman," he corrected her.

"Me sorry tu hear dat. Me here for yu if ya ever want tu talk about it, OK?"

"OK. Enough about her. I'm trying to move on."

"Good. Yu ca'an start by getting dressed and comin' ta church wit' me and me dawta."

"Ahhh ... all right. You coming to get me?"

"Yes." She nodded her head. "Wifey's gone and ya already want me tu come tu ya house. Ya must want me or sum't'ing?"

"Want? I mistakenly thought I had you."

"Not yet. But yu ca'an, depending on how down ya are for me." She threw out the bait.

Cody caught the hook, knowing that Tukey was trying to reel him in for something. Any other cop would have cut her off, but he chose to stay around and reap the benefits until he found out what she was up to.

Cody gave Tukey the address and informed her that he would be ready when they arrived. Tukey hung up.

"Mama's got a boyfriend. Mama's got a boyfriend," Mi'kelle chanted happily.

"Oh be quiet. Us still have not discussed dem boys dat ya have calling."

Mi'kelle hushed up and looked out the window.

"Yeah, dat's what me t'ought," Tukey said triumphantly.

* * * * *

Holding hands, she and Cody walked into the church while Mi'kelle lagged behind. The undercover hoes and so-called Christian women stared at them.

Tukey excused herself so she could take Mi'kelle to the basement to see her grandma. She didn't want Mrs. Banks to see her with Cody before she announced him.

Mrs. Banks was sitting behind her office desk preparing the Reverend's sermon when Tukey and Mi'kelle appeared in the doorway.

"Knock knock," Tukey said as they walked in. Mrs. Banks, still looking youthful, stood grinning broadly.

"My baby girl," she said, embracing Mi'kelle.

"Hi, granny," Mi'kelle said. She looked at her grandma's hair. "You've got gray hairs."

"I'm old, shit ... I mean shoot." She faced Tukey. "Hi," she said coldly. Mrs. Banks refused to accept the fact that her son had killed himself. She really felt that Tukey was behind it. When Tukey tried to give her some of the money that Keith left behind, she refused it. She would not spend the money that her son's blood was spilled for. In fact, she only spoke to Tukey because of Mi'kelle. The streets had claimed the lives of both of her sons, so her two grandchildren were all she had to hold on to.

"Hi, Mrs. Banks. Mi'kelle, would yu excuse us for a

moment?"

"OK," she replied. "Grandma, I'm spending the night with you, OK?"

"What about school?"

"I've got clothes over there. Paw Paw can take me to school." She looked at Tukey. "Besides, I wanna give mama a chance to be alone with her boyfriend."

Mrs. Banks looked at Tukey. "Oh, really?"

"Yep. He's cute, too. I'll be upstairs y'all." While she walked away, Tukey noticed that Mi'kelle already had a run in her stockings.

"She's getting so big," Mrs. Banks said as she stepped around Tukey to close the door.

"Yes her is," Tukey said timidly.

Mrs. Banks took a seat behind her desk, then glanced at her watch. "Services will be starting soon, so make this quick."

"Well," Tukey began slowly. "Me just wanted ya tu know dat me brung a frien' ... a male frien' wit' me today. Understand dat me doan expose Mi'kelle tu not'ing wrong dat me do. And me doan or have not brung any other men around her."

"What do you want from me, Tukey?"

Tukey's hands fidgeted. "Me want tu bridge de gap between us. And me doan just want tu be friends while Mi'kelle's around. Yu was like me mum when Keith was alive ... and me want tu go back tu dat."

"Tell me the truth. Why did my son," she paused and swallowed, "kill himself?" Mrs. Banks asked. Her unblinking eyes shot daggers at Tukey.

"Me swear me—"

"He was all that I had left!" she shouted, slamming her fist down on the desk. A tear rolled down her cheek. "Until you have the guts to tell me the truth," she glared at Tukey and continued, "the gap between us will only get bigger. You just better thank the Lord that I'm too much of a Christian to send you to join my son." She pointed a wrinkled finger at Tukey. "No one can ever explain to me why my son would up and kill himself, leaving me and his only daughter behind ... for no reason."

Mrs. Banks stood and walked over to the door. She opened it and said, "Now if you'll excuse me, church is about to start."

Tukey nodded slowly. On her way out she paused in the doorway and said, "Me sorry yu feel dat way, Mrs. Banks." Then she continued out the door.

An hour later, the tall, wide Reverend Teddy Taylor stepped up to the podium. He smiled, flashing a solid gold tooth that sat in the corner of his mouth as he glanced around the room at all his faithful followers. Opening his leather bound Bible, he began to speak.

Every time Tukey came to church, it seemed like the preacher was always directing his sermon toward her. Every word that would come out of his mouth would have something to do with what was going on in her life at the present time. And he would always be looking directly at her when he said it.

Reverend Taylor grabbed the microphone with his jeweled fingers, then stepped down off the podium. A wad of tissue was wedged between his thumb and the palm of his left hand. The church clapped and praised the Lord while he animatedly preached the gospel.

"Young people of today ... don't understand, nor do they believe in the word karma," he spoke in a loud, gruff voice. "The Lawd says that you reeepth ... whatever you soweth." He paused as he stared at the agreeing crowd. "Y'all don't hear me. In other words, what goes around," he made a circle with his finger, "comes ... right back on around. The Lawd also says that whatever is done in the dark will soon come to light."

From the front pew, Mrs. Banks looked back to see the guilty expression that was painted on Tukey's face. She had her arm around Mi'kelle's shoulders, looking out into space.

The preacher said, "It's a shame that a dead president's face printed on a piece of paper could cause one human being ... to kill another. You or me ... could lose our lives ... just because we possess more dead presidents' faces ... than the next man. Now, I've come up with a remedy for that." He wiped sweat from his brow.

"What's that preacher," a congregation member said between cheers and Amens.

"Give what you have," he shouted. "I said, give what you have ... to the church to feed the hungry. That way, you won't have to worry about the hungry ... killing you for it. Because you don't have it." The church chuckled briefly.

While they stood to applaud him, he took a minute to catch his breath. The loud claps brought Tukey back to reality. The last sermon that she heard him preach was about people of the same sex courting one another. At the time she felt like it was a shot toward her by way of Mrs. Banks. Now three months later, she pops up and he's preaching about something that happened in her past that she was trying to forget. Was it a coincidence, or was God trying to tell her something?

"Before I close this sermon," Reverend Taylor said, sixty minutes later, "I want you revenge seekers to know something. There is nothing ... nothing that another person can do to you, that is reason enough for you to kill him. When the Lawd said an eye for an eye ... he meant that the evildoer ... shall pay for his sins ... come judgment day."

Tukey noticed he looked directly at her as he continued, "He didn't mean kill him because your husband or boyfriend cheated on you. Or kill her because your girlfriend or wife cheated on you. Only God, and He alone, has the power to judge. And when judgment day comes, we will all kneel before Him, and be held accountable for our sins."

He held his free hand high in the air while his eyes swept the room. "For all of you gamblers out there. You know, the ones who take dangerous chances. The ones who throw rocks at the penitentiary. The ones who think they're too slick to be caught. The ones who seem to win every time they roll the dice. If you keep on rolling them, one day soon ... I say, one day soon!" he shouted. "Your luck ... is gonna run out."

Chapter 16

"Ooh! Ooh! Oooh," Peko moaned while Herm banged her to death. Soon he came and rolled over on the bed, panting.

"Goddamn! That shit was good. You wasn't lying either. Yo' shit is tighter than a mosquito's pussy."

Peko laughed while scooting up under him to feel his warmth. "Me warned yu about me Jamaican fuck, mon," Peko said, pleased with the outcome.

Reaching down between Herm's legs, Peko gently grabbed the tip of his condom and rolled it off his limp dick.

"How much yu want tu bet dat me ca'an get him back up?" She suddenly had a taste for some dick.

"I'll bet you five hundred you can't make me cum with your mouth," he said, knowing what she was getting at.

"Come on, rude boy. Me t'ought ya was a balla," she said, challenging his ego. "Bet two t'ousand dollars."

"Aw'ight, bet." They shook on it. Peko put her head down between his legs and sniffed. "Ew! Go take a shower first. Ya got cum juice runnin' all down ya balls."

Looking into her pretty dark brown eyes and baby face made Herm even more eager to fuck it. He hurried his bulk off the bed and rushed into the bathroom. As soon as she heard the shower come on, Peko picked up the phone and called Tukey.

Tukey was standing in line at Priscilla's purchasing some sexy lingerie for herself and Lateka. She was going to wear hers for Cody and Anitra, and Lateka was gonna wear hers for Tukey. Her triangle of sins had turned into a rectangle real fast.

Ciara's "*1, 2 Step*" started playing through her phone, alerting her that she had a call. Shantí, who was still shopping, held up a red lace nightie.

"How does this look?" she asked.

"Whorish," Tukey replied, then answered her call. Out of the corner of her eye, she saw Shantí brush her off. "Hello."

"Dis Peko. Me at de room wit' Herm."

"Good," Tukey said with a smile. "Yu know me doan trust him. Him called me and said dat he may need tu cop from us until him plug get at him. So feel him out a likkle bit. Ya know, engage in a likkle pillow talk."

"Gotcha." Peko peered at the closed bathroom door after she heard the shower shut off. "Me gotta go, gurl." She giggled. "Me about ta blow him head off."

"Ya nasty, gurl. How was him anyway? Could ya find it under dat big stomach?"

"It stuck out way past dat. If it's more under dere me doan wan it. Me gotta go." She hung up.

Herm stood at the edge of the bed, massaging his organ. "Dinner time. Come and get it."

On her hands and knees, Peko crawled over to him. Herm released his dick, letting it dangle before her eyes. Using her nose like a dolphin, she batted it up and let it fall into her mouth. He put his hand on her head, closed his eyes and prayed that he would lose the bet.

Several minutes later, Peko pulled his pulsating dick out of her mouth just as he came. The warm juice hit her on the chin and rolled down her neck. She hated the salty taste of cum.

Herm collapsed on the bed. Peko lay next to him, staring up at the ceiling. He looked over at her brown heaving chest. She felt his eyes on her. If he asked her if it was good, she was gonna be turned off. That was one of the lamest questions one could ask after sex. A man should be able to tell by a woman's loss of breath, her disfigured facial expressions and how many scars she left on his back if he'd done his thing well.

Herm asked, "Are you and Tukey real cousins?"

Peko gave him a look that said that should've gone without saying. "Ya cyaah tell me Jamaican? Duh!" She propped her left elbow up on the bed and held her head up with her hand. "Ya doan like Tukey or sum't'ing?"

"She cool. Just too arrogant."

That brought a smile to Peko's face. She stroked his nipple with her thumb. "Sometimes her is, but her good people."

"I ain't gon' doubt that. Shit, the bitch took—"

"Bitch?" she interrupted in a serious tone.

"Excuse me," he said, sensing her anger. "The broad ... won over thirty g's from me a few weeks ago, then started talking shit." He bit down on his bottom lip. "Man I wanted to beat that bi ... broad's ass."

Peko sneered. "Ya tu violent, Herm." She pulled her braids back out of her face. "Ya wouldn't try tu hurt her, would yu?"

"Nah," he replied. "She pisses me off, but I wouldn't take it that far. Tell her she ain't got to worry about me. My paper is too long for me to put some bullshit in the game."

"Speaking of paper," Peko said, "doan forget ya owe me two t'ousand dollars, mon. Or should me say, Mr. Quick Cum."

* * * * *

Three days later, Cody stood in a blue suit in the Jackson County Courthouse drinking coffee. His nicotine-craving lungs ached for a Newport. But it would be at least another hour before he would be able to smoke one.

Cody chitchatted idly with his fellow officers and a few attorneys that he knew. He tried not to appear nervous, but the new testimony that he was about to give made him a little jittery.

Cody couldn't believe that he was about to risk his career by changing his testimony for ten g's. Deep down inside, he knew that he wasn't doing it for the money. He would have done it because Tukey asked him to.

The prosecuting attorney, Richard Hulagan, stuck his shiny bald head out of the double doors that led inside the courtroom.

"Officer Brown, could you step inside for a minute, please?"

"Sure." He swallowed what was left of his coffee, then tossed the empty cup into the trashcan.

Inside the courtroom, Richard tried to prep Cody before the suppression hearing began. He had no idea that his star witness was about to alter his testimony in the defense's favor.

Brad W. Simon glanced at his watch for the fifth time while he impatiently paced back and forth in the courthouse hallway. He felt a sense of relief when he saw Tukey walking toward him with the defendants in tow.

"Well, I'm glad to see that you three finally decided to show up," he said sarcastically. "I said to be here early so we could go over a few things, like our strategy for one."

Tukey greeted him with a warm smile. "Chill out, and doan worry so much. Everyt'ings under control."

Brad eyed her suspiciously. "Oh? How can you be so sure?"

Tukey gave him an incriminating smile. Catching her drift, he put his hand on his forehead. "Oh no," he said disapprovingly. "Tukey ... why—"

"Shhh!" she said. "Just go in and act like yu an attorney."

Brad regarded Tiki and Peko, then turned back to Tukey. "If and when this thing blows up ... it's your ass. Am I clear on that?"

"Mr. Simon," she said, stepping closer to him. "Yu answer tu me. Me doan answer tu yu. Am me clear on dat?"

"Haven't we changed," he said, then walked into the courtroom.

Cody was sitting at the prosecutor's table while Richard stood over him discussing the case. Peko and Tiki took seats at the defense table next to their lawyer.

Tukey, sitting in the front row, faked a cough. Cody looked up and around at her. Hulagan continued talking about the case. She discretely nodded toward the door. He acknowledged her.

"Could you excuse me for a minute, Richard?" Cody said as he stood up. "Coffee is running through me."

"Sure, sure." Richard glanced at his watch. "We still have a few minutes."

"Be right back."

Tukey waited until he left before she trailed behind him. She caught up with him in front of the men's restroom.

"What's up?" he whispered.

"Just making sure yu not gonna back out on us."

Cody's eyes explored the hallway making sure that no one was coming. "Don't worry. By the time we leave the courtroom, Richard will be so mad that he'll be ready to quit."

Tukey sucked on her platinum teeth. "Good! When ya finished, ya money will find ya."

"Thank you. Now get back in there before old bald head becomes suspicious."

* * * * *

When Cody took the stand, he was asked to explain to the judge what happened that day. His story basically remained the same, except when he said that he pulled the two women over under false pretenses. He said that he never saw a bottle of alcohol, and he only pulled them over because he suspected that they were the two suspects that shot at him the week before. Who could fault him for following up on a hunch? Police cracked some of their biggest cases following their gut feelings.

Several times, Richard attempted to shut him up, but he kept on talking. Cody testified that after a ballistics check, the gun they found came back with negative results of being the weapon that fired three rounds into his police cruiser.

After thirty minutes of Cody's testimony, the judge had heard enough. He threw out the case and adjourned the court in time for lunch. The women gladly exited the courtroom along with Brad.

Cody stood to shake Richard's hand but he declined. While Richard angrily stuffed papers into his briefcase, Cody quietly made an exit. He felt bad for having to betray his trust, but the money that awaited him would lift his spirits quickly.

Richard furiously watched Cody leave the room. He had seen Tukey when she followed Cody out of the room before the hearing started. At first he thought nothing of it, but Cody's sudden change of testimony made him suspicious.

Cody happily stepped outside to his Suburban. His cold hands shook while he unlocked the truck. He was cruising up Pasco Boulevard when a red Magnum pulled alongside him. The driver signaled him to pull over. Cody followed it into an Amoco gas station. Anitra parked and got out. He watched as the attractive female strolled over to his truck and opened the passenger door.

"Can I get in?" she asked.

"Yeah, climb on in," he replied, still not knowing what she wanted.

Out of the pocket of Anitra's leather bomber, she produced a stack of bills that were bound by a rubber band.

"Tukey sends her regards," she said as she handed it to him. Anitra gazed at his handsome features. She had been gay for years, but she still found herself attracted to him. The vibes were so strong that she had to exhale.

"Thank you," he said, flashing a white smile. "And you are?"

"Huh?" She came back to reality. "Anitra. I'm Tukey's ah ... partner."

Cody gave her a knowing look. "Partner, huh? Well, you're

a fine one."

"Thank you," she replied bashfully. They gazed at each other not knowing what to say next. She cleared her throat. "Um ... well ... I guess I'll get going."

"All right now. Thanks again," he said, holding the money up.

Anitra put a little swing in her hips on her way back to her car because she could feel him watching her. She looked back just to be sure. He was. She smiled and continued on.

She's sexy, Cody thought while he watched her. Anitra's ass wasn't fat, but she had enough to shake. Her chest was near flat, but she had enough to suck. *I'd fuck her.*

"Let me stop," he said to himself, "before I let my dick fuck shit up for me." He pulled away.

* * * * *

Dulow and Dickey were on duty, but it was time for their lunch break. After grabbing a bite from Wendy's, they parked in the parking lot and began to eat.

"Sonsabitches got my check fucked up again," Dickie complained. "I'm getting sick of that shit!"

Dulow swallowed a piece of hamburger. "You can complain all you want. They're still gon' do it." He took a sip of Sprite. "If I was one of them white boys who knew something about computers, I'd be doing white collar crimes."

"Why?"

"Because, man. They can hit a big company for millions and only get a year or two if they get caught. We bust a crack dealer and he gets ten or better."

"Where is all this coming from?"

Dulow sighed. "What I'm saying is this. We are out here rounding up our own people ... excuse me, capturing our own kind for the white man to confine and make slaves out of. And the same laws that we enforce are designed for the whites to escape with a slap on the wrist. I don't know how we get any sleep at night."

Dickie smirked. "I sleep like a fed baby."

"Not me. And I haven't for the past couple weeks. Matter of fact, from here on out, I refuse to make another crack arrest."

"What are you gonna do then?"

"If I catch'em with crack, I'ma take it."

"If you gon' do all that, you might as well find a buyer for what you take."

"That ain't a bad idea," Dulow said seriously.

"Well," he said, chewing his food, "Count me in on whatever plan you come up with." He burped. "Casey, too." Casey was another close cop friend of theirs. Though he was white, he suffered from financial problems, too.

Knowing where his friends would be that time of day, Cody pulled into the parking lot. He was grinning broadly as he pulled alongside of them.

Dulow let down his window. "How did court go?"

Cody tossed the bundle of money at him.

"Like a charm," he replied.

"What's this?" Dulow examined the money.

"Hush money."

"Hush money?"

"That's what I said. Let me go inside and grab a baked potato real quick, then I'll tell you everything."

Chapter 17

Phones ringing, fax machines buzzing, keys being typed and officers consulting with one another were all that could be heard inside the 63rd Street Police Station. Detectives wracked their brains trying to piece together the clues of the latest homicide.

With a steaming hot cup of coffee in his hand, Cody stood in front of the copy machine flirting with a female officer. She was in her mid-thirties and wore a bad wig, but she still thought she was hot.

Cody was complimenting her on her new glasses when Captain Kirby stuck her head out of her office and yelled, "Sergeant Brown! Get in here, now!"

Handing Debra his cup, he went to see what was up.

"Have a seat," Kirby commanded. She marched around her desk and took a seat. "What's this shit I'm hearing about you changing your testimony in the middle of a drug hearing?"

Cody took a deep breath before responding. "I ... ah ... did what I thought was right." He chose his words carefully. The whole thing had taken him completely off guard.

Twila jumped up. "The right thing? Sergeant Brown, I don't believe I have to tell you how suspicious you made yourself look."

"Suspicious?" he said angrily, pretending to be offended. He raised his voice. "I made a bad and personal decision to pull those girls over, based on the fact that I *thought* they were the suspects that I was seeking."

"Big deal. You're not the first and won't be the last cop to take this job personal."

"Speaking of job, I wasn't on duty as a cop that day. I was working security for Friendship Village."

"And that's exactly why," she said, pointing a finger at him, "I'm not confiscating your badge and gun right now."

Cody stood glaring down at her. "That all?"

"No! The next time you pull a stunt like that, I will have you placed under investigation ... and suspended." She had a disappointed look in her eyes. "Now get outta my office, Cody."

* * * * *

In a barred-up, abandoned-looking house located in the mid part of Kansas City, Tukey, Tiki and Anitra sat around a table counting and bundling money to be stashed in the safe. There was so much money around that it made Anitra scared. Anything could happen when you were dealing with six and seven figures of illegal money. The feds could kick in, or worse, a thirsty group of niggas could be waiting on them to slip up.

Tukey wasn't worried. Unbeknownst to the rest of the clique, Dulow and Dickie were patrolling the perimeter, making sure that no one bothered them while they were doing whatever they were doing. They didn't know her exact location. She would never reveal that. Their job was to stay within a ten-block radius in case something popped off. If trouble came, she would hit a text on her phone that already had the address stored into it and they would come to the rescue.

Tukey's bling tone started playing.

"Hello."

"Hey, rude gurl. Is everyt'ing ready?" Dave quizzed.

"Tell ya driver tu hold up, unc. Me got t'ree of me own people dat's gonna come get it." She tossed a wrapped bundle to Peko.

"Me doan follow yu."

"Tiki will explain everyt'ing when her get to LA."

"Tiki's coming here?" he asked, confused.

"Yes. Me came up wit' a safe way tu move t'ings. But us will split de cost fifty fifty. Tiki will explain it all."

"Ca'an yu trust dem?"

"Me t'ink so. If not, us in deep shit."

"Well, if yu cool wit' it, me am tu. Ya know what me sayin'? Me gonna send ya a batch of ganja tu blow ya top." He broke out in laughter. "Yu gonna be so high dat ya gonna be seein' shit."

"In dat case, send a hundred pounds of it, de pills and de blow. Me will have ya money in no time at all."

"OK. Send dem down."

Tukey hung up and called Cody.

"Hello," he answered with hostility in his voice.

"Cody, it's me, Tukey."

"Oh, hey love." He was walking to his truck.

"Ya guys still have de next couple days off?"

"Yep. And we're ready to go."

"Cool. Me gonna put y'all on a plane tonight along wit' Tiki. Her will do all de business when ya touch down, den ya bring me stuff home safely."

"Don't worry. We'll do just that." Cody opened the door of his Suburban and climbed in. "Just make sure that you have our cash waiting. We're taking a big risk here."

"Me know. Just trust dat me gonna mek it worth ya while in more ways den one, mon. Ya hear me?"

"Yeah," he said coolly. "I'll hit you back in a minute." After Cody ended the call, he sat for a moment to think. If things went wrong, he would end up in prison forever. He had to be sure that he was ready to take that chance. While he was pondering it, his phone rang.

"Yeah."

"What's happening?" Dulow inquired. "After Tukey finishes whatever she's doing, me and Dickie are gonna clock out."

Dickie was also scared about the possibility of something going wrong. If his partners changed their minds about wanting to go through with it, it was cool by him. If they didn't, he would go along because he didn't want to miss out. He hoped he wouldn't end up regretting it.

It took Cody a few minutes before he made up his mind.

"Let's do it."

"All right, we'll call you after we clock out."

* * * * *

Tiki and the three cops boarded a plane to Los Angeles. She purposely sat beside Dulow because she noticed that he had been avoiding her lately. When the plane took off and they cleared through the turbulence, Tiki began to relax. The cops had to chew some TUMS to get rid of the bubbling feeling inside their stomachs.

Tiki looked over at Dulow who was gazing out the window.

"Yu mad at me or sum't'ing?" she quizzed.

"Why would you say that?"

"Because, yu been actin' funny all week."

Dulow grunted and said, "Shouldn't I be?"

Tiki scowled. "Speak ya mind when yu talking tu me, mon. Me doan play de guessing game."

Dulow faced her. "You used me."

"For what?"

"To get next to Cody, so he could help you and your sister beat y'all's case."

Tiki took a deep breath. "So ya not talkin' tu me because of dat? Dat's fucked up, mon."

"Naw, what's fucked up is that you get off ... you know what? Fuck it!"

They rode in silence for a while. Tiki was first to break the silence.

"OK. Yu right. Me did use y'all, but dat doan mean dat us cyaah still fuck from time to time. Shit, me not mad because yu gotta wife."

"What the fuck that mean?"

"It means dat all me am is a fuck tu yu. It's not like yu plan on or will leave ya wife and kids tu be wit' me. Does it?" He didn't respond. "Me know. Like me said, all me is is a fuck tu yu. Just like yu are ta me. Only me doan let feelins get caught in de mix, like yu tender-dick ass." She took out her lip-gloss and applied it to her lips.

Dulow gave in. He nudged her elbow.

"Doan touch me, cry baby," she said jokingly.

"All right."

After they landed in LA, they were greeted by Tiki's cousin, Sean Paul, who was waiting for them at the front gate. They piled inside his Denali XL and were taken to meet Dave. He wanted to meet the dirty cops and get to know them on a personal level before any business could be done.

Sean Paul took them to Dave's favorite eating spot, Sir Graham's. It was a combination of both a restaurant and a nightclub. When the host led them to his table, Tiki rushed to embrace him. The three cops stood patiently until one of the two bodyguards who stood on both sides of Dave instructed them to be seated.

Throughout the duration of his meal, Dave said not one word to either of the cops. The three of them twiddled their thumbs while Dave and Tiki spoke in their native tongues.

About forty minutes went by before Dave finished his meal. He wiped his mouth with a cloth napkin, then sucked his teeth. Cody surveyed the room, trying not to appear nervous. He didn't want to spook the man before they formed the partnership.

Sitting in a dimly lit part of the restaurant surrounded by

three beautiful women, one of whom was white, was the actor/comedian, Eddie Griffin. At least that's who Cody thought it was.

Dave leaned over and whispered something into one of his bodyguard's ears. The big black man nodded, then approached Cody. He and his crew were searched for wires and weapons, then the guard resumed his position to the right of Dave.

"So," Dave said, finally speaking to them, "who is it sittin' in front of me?"

Cody sat up in his seat and introduced them. "I'm Cody." He turned to his two friends. "And this is Dulow and Dickie." They both nodded.

Dave said, "Cody, since yu seem ta be de leader of dis posse, let me ask ya sum't'ing."

"Shoot."

Dave stuck a Newport between his lips. He wasn't going to light it. He just liked to pull on it to taste the menthol flavor.

"What are ya motives here?"

Cody looked him straight in the eyes and simply said, "Money." He stuck a Newport between his lips as well. "You see, in our line of work there isn't much of that involved, Mr. Tosh."

"Especially for the risk we take," Dulow added.

Then Dickie said, "So we decided to cross over."

"That's right," Cody said. "And I know for a fact that our services will make you a whole lot more than what we'll be getting." Cody held up a lighter. "May I?"

Dave leaned over so Cody could light his cigarette. "Like I was saying. Between me and my partners here, we have seven kids and three wives." He shrugged. "And they want nice things. We promised them the world in our vows ... now it's time for us to produce it."

"You can't even buy a good house for thirty-three thousand, let alone the world," Dulow said.

"T'irty t'ree t'ousand? Dat what yu mek a year?" They all nodded. "Den dat's what me will pay ya per run. T'irty t'ree t'ousand a piece. Half now, half when de stuff hits Kansas City."

Cody smiled agreeingly. "So we have a deal?"

"Yes." Dave smiled. "Ya sold me on de family t'ing, mon. Me got kids ta feed, tu. Now let's feed ya, mon."

Cody wanted to impress Dave by ordering the house's best champagne. When it arrived, he poured everybody drinks.

Dave proposed a toast. "Dis is tu us, de cops and hustlers unitin' toget'er. Me cyaah pay yu enough money tu buy de world, Cody. But me ca'an mek sure dat ya mek enough ta buy a lot of what's in it."

* * * * *

The next day, the three cops dressed in their police tactical gear and stashed themselves in the back of an eighteen-wheeler. On the outside of the big rig, painted in big red letters, were the words "Dan's Fresh Fruits." But instead of apples and oranges, Ecstasy, cocaine and marijuana were packed inside the crates.

Tiki was behind the wheel headed northeast on I-15. She wasn't worried about getting busted because she had the law on her side. The truck wasn't what looked peculiar to the other travelers on the highway. It was the woman behind the wheel bobbing her head like she was driving a car.

After Tiki jumped on I-70 headed east, she saw a sign that read "Weigh Station Ahead."

"Oh, shit!" she exclaimed. Tiki picked up her walkie-talkie. "Cody. Me have a weigh station comin' up ahead."

"OK. Just pull into it and hand them the paper. If trouble comes, I'll handle it." He faced his men. "Showtime."

The first things that Tiki saw after she pulled into the weigh station were two highway patrol cars. Her heart instantly sank to the pit of her stomach. Somehow she managed to hold a smile on her face while she nervously exited the truck with a clipboard in her hand.

Tiki had on faded jeans, a plaid button-up shirt and a long john shirt on underneath.

"Howdy," she said in a Southern accent. A fat gray-headed white man wearing coveralls with a cowboy hat on his head stood next to two highway patrolmen. "Tryin' ta get dis here fruit tu de big city before it ain't fresh no more." She smiled, but they didn't.

The gray-headed man took the clipboard, then walked over to the truck. Tiki timidly nodded at the two patrolmen.

The fat man came marching back with a suspicious look on his winkled face. One of the patrolmen recognized the look, then popped the button on his holster.

"Problem?" Tiki asked in a shaky voice.

"Load's too heavy," he said. He spit a gob of tobacco onto the concrete. "What ya got back there besides fruit, girl?"

Tiki unclipped the walkie-talkie off her hip. "Sergeant Brown, we have a problem out here."

The two patrolmen became alert when they heard the cargo door open. Out leapt three men dressed in black tactical gear. Everything but their duty boots had "Police" written on it.

"Wha'ta hell?" the fat man mumbled.

Cody flashed his badge and police identification.

"KCPD. May I have a word with you, gentlemen?" He spoke in an authoritative tone.

"Just what in Sam Hill is going on?" the fat man inquired.

"This woman here," Cody gestured toward Tiki, "is a part of an important drug sting that's about to go down tomorrow. We had surveillance on her all the way to Los Angeles, where we observed her picking up a truck full of narcotics for an unnamed subject. After we made the bust, she agreed to cooperate by leading us to her contacts."

"So what now?" one of the patrolmen asked.

"It should be obvious. You country boys got all this dope

traveling down y'all's highways and you don't know jack shit."

"Well, why don't you inform us on what we dummies don't already know?"

"This cooperating witness is going to lead us to the people for whom she's allegedly working."

"Say, y'all wouldn't mind if my partner and I tagged along, would ya? We'd kinda like to get our picture in the paper, too."

"Negative. And this is not a game, officer." Cody handed the man a card. "This is the number where my superiors may be reached for questioning."

"Well we—"

"Back in the truck," Cody ordered Tiki and his crew.

"Now wait just a minute. I reckon I'ma have to call and verify this."

"Very well."

The patrolman hurried over to his car where his cell phone was. Dulow got on his cell phone and texted Casey the words "DO YOUR THING."

Sitting down the deck of cards that he was playing solitaire with, Casey hurried over to the Captain's office. Captain Kirby was on the Internet logged onto a gay porn Website. Hearing Casey knock on the door spooked her, and she quickly hit the "Esc" button on the keyboard.

"What is it, Spratt?" she asked in an irritated voice.

"Captain Kirby, on my way in today I observed that you had a busted tail light." He had done it himself when he arrived at work. "I just wanted you to know."

"What?" she shouted, jumping up from her chair. "Watch my office. I'll be right back." She grabbed her blazer and left. "As if my car ain't already raggedy enough."

The phone rang.

"Captain Twila Kirby speaking," Casey answered.

The highway patrolman was surprised to hear a man's voice come on the line. "I didn't know they named men Twila," he said. "Y'all must believe in gay rights over in Missouri."

"Very funny. What can I do for you?"

"Officer Pittman. Listen here, Twila. I got a group of officers here in a fruit truck claiming that they're a tactical unit on assignment under your orders. Is that correct?"

"Yes sir. And they are not to be detained or delayed by any of your men."

"Well, Twila, I figured they were legit when they produced their identification."

"Well, let them go immediately, or are you country boys down there too dumb to read badges?"

He chuckled. "Now you listen here. Don't sass me because your name is Twila. Your mama ... Hello? Hello?" The line went dead in his ear. "Fuckin' faggot."

After Cody and his crew were released, the two patrolmen and the fat man watched in disgust as the big rig took off down the highway.

"Fuckin' niggers," the fat man said. He spat tobacco on the ground.

Chapter 18

Peko stood inside the garage of A Touch of Class paint and body shop while Tukey bitched to the owners about her cars not being ready. Her cell phone was ringing off the hook by people who were trying to cop some Ex pills. She wanted to tell Tukey to shut the fuck up and let's go, but it would do no good.

They were waiting on a cotton-candy pink chameleon paint that turned rose red in the sunlight for her brand new Chevy SSR. The Dodge Magnum that Peko wrecked wasn't even close to being finished.

"Tukey, let's go!" Peko said, becoming impatient. "Me got people tu see."

Tukey nodded, then said to the owner, "Hurry up!"

The two girls were riding up 59th Street in Peko's royal blue Chevy Caprice. They both sat low in the Burberry-covered seats, chopping on their cell phones. Cody was informing Tukey that everything went as planned. Peko was telling one of her customers that she was on her way.

"Me cyaah wait tu see dem bitches down in Texas faces when us pull up in de SSR wit' Lamborghini doors. Dey gon' be like no ... no ... no ... no dey didn't." They both laughed.

Peko saw the black Blazer that belonged to the guy who she was supposed to be meeting. The white Tahoe that was parked beside it suddenly pulled off. Peko parked behind Manhattan Cleaners, then hopped into the Blazer while Tukey went inside to pick up Cody's clothes.

"Who was that inside the Tahoe, Eight Ball?" Peko asked.

Eight Ball had driven over from St. Louis and didn't know many people in Kansas City, so the Tahoe made her suspicious.

"Another one of my plugs," he said regretfully. "I've been waiting here for an hour while you kept lying like you was on your way, Peko."

"So ya got me ridin' around wit' five t'ousand pills for not'ing?"

"Man, look. What's done is done, ya know."

Peko and Eight Ball had met at Lincoln College's homecoming back in October. He was thizzin and she was thizzin. When the two crossed paths, you know where they ended up – the motel.

"Yu know what, Ball? Fuck you! And doan call me no more." She got out of the truck.

"Peko!" he called out, but she kept walking as if she didn't hear him. "Peko!"

Tukey was inside the cleaners' examining Cody's clothes. The cleaners sometimes fucked up people's shit, so she wanted to be sure that they were done right before she left. She suddenly felt someone walk up behind her and turned around.

"Hi," she said, taking in the familiar face.

"Tukey?" Tiera said, unsure if it was Tukey or not.

"Tiera?" Tukey asked, now well aware of who she was.

"It's me." Tiera smiled. "Girl, look at you."

Tukey was sporting a bronze Baby Phat jacket, brown Triple Five sweats and brown Yves Saint Laurent boots. She hadn't seen her since high school and was glad she looked up to par.

"Nevermind me," Tukey said, letting her catch a glimpse of the pink diamonds in her grill. "Look at yu."

Tiera was sporting a pink and gray Rocawear sweatsuit, gray

and pink Air Force 1's and pink Gucci glasses. What Tukey noticed most was the diamond ring on her finger.

"Yu married?"

"Girl," Tiera said, looking at the ring Kenny gave her. She had put her gold wedding band in her jewelry box. "I'm going through a divorce and an engagement." She hoped that her makeup covered the bruises on her face from Kenny hitting her.

"Who's de lucky man?"

"You remember Kenny, don't you?"

"Yeah, I know Kenny. Him come by me club all da time." She had to mention her club.

"What club you own?" She tried not to show her envy.

"No Draws."

"Damn! You doing the damn thang, girl."

"Yeah, me doin' a lil sum't'ing." She shrugged. "Me doan like tu brag about it."

Don't like to brag, huh, bitch? Tiera thought. *This ho ain't doing nothing but fronting. Bitch probably strips there.*

Peko sat in the car chewing gum and talking on the phone when Tukey and Tiera walked out. They both wore false smiles while they chatted. After about a minute of conversation, they parted ways. Tukey noticed that Tiera was getting in an Infiniti, and Tiera saw Tukey get into the passenger side of an old but clean Caprice.

With the exception of the beatings, Tiera was happy to be with Kenny. He bought new clothes for her and the kids and let her keep his whip.

"Who dat bitch?" Peko inquired.

"Some gurl me used ta know."

Peko continued to talk on her phone. "Me will be dere in ten minutes. Doan have me come for not'ing."

"Ya pissed off or sum't'ing?" Tukey asked.

"Fuckin' Eight Ball's punk ass had me bring dis shit all de way over here for not'ing. De dude in de Tahoe was another one of him connects."

"Mpf! Doan sweat it, gurl. From now on de Ecstasy trade in dis city is gonna belong tu us. Me didn't train our police dogs for not'ing. Me gonna sic 'em on whoever's moving against us."

Peko was awed by Tukey's keen mind. "Gurl, dat was ya plan from de very beginnin'?"

"Damn right!" she admitted. "And dis is just de beginnin'."

Peko drove down Swope Parkway grooving to 50 Cent's "*Candy Shop*" that was playing on Hot 103.3.

"Hey, me love dat song," Tukey said, cranking up the beat. "Fifty's my negga, mon."

Peko cut it back down. "Me know who else ya like."

"Who?" Tukey asked curiously.

"Cody."

Tukey gazed out her window. She wasn't for sure how she felt about Cody. Was he just her project or was she starting to fall for him? Really she wasn't ready to give her heart to another man. Not after all of the drama that she went through with Keith. But if he stole her heart, there would be nothing she could do but accept him.

"Me not sure how me feel about dat mon," she finally said.

"Ain't him married?"

"Sum't'ing like dat. Dey goin' t'rough some t'ings."

"Well, whatever yu do, doan let ya heart stop ya from carryin' out ya plan."

"Believe me, when me put a plan into effect, not'ing will stop me from gettin' it done. Just ask Keith." She regretted saying those last words the moment they passed her lips.

"Yu a durty gurl," Peko said, referring to her last statement.

"What Jamaican ya know dat ain't? A mon ca'an cross me once. Maybe even twice. T'ree times him have tu pay de Tukey way. Ya hear me?"

"Not only do me hear yu, me wit' ya all de way."

"Good. After yu finish mekin' ya runs, swing by de police

station."

"De police station? For what, mon?"

Tukey smiled wickedly. "Time for plan B."

"What's plan B?"

"Tu tek command of de 63rd Street Precinct."

* * * * *

It took Peko about two hours to make her runs and stop by her apartment to drop off the cash. It wasn't until later on that evening that they finally made it to the police station.

"Wait here," Tukey instructed her.

When Tukey entered the police station, she saw two clerks sitting at the front desk. They were both tired looking white women. One was frowning while being cussed out by a black woman about her son being locked up.

"May I help you?" the other clerk asked.

A quick glance at her name tag informed Tukey that her name was Bruner.

"Yes," Tukey said in a pleasant voice. "About a week ago, me was walking down de street when all of a sudden dis big man came up behind me and snatched me purse, knockin' me down. Den dis officer dat me like tu call Super Cop came out of nowhere, caught de purse snatcher and returned me purse. So me came here today tu inform him boss about de heroic act."

The clerk took out a pen. "Do you remember the officer's name?"

"Yes. It was Sergeant Cody Brown."

Bruner raised her eyebrows. "This is a first. Usually when people come in here asking to see the boss, it's to file a complaint against one of our officers." She picked up the phone. "Captain Kirby is gonna love this." After about ten minutes of conversation, she hung up and said, "She'll be out in a minute."

"T'anks."

Police cars came and left the parking lot. Seeing all of the blue suits and badges made Peko uncomfortable. She glanced at her Lil' Kim watch, wondering how long Tukey would be in there.

Back home in Kingston, Jamaica, one stayed as far away from the police as possible. There, the police would kill you for possessing a firearm. And the crime rate was too high not to carry one. That's why in Jamaica the police and the citizens stayed at war like the Bloods and Crips.

Twila seemed to be walking in slow motion when Tukey saw her walk through the door. She had small legs and a big upper body. Her breasts seemed to stick out a foot in front of her. She whispered into Bruner's ear, then faced Tukey.

"Hi. I'm Captain Kirby." She stuck out her hand.

"Tukey Tosh." They shook hands. "If dis is a bad time, me could come back."

"No ... no. I'll be leaving in a couple of hours."

Tukey glanced at the clock on the wall and saw that it was just after six. While she spoke to the Captain about Cody's brave act, she recorded in her head what made Kirby stick out from the rest of the cops. For one, she wore a white shirt and she had silver bars on her collars.

After Tukey got back to the car, she took out her cell phone and started dialing numbers.

"Watching Eye, this is Rocky speaking." The man's voice sounded like Tone-Loc's.

"Me got a job for ya, Rock."

"Well, we're kinda tied up right now ..."

"Doan yu feed me dat shit, mon. It's not no big demand for private eyes since dat show '*Cheaters*' started."

"Girl, you know how that accent turns me on," he said, changing the subject. "I swear I get hot every time I talk to you. HA! HA!" he laughed.

"All de money in de world couldn't get ya none of dis pussy, Rocky."

Rocky fired up a cigarette. "All right, now that we got the

foreplay out the way, how can I fuck you ... I mean help you?"

"Me want yu tu get down to de Sixty T'ird Street Police Station by eight. De subject us lookin' for is a white female wit' red hair. Her a cop—"

"A cop?"

"Just listen. Her de Captain so she'll be wearin' a white shirt wit' bars on de collar."

Rocky took down the information. "Her build?"

"Top heavy. About five seven or eight."

"What am I looking for?"

"Anyt'ing and everyt'ing yu ca'an, good or bad. Get tu know her personal life. Where her hang out? Who her dates? T'ings like dat."

"What kinda shit you on, Tukey? Wanting me to surveil a cop. A Captain at that."

Peko was wondering the same thing.

"If yu doan know, dey woan ask yu tu testify if me get caught up."

"Fair enough. I'll start the investigation tonight and have the report ready in a week."

"T'anks, Rock." She hung up.

Peko said, "Yu have tu be de sneakiest, most devious and unpredictable bitch me know."

Chapter 19

Late the next evening, Tiki pulled the truck into the alley behind the club. Sluggishly, she leapt from her seat down onto the concrete. Stretching, she took in the familiar surroundings and was glad to be back.

After knocking twice, she lifted the cargo door. The cops squinted their eyes like they hadn't seen daylight in months.

"I feel like I been in there for a year," Dickie said.

"It's all gonna be worth it. You know why?" asked Cody. "Because it's payoff time. Let's go get paid."

Anitra, Peko and Shantí were inside the office drinking Alizé Red. They giggled while they watched the two Kid 'N Play look-alikes on the dance floor through the two-way mirror.

"I can't believe these clowns," Anitra said, laughing. "What'n the hell was Guru thinking when he let those idiots in?"

"He probably thought they were the real Kid 'N Play," Shantí said, unable to hold back her laughter.

Peko said, "Me doan know who Kid 'N Play is, but dey look stupid in dem cheap suits."

Tiki walked in looking tired, followed by the three cops. They also looked fatigued.

"Hey, sister," Peko said, sitting her drink down to go hug her sibling. "Yu made it." They kissed on the lips.

"Damn right we did," Cody said. "Now it's time to collect." Anitra felt that vibe again. It was the same feeling that she had the first time they met. She took a deep breath, then slowly exhaled. Her brain was telling her to leave the room and get out of Cody's presence, but her legs weren't responding.

Anitra spoke up. "Did Dave give you his half, Tiki?"

"Him did," she replied, breaking the embrace. "Him gave me fifty t'ousand. T'eir fee is ninety nine."

"That's a lot of money to pay a bunch of mules," Anitra said insultingly. She wanted to seem cold on the surface, but her inner body wanted to get to know him. She fought the feeling. Her body was feeling like it hadn't felt in years. Submissive.

When Cody looked into her green eyes, she looked away.

"Mules, huh? Let me ask you a question." He stepped close to her. Her body tensed. "Are you being mean because you're arrogant?" He paused, moving his head to the left so his eyes could meet hers. "Or because you're sweet on me?"

"Please!" Anitra exclaimed. She stepped around him, walked to the doorway, then turned around. "Pay these jerks and get rid of 'em." Then she left the room.

Peko laughed to break the silence. "Let me let ya in on sum't'ing, Cody. No use in flirtin' wit' her, mon. Her is strickly undickly." They all laughed.

"Unless it's made of rubber," Shantí added.

"Yeah, well," Cody said, "you never know. Even fags stick their dicks in something every once in a while."

"Enough with the jokes," Dulow said. "Let's talk turkey."

Shantí removed Mi'kelle's picture that hung on the wall behind Tukey's desk, revealing a maroon safe with a gold handle. When she opened it, Dulow whistled at the stacks of cash that it held.

They never kept more than they needed inside the safe, so

who cared if they saw it? Tiki left to get the money that Dave had given her out of the truck. When she returned, she dumped the money on the table next to the five ten-thousand-dollar stacks that Shantí sat on the table.

Shantí said, "That's a hundred thousand. Keep the change."

Cody picked up a stack and held it up. "Huh? Huh? I told you, Dulow, that it was gonna get greater later."

"Yes you did, man." Dulow took the stack out of Cody's hand, then tossed it to Dickie.

Dickie held it like it was too heavy to hold. "Wheeew!" he shouted. "Don't forget ten grand of this goes to Casey. He's part of this group, too."

"That's cool by me," Cody agreed. "Now you two better get home to your families and get some rest. We gotta be at work in the morning."

Tiki tossed Shantí the keys to the truck. "Y'all handle dat. Me gonna catch a ride wit' Dulow."

Alf and Rhyme pulled Cody's Suburban and Dulow's Bravada around the front. Dulow and Dickie hopped in his Bravada and Cody got into his truck.

Dulow was about to pull off when Tiki came running out, flagging them down.

"Wait for me!" she yelled. She jumped in the backseat.

"Where you going?"

"Hanover in de Woods," she replied, reciting the name of her apartment complex. "And me doan want tu hear ya bitchin', mon. Just drive."

Cody put the heater on inside his truck and waited while it warmed up. His phone beeped, signaling him that he had a picture message. It was a picture of Tukey lying across her bed in a black lace and satin chemise with a matching thong. Her address followed it.

Cody blew his horn at Rhyme.

"What's up, my man?" Rhyme quizzed.

Cody handed him two c-notes. "Bring me a bottle of something that'll keep the yang up. And a couple Ex pills."

* * * * *

Tiki punched the code in so they could get through the front gate at her apartment complex.

"Y'all want tu come in for a night cap?" Tiki asked.

Dulow said, "I have a wife, remember?"

"Oh yes. How could me forget." She looked at Dickie. "Ya wife expectin' yu, tu?"

"Not 'till tomorrow."

She whispered in his ear, "Me will be here if yu decide ya want tu come back."

Dulow's face tightened with anger. Inside, he prayed that Dickie would turn her down. One look at Dulow's face told Dickie what was going through his mind.

"Nah, I'm a little tired."

"Ya sure?"

"Ye ... yeah, I'm sure."

Dulow opened up his door. "Tiki, let me talk to you outside," he said harshly.

"Me'll be here if yu change ya mind," she said to Dickie.

Outside the truck, Tiki said, "What is it?" She flung her braids over her shoulder and stared up at him.

"You trying to embarrass me or something?"

"Yu embarrassed me, talkin' about ya wife and shit."

Dulow grabbed her arm and roughly pulled her toward him. "Don't play with me. I'm warning you, Tiki."

"Us kill crooked cops where me come from."

Dulow violently shook her until her brain rattled inside her head, then released her. "Remember what I said."

He got back inside his truck and pulled away.

"Next time doan fall in love so quick!" she yelled.

* * * * *

Cody got lost twice before he found the right house. They

were all gorgeous Tudor homes, so it was hard to tell which looked like it would be hers.

Roof! Roof! Roof! He heard dogs barking through the door.

"Be quiet!" Rose commanded as she clapped her hands. "Sit!" The well-trained dogs did as they were told.

Cody leapt backward after he laid eyes on the two biggest Great Danes that he had ever seen.

"Get back, Fifty!" Rose yelled. Fifty was white and black. When she struck him, he took off running. "You too, Luda." Luda was brown and white. He ducked and ran.

"I'm so sorry," Rose apologized. "C'mon in."

* * * * *

After Anitra finished doing the books, she told Peko and Shantí to take the truck to the storage house. She wouldn't be far behind them. But she changed her plans after she repeatedly called Tukey without receiving an answer.

Anitra jumped in her car and left. When she reached their block, she cut the lights and pulled into the driveway behind Cody's Suburban. Fifty and Luda recognized the smell of her perfume and didn't budge when they heard her come in. She tiptoed up the circular staircase headed straight for their bedroom. The bed was empty.

Quietly, Anitra cat-walked down the hall to the guest room. Peabo Bryson could be heard singing, "Can you stop the rain ... from falling?" Gently, Anitra turned the brass handle and slowly pushed open the door.

The pink bottoms of Tukey's feet and Cody's black ass were the first things that she saw. Part of her wanted to run over there and snatch Cody out of her pussy. The other part of her wanted to be up under him getting hit with deep, hard thrusts.

Subconsciously, Anitra's hand slid down to her crotch and her breathing started to accelerate. She went into a daze. In her mind, Cody was eight inches up in her while she clawed his back and begged for more. Her pussy was just about to squirt cum inside her panties when she felt Rose touch her shoulder. Flinching, she cupped her mouth with her hands before she let out a soft yelp. Rose regarded her curiously.

Anitra put her finger up to her lips then gently closed the door.

"You didn't see me, Rose," Anitra whispered. She pulled out some money and handed it to her.

"Me no see nothing," Rose said softly.

Anitra went outside to her car, honked the horn to stir up the dogs, then came back inside the house. When she peeped into their bedroom, Tukey was lying in the bed, mocking sleep.

* * * * *

Ten minutes after Dulow dropped him off, Dickie threw his bag into his F-150 and drove back to Tiki's place. He was careful not to wake his family when he walked inside his house to fool Dulow into thinking that he was in for the night.

Dickie ended up sitting outside the gate for eight minutes before another car showed up. They punched in their code, waited for the gate to open and they drove through it. He eased in before the gate closed back.

From the parking lot of the gas station across the street, Dulow could see Tiki's apartment. He observed her open up the door wearing nothing but panties to let Dickie in. He angrily threw his cigarette on the ground, got inside his truck and sped away.

An hour later, Tiki rushed into her bedroom where Dickie was sleeping and jumped on the bed, shouting, "Dickie! Wake up! Somebody just broke into ya truck."

The truck's alarm was going off. When Dickie put on his pants and hurried outside, there wasn't a thief in sight.

Chapter 20

Rocky pulled his Lincoln LS into Tukey's driveway. Looking in the mirror, he ran his hand over his short graying head and licked his lips. He rang the bell a couple times, straightened his collar and waited for an answer.

Tukey was lying across the sofa in a pair of boy shorts and a bra. Anitra was sitting on the floor while they watched the movie "*Ray*" on the plasma TV.

"He is so crazy," Anitra said.

"Me didn't know him was on drugs and stuff."

When they heard the doorbell ring, Tukey got up, pulled her shorts out of her booty and went to go answer it. Rocky looked down at her crotch and saw her kinky bush bulging through her shorts.

"Damn, yo' pussy fat," he said, laughing and showing his nicotine-stained teeth.

"Get ya perverted ass in here."

"Goddamn!" Rocky exclaimed, taking in the big house. "You living awfully lavish. I might have to charge you extra." He peered at her jiggling ass while he followed her. "You've got something better than money right there on your back."

Rocky took a seat in the platinum chair made of Royal Hide. Tukey sat on the floor by the table while he removed photos from his briefcase.

They were photos of the Captain with young women. While Rocky took his time, Tukey anxiously waited to hear some dirt. After cutting the TV off, Anitra crawled over by Tukey.

Tukey picked up the stack of photos. While she looked them over, Rocky explained what she was seeing.

"That photo in your hand," Rocky said, "is of the Captain leaving the gay club with a young girl. Every night for the past five days, she would come home, change into some tight leather clothes, then hit the club. She'd have a couple of drinks, then leave after she found her prey."

"OK? She's gay, so what. We are, too," Anitra said.

Rocky pointed at the picture that Tukey had in her hand. "Look at that picture closely, Tukey," he said.

Tukey saw a young white girl storming out of the Captain's house with an angry look on her face while the Captain stood in the doorway looking disappointed.

"What am me looking for, Rocky?" Tukey inquired.

"What they all have in common?"

Glancing at all the pictures, Tukey noticed that all four women seemed to be angry after they left Kirby's house.

"Dey are all angry about sum't'ing," Tukey said.

Rocky smiled. "Correct. Perhaps they are mad because she's asked them to do something that made them feel uncomfortable." Tukey smiled. "So I did some further investigating, like going through her trash, peeking through windows and shit like that."

"And what did ya find out?" Tukey asked anxiously.

He simply said, "Bondage. She's into sex games - S&M. Likes to be beat and shit on, and shit like that." Rocky took a deep breath. "Other than that, she's as clean as your Hummer."

Anitra wondered what Tukey's motives were behind all this.

Tukey paced the floor in deep thought. The information

that Rocky had could be useful. But how?

"Rocky," Tukey called out. "Did she hit on any black women?"

"Not that I can remember. If she did they were probably so light-skinned that I didn't notice." Tukey stopped in her tracks, then gazed down at Anitra.

"What?" Anitra quizzed. Tukey didn't say anything, she just continued to stare with a big smile on her face. "I'm not getting involved in that shit, Tukey, if that's what you're thinking."

Falling to her knees, Tukey said, "Please! Pretty pretty please, Anitra."

"Hold it!" Rocky said, holding his hand up. "I don't wanna hear no more. Pay me and let me go before y'all start plotting and shit."

Tukey got up and grabbed her Coach bag off the mantle. "Me only have eighteen hundred," she informed him.

"Bullshit! You owe me two grand."

Tukey stared at him unbelievingly. "Come here, Rocky." He walked over to her. She grabbed his cheek and planted a kiss on his lips. "Dat's for de ot'er two hundred."

Rocky took the money and stuffed it inside his pocket.

"Taste like you've been kissing on something more than lips," Rocky said, laughing. Tukey hit him on the shoulder. "Nah, I'm just joking. I'm out of here, y'all."

After Tukey walked Rocky out, she returned to find Anitra sitting on the couch, looking at the photographs.

"What're you up to, Tukey?" Her gaze remained on the pictures.

Tukey sat next to her. "Me t'inking about startin' me a drug task force."

"Girl, are you talking crazy?"

"It's only crazy if impossible. But me came up wit' a plan tu mek it happen."

Tossing the pictures on the table, Anitra asked, "Say that

you did manage to do it. Why are you doing it?"

"Because, Anitra. Me tired of all dese hating-ass niggas playin' me because me a woman."

"I told you that we need to quit this shit."

"And do what? Me doan want tu live a regular life." She stood up, walked around the table, then faced Anitra. "Me grew up around dis shit, wit' me daddy, me Uncle Ben and Keith. Now me doin' me own t'ing."

"Why?"

"Because it's fun."

Anitra stood. "You're either gonna get us killed or put in jail."

"Den me will do it alone."

"Do what alone?"

Tukey got up in Anitra's face. "Just t'ink, if a nigga is movin' more Ex dan us, us will send our team of dogs over tu tek dere whole supply and bring it tu us. Den us ca'an give dem a t'ird of what de shits worth. What do dey know?"

"What if they're placed in a position where they might have to kill somebody? Do you think they'll do it?"

"Me freaked Cody's mind, Anitra. So him ass will follow anyt'ing me seh, ya hear me?" She put her arms around Anitra's waist. "But me need yu tu be involved in order for it ta work. Are yu wit' me?"

Anitra peered at her serious eyes and said, "Yes, but I promise you that it's gonna blow up in our faces."

* * * * *

"You spent any of your money?" Cody asked Dickie. They were inside the men's restroom, peeing.

"I took my family shopping and bought me a watch. How about you?"

"I ha—"

Another cop walked in interrupting Cody.

"Gentlemen." He was actually a detective.

Cody said, "Hey." He zipped his pants and walked over to the sink. "You doing all right?"

"Fuck no!" he replied. "Every time I get my caseload down, bam! Something else pops up."

"What're you working on now?" Cody wiped his hands. Dickie was washing his as well.

The detective zipped his pants. "I've got a double homicide that happened at a gas station. A young woman and a known felon were both killed by gunfire. What pisses me off is that I know the young lady was killed for one simple reason."

"Because she wanted to hang out with gangsters," Cody said for him. "Damn shame, isn't it?"

"Sure is." He wiped his hands while staring at his handsome reflection in the mirror. "Anyway, the female victim's best friend was there also."

"She's a witness?"

"Yeah. Said the shooters drove a white Infiniti with those pretty rims that black guys ride on."

"Black guys?" Dickie quizzed.

The detective turned to Dickie. "Yeah. Black guys. What? I say something wrong? If I did, my mouth's not bleeding."

"It's gon' be bleeding if—"

"Hey! Hey! Hey!" Cody said, trying to stop it before it started. "I'm sure Detective Gere didn't mean nothing by that. Did you, Detective?"

"You know I didn't. Dickie knows I was just busting his balls."

"There you have it." Cody slapped Gere on the shoulder. "Continue what you were saying."

"Anyway, the witness stated that she saw two guys inside the car. The driver was brown-skinned with braided hair. The shooter wore a low cut, was dark-skinned and looked familiar to her."

"Really? You do a follow up yet?"

"No, but I'm on it."

Cody sighed. "Well, let me know how it turns out." He faced Dickie, then nodded toward the door. Dickie glared at Gere as he walked out.

"Freakin' jerk off," Gere said under his breath.

Cody and Dickie stopped by the lock boxes to get their weapons.

"You've got to calm that attitude of yours," Cody said while holstering his weapon. "We got to start keeping a low profile." They were about to walk out the door when Dulow walked in.

"Hey, Cody. What's up, Dickie? Buddy, old pal."

"What's up?" Dickie said sheepishly.

Dulow said, "I heard somebody broke into your truck and stole some of your equipment."

"They stole my badge and radio."

"I can't believe somebody done that at your house as long as you been living there." Dulow wanted to see if he would lie about it.

Dickie didn't want to lie to his buddy, but he didn't want to hurt him either. He knew Dulow had feelings for Tiki, but he went ahead and fucked her anyway. Shit, Dulow was a married man and had no right to get mad because Tiki gave him the pussy.

"It happened over Tiki's crib."

Cody raised his eyebrows. "Really?" he quizzed. "You fucking Tiki?"

Dickie shrugged. "It ain't no fun if your homies can't have none. Right, bro?" He nudged Dulow's arm.

"If you say so," Dulow replied coldly.

Cody could sense the tension between them. "Look here, fellas, what's done is done. It's just a ho and you both are married. So no harm, no foul. Now shake hands."

For the time being they settled their differences and shook hands.

Chapter 21

"So what's next on your agenda?" Cody asked Tukey.

They were walking the track in Loose Park while her dogs chased each other around.

"Why yu ask me dat, Cody?" She pulled her pink Kangol skull cap down over her ears.

"Because, now that you've got us in your pocket, I know you're gonna take advantage." He tossed a pebble into the small pond. "Besides, I'm like a vicious dog that just had his first taste of blood. Now I'm hungry for it."

Tukey smiled. "Yu mean ya money hungry." She put her cold hands inside her pockets and started walking ahead of him.

"I know you're not just gonna leave us out in the cold," he yelled after her.

Tukey stopped and turned around. "Just promise if me help yu get money ... ya woan change on me."

"Change?" He chuckled. "All we want to do is live well, Tukey. Nothing more, nothing less."

"OK." She took a seat on the nearest bench. He joined her. "Yu right. Me do have an agenda."

"See there, I knew it. What is it?"

"What me got planned has no room for cowards. Yu might even have tu kill." He nodded. She waited for an elderly couple to pass before she went on. "Me want yaself, Dulow, Dickie and Casey tu form a drug unit."

"We can't do that without authorization from our Captain. Stuff like that has to be approved by her, and believe me, the way me and her ... let's just put it this way. I'm not in the position to ask her for nothing. Especially for something like that."

"What if me ca'an persuade her tu agree tu it?"

Cody looked at her with a serious look on his face and said, "You think you're that cold?"

Tukey caressed his cold cheek. "Baby boy, ya should know by now dat me capable of doin' many ... many difficult t'ings, mon."

"That I do know." He peered at Fifty and Luda who were barking up a tree. "If we get the approval, what will be our objective?"

"Ya objective would be tu search and seize on me command. All us need is ta find a snitch dat will provide us with substantial information for us tu get warrants."

"How do me and my partners benefit?"

"Me will pay ya a set rate for each job ya do for me. All drugs and cash will be brought tu me."

"What about the arrests? Don't you think they would tell? What if we find more drugs and money than you're paying us?"

"Come here, Fifty," Tukey called out. The dog quit barking and immediately ran over and knelt down beside her. "Dat's a good boy," she said, rubbing his head.

"Well?" Cody asked impatiently.

"If ya kick in a drug dealer's house and find ten kilos of cocaine, him would be very grateful if yu doan arrest him. It's better for yu tu tek it rather dan t'row him in jail for ten years. But yu will have tu mek an arrest in order tu cover y'all's and de Captain's asses. But when yu do, unless instructed by me tu do ot'erwise, turn dem in for money or cocaine. No crack."

Cody nodded.

" ... Now in regard tu ya last question. Me will be willin' ta pay ya one t'ird of whatever de narcotics dat yu bring me are wort'. Yu get paid even if yu doan find anyt'ing."

"I'll have to think about it."

"T'ink about it real good, mon." Fifty saw a squirrel digging in the grass a few yards away from him. His ears stood erect as he began to growl. "Sssss, sic 'em, bwoy." The squirrel saw him coming and quickly darted up a tree. "But let me tell yu dis, Cody. And me only tellin' yu dis because ... because me startin' tu develop some feelings for yu. If me find out dat yu been holdin' back on me ..."

"Holding back?"

"What me mean by dat is, not reporting everyt'ing dat yu find tu me. If yu caught doin' dat, our deal is terminated. Yu ca'an still get de pussy, but our business will be finished."

Cody was confused. "But I can still fuck you, huh?"

"Business and pleasure should always remain separate. Unless yu use pleasure tu get de edge on ya business partner." A wicked smile crossed her face.

Cody looked into her eyes and said, "I don't know why you're the way that you are, but I'm glad I'm on your team."

Chapter 22

Cody, Dulow, Dickie and Casey took off and flew to Vegas for the weekend. They wanted to do some heavy drinking, gambling and buy some expensive pussy. It was their first time having big money to spend and they wanted to see what it felt like to blow it all. Fuck it! There would be plenty more to come.

Tiera called before Cody left so he could speak to his children. He offered money, but she declined. She bragged that they were being well provided for and weren't in need of his assistance. He wasn't even allowed to know where his kids were staying, which was fine by him. Cody needed a break from all of them anyway. He couldn't wait until he came up so he could floss on Tiera's punk ass. Cody didn't go to Vegas just to kick it. He was grooming himself for a new life that he was about to live. He would stand in the mirror with his hat cocked to the side and see that he was meant for it. In Vegas, he would get hip for it. Maybe he could add a little swagger in his walk for it.

* * * * *

Club No Draws was jumping. Everybody in the club was getting tipsy and thizzed out. Bitches were on the floor with their skirts pulled up to their waists showing off their colorful thongs and thick thighs.

The strip club had a titty cockfight going on. Naughty and

Hpnotiq were slapping their big tits together on stage while the crowd cheered them on. Petey Pablo's "*Freek-A-Leek*" had the girls going wild, especially the white ones. They showed their perky titties to everyone who came within flashing distance, both male and female. The black girls were upset because the freaky-ass white girls were receiving the most attention because they were taking it all off.

Two strange faces entered the club and took seats at the bar.

"Bartender," the shorter of the two called. "Get me a Crown and Coke. And get my guy here a ..."

"Long Island Iced Tea," the other one said.

The short one balled up his face. "A Long Island Iced Tea? What kind of drink is that for a man, Ray?" He spoke in a slick, low tone of voice.

"Let me do me, Pone," Ray said. "And don't call me Ray up in here, nigga. Call me Duck."

"Duck, Ray, I don't give a fuck what you go by. I do give a fuck that you're up in the club with me drinking tea."

"Shut the fuck up!" Duck saw two white girls on the floor feeling each other up. "Let's get on them hoes."

Pone shook his head. "We can't let them bitches get us off our square. We're here for a reason. So let's just hang around for a minute until we can get a good look at the bitch we came to see."

"All right. Let's shoot a few games of pool then." Duck paid for the drinks, then they went to get a table.

Mocha Cream was busy performing a lap dance on a guy who they called White Rich. Rich had a white exterior, but his interior was as black as any other nigga in the club. She danced with him for four songs and was ready to dig deep into his pockets.

After the song went off, Mocha stood up, pulled her thong out of her crack and pretended like she was about to leave.

"Wait a minute, baby. Where you going?" He grabbed her

hand. Rich stayed so thizzed out that he could barely part his lips when he spoke.

Rich dealt Ecstasy also, but instead of locally, he sold Ex in large quantities to people in different states. In the Ex business, he was where Tukey wanted to be.

"Your dance is finished, sweetie," Mocha said. "Now I have to go make some more money, baby."

Rich pulled out a knot of bills. He sat back in his seat watching her through tinted Cartiers and said, "Bitch, I'm White Rich. I can buy yo' ass for the year if I want to."

With a greedy smile on her face, Mocha straddled him and said, "I don't know about the year, but I'm already priced to sell for the night." While she kissed his neck, she reached over and took the whole wad of cash out of his hand.

"Let's head to my crib then," Rich offered.

Tukey sat in her office watching the whole scene on the security screens. She smiled when she saw Mocha lead Rich away.

"Gotcha!" she said. She dialed Mocha's number.

Mocha led him into the women's locker room so she could change. When they entered the room, he saw ass and titties of all shapes and colors. Surprisingly, not one of the women flinched or tried to cover her naked private parts. They kept right on doing what they were doing.

Mocha had just opened the locker when she heard her cell phone ringing inside her Fendi bag.

"Hello," she answered.

"Doan let him tek yu tu a hotel room. Eit'er y'all fuck at his house or nowhere. Mek sure ya get dat information out of him."

"Just make sure I get paid this time, Tukey," Mocha said. Then she hung up. "Black-ass bitch!"

After they left the club, Tukey came out of her office and showed her pretty face. She sucked on her platinum teeth while she scanned the room looking for Herm's big ass. He was at bar

#2, wining Peko, when he saw Tukey looking around the club. He looked across the room at Pone and Duck who were already looking in his direction, then nodded toward Tukey.

Pone got a good look at the woman and nodded his head in response.

Duck asked, "Did you get a good look at her?"

Pone smirked at his friend while he chalked his stick. "I don't have to," he replied. "I already know the bitch."

Tukey spotted Herm at the bar feeding Peko drinks. When their eyes met, she motioned for him to come to her.

"I'll be right back, babe," he said to Peko. Picking up his drink, he left to talk to Tukey.

Tukey led him back to her office where she fixed herself a drink and sat in her wingback chair. Taking a sip out of her pimp glass, she motioned for Herm to have a seat.

When Tukey finished, she smacked her lips and said, "Me hope ya didn't come tu waste me time, Herman."

Herm chuckled. "Herman, huh? Well, Tukey, I should inform you that I wouldn't be here ... if I couldn't be here." He sipped his drink.

After kicking off her heels, Tukey put her stockinged feet up on the table in his eyesight. "Now, what is it dat ya come for?"

"I want every key that you got," he said proudly.

Doing some figuring inside her head, Tukey took the sixty and deducted twenty for Fuzzy and Black, which would leave her with forty. Then she deducted another fifteen for Kenny and Paper Boy. And, aw yeah, Tiki had taken six of them to play with. That left nineteen.

While Tukey did the math, Herm sat back in his chair and admired her. The young, fine female that sat before him had it all. A business, houses, cars and money. And to top it all off, here he was, Big Herm, the man who pushed more keys than a pianist, about to cop from her. He didn't know exactly how she got on, but she deserved her props.

Tukey cleared her throat first, then said, "Me ca'an sell yu nineteen units for sixteen a piece."

"All right. Give me two days."

"Good." She removed her feet from the table. "Me'll call yu after church."

* * * * *

While Tukey ran the club, Anitra and Shantí were on a mission to reel in Captain Kirby. Dressed in a tight pair of black leather pants, a leather vest with a spiky choker around her neck, a biker's hat and knee-high riding boots, Anitra sat alone at the end of the bar inside the gay club.

Anitra was forced to turn down some very attractive lesbian broads who approached her. Shantí was over by the stage sticking dollar bills into the G-strings of the drag queens who were dancing. This was her first time witnessing something like this and she was really enjoying herself.

A tall, muscular redhead entered the club. She had on a black leather biker jacket, a short leather skirt, fishnet stockings and thigh-high boots. She strutted up to the bar and ordered a gin and tonic.

Anitra immediately recognized her from Rocky's photographs. It was time for her to perform. She didn't smoke but she had to pretend to in order to carry out her plan. Taking out a pack of Marlboro Lights, Anitra took one out and stuck it between her lips.

Stirring her drink, Captain Kirby bobbed her head to the beat of Gwen Stefani's *"Rich Girl."* There were some pretty ladies in the place, but none seemed to grab her attention. Quickly, she spun around on the heels of her boots after she felt someone tap her shoulder.

Anitra stood in front of her with a hard look on her face and a cigarette dangling from her mouth. She stared at Twila from head to toe.

Since the Captain was into sex games, Anitra assumed that

she liked it rough. "You gotta light, bitch?" Anitra asked harshly.

Twila went into her submissive mode. "Yes."

"Well, what the fuck are you waiting on?"

Reaching into her pocket, Twila pulled out a lighter and lit the cigarette. Anitra's eyes teared up while she desperately tried to hold back a cough.

After Anitra regained her composure, she blew the smoke into Twila's face and said, "Thanks, bitch," then walked away.

When Shantí took a break from giving away money, she turned around in time to catch Anitra's signal. Anitra rolled her eyes upward, letting her know that their victim was behind her. Shantí nodded, then continued on with what she was doing.

Anitra took a seat at the table that Shantí had held down especially for the two of them. Out of the corner of her eye, Anitra could see Twila coming her way. To look more attractive, Anitra crossed her legs and starting puffing on the cigarette.

"Mind if I join you?" Twila asked timidly.

Anitra looked at her like she was covered in shit, then said, "It'll cost you a few drinks."

Twila placed her wallet on the table before Anitra.

"I never leave home without it," she said, smiling. She sat in the seat across from her.

"Waitress," Anitra called out. Shantí strolled over to the table. "Get me four shots of tequila and a whole lemon." She handed her Twila's whole wallet.

"Coming right up," Shantí said happily. Before she returned from the bar with the drinks, she copied Twila's address off her driver's license so she wouldn't have to follow them to Twila's house. Shantí would be waiting when they arrived.

For half the night, Anitra and Twila sat, talked and repeatedly downed shots of tequila and gin. After they got to know one another's sexual pleasures and fetishes, Anitra agreed to go home with her.

Drunkenly, they both staggered out of the club with their arms wrapped around each other's necks. Since Anitra had the better car, she was the one who drove. Twila left her car there for fear that Anitra might get away from her. She had been longing for someone like Anitra and had finally found her. Her vagina spasmed as she thought of the beating that she was about to receive.

Shantí and Derrius were sitting in his car, parked up the street from Twila's home in Independence, Missouri. Her body was too ill to respond to Derrius' teeth as they bit down on her nipples. But it got him aroused so she allowed him to do it. Every few seconds she would moan so he wouldn't become discouraged. If Shantí tipped her hand to him about how weak she had been feeling lately, he would probably dump her.

"Stop it, Derrius!" She saw Anitra's lights coming up the block.

"Huh?" he said, lifting his head.

"They're coming. Get the camera ready."

The two drunken women exited the car and stumbled up the steps. It took six tries before Twila found the right key that unlocked her front door. Anitra removed her vest while Twila disabled the alarm.

"Hurry up, you trifling-ass bitch!" Anitra commanded. Twila deactivated the alarm and returned to the living room.

"Yes, Master," she said obediently.

Anitra drew back, then viciously smacked her across the face.

"Ouch!" Twila screamed as she fell to the floor.

"Get in there, whore! And get ready for your spanking." Twila was too slow getting up, so Anitra kicked her in the ass to help her get going. "Get!"

Shantí and Derrius crept up on the screened-in porch. Quietly, they opened the door and entered the house. They could hear Anitra in the back screaming at Twila. Shantí cut the camera on and pushed the record button. Following Anitra's loud voice, they were led to the bathroom. The door was wide open so they stashed themselves in a dark corner and zoomed in on the two freaks.

Anitra stood topless inside the bathtub with a whip in her hand and a mask over her eyes. Twila was sitting up on her knees buck naked with her hands tied in front of her.

"How you want it first, tramp?" Anitra asked harshly.

"Ooh, pee on me. Please, Master," Twila begged. Anitra undid the zipper on the front of her pants that went all the way down between her legs. While Twila eagerly awaited the golden shower, Anitra positioned her hips so that her hole was facing Twila, then released her urine. "OOOH! OOOH! OOOH, baby," Twila moaned as the hot liquid hit her face and ran down her body.

Derrius shook his head while he watched the disgusting scenes on the camera's flip screen. "She's a sick woman."

"Ummhm," Shantí murmured in agreement.

After Anitra rinsed the piss off her, she chained her with a dog leash and made her walk on all fours to the bedroom.

"Heel, bitch!" Anitra commanded. Twila sat back on her hind legs like a dog.

Anitra placed a ball inside Twila's mouth and tied the straps around her head. Then she helped her up and tied her hands to two ropes that hung from the ceiling. From the dresser Anitra got a jar of Vaseline that she used to prep Twila's ass cheeks for the beating that they were about to take.

"Now," Anitra said, standing behind her. She popped the whip. "Are you the Captain of the police force, or are you a shit-eating dog?" Anitra popped her on the ass with the whip.

"OOW!" Twila screamed as she bit down on the ball.

"Tell me, you filthy ... trrramp!" Anitra popped her again. Twila screamed and mumbled something unintelligible.

After three more lashes, she saw Twila's legs begin to tremble as she began to release her orgasmic fluid. So it was true. A person could actually get off by being beaten.

For the next act, Anitra positioned herself on the bed, doggy style, while Twila licked her asshole clean. Every chance she got, she would strain out a fart so Twila could get a mouthful of polluted air.

"Lap it up, you dog, you," Anitra commanded. "Dig in my ass with your taster. Now, are you the Captain or a female dog, bitch?"

Twila stopped long enough to bark three times, then continued to suck farts out of her ass.

"Yeahhh, that's a good bitch," Anitra said, panting. It started feeling so good to her that it wasn't long before she felt her own cum oozing down her thigh.

Chapter 23

Tukey sat in the back seat of her Hummer, talking on her phone to Mocha with the Xbox controller inside her hands. Tiki was driving while Peko sat next to her playing a boxing game. They rode cautiously down Woodland trying to reach 39th Street safely. Fifteen kilos of cocaine were inside two bags on the backseat floor. Every time Tiki saw a police car, she would flash back to the night that she shot at a policeman.

After they arrived at their destination, Tiki and Peko checked the chambers of the two Bulldog .44s that they had brought along for protection. Tukey grabbed the two bags and they emerged from the vehicle.

Kenny's white Infiniti was parked in the driveway behind Paper Boy's Cadillac. The house was in need of a couple coats of paint and the yard was sixty percent dirt. Tukey waited by her truck while Tiki cautiously walked up on the porch and knocked on the door.

Paper Boy opened it. "What's up?"

"Everyt'ing cool?" Tiki inquired.

"Yeah, girl. Tell Tukey to come in."

Kenny was sitting on the couch in front of a pile of money on the coffee table. His bandaged arm rested inside a sling.

"What's up, Tukey?" he said groggily.

"Hey, Kenny," Tukey said. "Wha'sup, Paper Boy?"

Tiki and Peko stood by the door while Tukey made the sale. Paper Boy took a brick out of one of the bags, then went to the kitchen to test it. Tukey thumbed through the cash on the table.

Ten minutes later, Paper Boy came back and gave Kenny a thumbs up.

"What happened tu ya arm, Kenny?" Tukey inquired.

Looking down at it, he said, "I got into it with Herm."

"Yeah," Paper Boy said, "them bitch-ass niggas jumped on me outside your club." He looked inside one of the bags. "The fight was over by the time your security showed up."

Tukey was loading cash into one of the bags that Paper Boy emptied. "Don't blame us for what happened."

"I ain't tripping," Paper Boy said. "We got at they ass that same night."

A thought hit Tukey. "Aw yeah, Kenny, me met ya fiancée at de cleaners."

"You remember her from school, don't you?"

"Mm hm. Us talked for a likkle while. Me invited her tu come tu de club some time."

"Please. You just trying to stunt on my girl because y'all know each other from Metro."

Finished loading the bag, Tukey stood up. "Why would me do such a t'ing, Kenny? Yu should know me better dan dat."

Kenny turned up his lips. "Yeah, right. Tukey, don't even talk that shit to me. You know I know."

Tukey put her palm up at him. "Whatever." She stepped toward the door, then turned around. "Me just curious, but who was her married tu before y'all got engaged? Did him go ta school wit' us, tu?"

Kenny stretched his long frame. "Yep. You remember Cody Brown, don't you?"

"Um hm," she said slowly.

"That buster-ass nigga."

"He ain't the buster," Paper said. "That nigga got you taking care of his wife and kids, and you calling his kids yours. Now you and that bitch engaged."

"Fuck you! You just worry about that bitch that dogged you out while you was locked up. Who you still with."

Tukey cut in. "Let me get dis straight. Did her leave him because of yu, or because she suspected Cody of doing sum't'ing?"

"I took her from him," Kenny bragged. "I help her out with the kids because he ain't got nothing."

Tukey became angry hearing him talk about Cody like that, but she didn't show it. "What are yu and Tiera doing dis weekend?"

"We shooting over to the Lou to catch the Cory Spinks fight. You going?"

"Supposed tu," she said, smiling. "Me and me boyfrien'."

Kenny's eyes widened. "Yo' boyfriend? What about Anitra?"

Tukey grunted. "Me ca'an fuck two birds wit' one coochie."

Kenny raised his hands, mocking surrender. "Whatever floats your boat."

* * * * *

After they left, Tukey received a call from Anitra. She told Tukey to meet her at the mall because she had some good news for her. Tukey dropped the bag of money off first, then they shot out to Independence Mall.

Tiki and Peko hit up the stores while Tukey met Anitra at the food court. She found her sitting alone, devouring a slice of cheese pizza.

"Where's Shanti?" Tukey asked, taking the seat across from her.

Anitra finished chewing her food before she said, "She's in the jewelry store. Don't say nothing, but I think she's shopping for Derrius."

Tukey giggled. "Her already trickin' for de dick."

"Un huh." Anitra wiped her mouth and hands and pulled the camera out of her bag. "Check that out."

Tukey flipped the screen open and pressed play. It took her eyes a second to conceive what they were seeing. Anitra was standing over the Captain, peeing on her face. She had her nose wrinkled up the whole time that she was viewing the tape. Just by looking at the woman, you wouldn't think that she was that kinky.

The tape wasn't near finished when Tukey shut it off and sat it on the table. She had seen enough. Her chocolate face wore a devilish smirk while she sat there shaking her head.

"Gurl, yu sure ya never done dat before?" Tukey asked jokingly. "Because yu played de part well."

Anitra threw a piece of crust at her. "Fuck you! I should get an Oscar for that act."

"Well, me hope yu didn't enjoy it so much dat yu t'inking about doin' dat wit' me."

"Whatever." Anitra put the camera back inside her bag. "Now what?"

"Now it's time to mek a deal." She stood and peeped at her watch. "Come on. Us still have time."

* * * * *

Hours later, Captain Kirby grabbed her jacket and clocked out for the day. When she reached her car, she noticed something stuck under her windshield wiper.

"What the hell?" she said, picking it up. It was a DVD. It came with a note that said "PLAY ME."

Twila drove home, entered her house and anxiously popped the DVD in. Picking up the remote, she sat on the couch, preparing for what was to come. Twila's heart rate sped up when she saw herself and the woman that she left the club with on the screen, committing kinky sex acts.

Twila watched herself get beaten, cussed out and treated like a dog. Under different circumstances she would've enjoyed watching the tape, but after seeing it this way, she could only imagine how sickening it looked to whoever recorded it.

If the DVD were to go public, Twila would be humiliated. She would never be able to show her face at the police station again. Those whom she commanded would laugh and talk behind her back when she wasn't around. But what scared her most was the respect that she would lose as a superior officer.

"Lap it up, you dog, you," Twila heard Anitra saying on the screen. "Dig in my ass with your taster. Now, are you the Captain or a female dog, bitch?" When she heard herself barking, she shut off the TV. Crying now, she put her face inside her hands and began to sob.

There was a knock on the door.

Quickly, Twila began wiping her eyes with the sleeves of her shirt. "Who is it?" she hollered, trying to hide the stress in her voice.

"Anitra."

Twila withdrew her nine-millimeter from her holster, then snatched the door open. Anitra and Tukey put their hands up after they saw the shaking gun pointed at them.

"Whoa!" Tukey exclaimed. "Us just came to talk."

"Talk, huh?" Twila pointed the gun at Anitra's nose. "You tricked me, you little bitch! I oughta shoot you right now."

"Before yu do, let me suggest dat yu look tu de right," Tukey warned. "Den slowly tu ya left."

Slowly, Twila turned her face to the right and saw Tiki standing on the outer side of the screen, pointing a gun at her. To the left was Peko doing the same. Both were ready to fire if necessary.

Securing the gun with both hands, Twila said, "I could kill her before they get me."

"Just ... calm ... down," Tukey said slowly. "Nobody has tu die, let's go inside and talk first. OK?"

Hearing Tukey's accent sparked Twila's memory bank.

"You. You're the girl who came to the police station."

Tukey nodded. "Now put de gun down and let's talk."

"What do y'all want?" she yelled.

Anitra said, "The sooner you put the gun down, the sooner you'll find out."

"OK," Twila agreed. "But if y'all try anything funny," she pointed to Anitra, "she'll be the first to get shot."

"Fair enough," Tukey said.

While the three of them went inside, Tiki and Peko watched the front. Tukey explained to Twila that they did not wish to use the DVD unless they had to. Twila sat and listened intently while Tukey explained her plan. She informed her that she wanted to form a drug task force that would be called the D-Unit. Then Tukey mimicked the conversation that she and Cody had at the park. If Twila refused to cooperate, the DVD would find its way to every news station in America via the Internet.

"What's in it for me?" Twila asked to their surprise.

"First of all," Tukey said, "yu woan be humiliated in front of de world. And second ... ya gonna get a piece of de pie."

"And judging by the look of this place," Anitra cut in while she surveyed the room, "I think you could use it."

Sniffling, Twila stood up and walked over to the window. It was a very risky thing to do, but they had her in a tough spot. Every night Twila prayed that God would make her life better. Was this his way of answering her prayers? Even though it was the wrong thing to do, the money sure sounded good.

"Now, what's it gonna be?" Tukey asked impatiently. "Public humiliation or a new house, car and money in de bank?"

Twila turned around to face Tukey. "I'll do it," she said. "But you have to be responsible for my payment." Tukey nodded. "And I want ten grand up front or no deal."

Tukey took a deep breath, then slowly released it. "OK, but me want dis t'ing tu happen immediately."

"Fine. But the DVD stays between us."

* * * * *

The next day, after Tukey and Mi'kelle left church, she called Herm up and told him to get the money ready. He told her that he only felt comfortable meeting at the motel next door to Niecy's on Blue Parkway. Her first mind told her not to, but since it was a public place, and Herm did have plenty of money, Tukey went against her first thought and agreed to meet him there.

Tukey called Tiki and Peko for backup but neither of them could be reached. Tiki was at the mall and her phone wouldn't pick up a signal inside the store. Herm had picked Peko up late last night, got her fucked up and stole her cell phone. At that moment she was passed out in Herm's bed, sleeping the high off. By coincidence, Shantí had become sick and Anitra rushed her to the hospital. Tukey told Anitra that she would be there as soon as she finished.

First, Tukey stopped by Taco Bell to feed her daughter, then dropped her off at home. After she picked up the dope, she drove to the motel. Pulling into the rundown place, Tukey spotted Herm's Denali parked at the far end of the motel. There were only six other cars inside the parking lot. But it was enough for her to feel safe. If she did get robbed, with other people nearby she stood a good chance of living to tell about it.

Tukey parked beside his truck then called him up.

"Wha'sup?" Herm answered.

"Me outside. Is everyt'ing cool?"

"Yeah," he said convincingly. "I'm in here getting your paper together."

"OK. Here me come." She hung up.

Armed with a Glock 9 in her coat pocket, Tukey picked up the two bags and walked up to the door.

Pone and Duck were on the side of the building ready to rush in behind her. With their guns held down to their sides, they listened for the door to open. Then they would make their move.

Tukey knocked twice, then stuck her hand inside her pocket that concealed her weapon. Herm answered with the friendliest smile on his face.

"Hurry in here before the police pull up," he said, stepping aside.

Tukey had just crossed the threshold when she was struck in the back of her neck. Her knees weakened and she fell to the floor, dazed.

Herm hollered, "Wait a min—"

Duck smacked him upside his head with the gun. He fell to the floor, unconscious.

Squirming on the floor, Tukey desperately tried to reach her weapon, but Pone kicked her in the stomach. Duck shut and locked the door. He reached inside her pocket to see what she was reaching for. Just as he expected. A pistol.

"Was you gon' shoot me? Huh, bitch?" Pone said, then kicked her again.

"Oow!" she cried. "Tek de shit and leave me alone."

Duck opened the bag and smiled at its contents.

"It's all good, baby," he said happily.

"That's good," Pone replied nonchalantly. He peered down at Tukey holding her stomach. "You remember me, don't you, bitch?" He knelt down, grabbing her dreads. "Take a good look."

Tukey peered up at the unfamiliar face through teary eyes and shook her head no. But somehow she did know him.

"I used to work for Keith," Pone reminded her. "I was one of the niggas that you set up at them apartments over in Kansas."

Yes, Tukey remembered that incident well. That day she orchestrated the demise of Keith's whole crew. All because of a beef that she had with Keith. Everyone around him had to pay.

Now Pone was about to make her pay for his three and a half years of incarceration.

"What we gon' do with this bitch, Pone?" Duck inquired.

Pone pulled out a package of rubbers and said, "We fit'na fuck this bitch in every hole that she got."

"Noooo!" Tukey screamed, then Pone punched her in the mouth. "Keep quiet, whore."

Duck snatched off Tukey's shoe, then used her stocking to gag her mouth. Once they got her inside the bathroom behind the closed door, they ripped off her clothes, tied her hands, then took turns raping her repeatedly.

Chapter 24

Cody and his crew returned home from Vegas that night. Instead of blowing their money, they bet big and ended up with more than what they came with. He couldn't reach Tukey, so he caught a cab home so he could rest.

The next day, Cody showed up for work a little late. After he clocked in, he fixed himself a cup of the bad coffee and took a seat behind his desk. Leaning back in his old, creaking chair, he had just closed his eyes when he heard his name being called.

"Cody!" Debra yelled, coming his way.

"What?"

"Cap wants you in her office, now," she told him. She patted her new wig, hoping that he would notice how good she looked.

Cody gazed at her smiling face while she patted her wig. "What's the matter with you?" he asked. "Your wig itching or something?" He walked away leaving her standing there with her feelings wounded.

Casey, Dulow and Dickie were all seated in the Captain's office when Cody walked in. Twila was sitting behind her desk with her arms folded across her chest.

"You wanted to see me, Captain?" he asked nervously as he

peered at his fellow officers.

"Yes I did, Sergeant Brown. Have a seat." She took a sip of coffee to wet her gullet. When she finished, she stood, picked up a stack of folders off her desk, then passed them out.

The folders had "D-UNIT" written across the front of them. They began reading through them.

Twila sat back down. "Sergeant Brown, I trust that while you were away in Vegas, you briefed your co-workers on your friend's plan?"

Cody was confused. "My friend?" Twila shot him a knowing look. "OH ... yeah ... my friend. She's contacted you?"

"Yes she did," Twila confirmed. "And may I add that she is a very clever one."

Cody cleared his throat. "I did brief them while we were away and we're all in agreement on this." He couldn't believe that Tukey had gotten Captain Kirby to cross over. "You're backing us on this?"

Twila nodded. "Just keep it as clean as you can and try not to use lethal force. If it does come to that, you'd better make damn sure that it appears justifiable. Do your thing, but in the meantime ... make me and yourselves look good. You're in with the other side, and I want y'all to use it to further all of our careers."

"What about warrants?" Dulow quizzed.

The Captain said, "All I have to do is tell the judge that we have a reliable informant who's feeding us information and he'll sign them. Meanwhile, you guys need to find us one."

As soon as they left her office, Twila picked up the phone and placed a call to her most trusted employee, Lieutenant Harris.

"Harris here," he said, answering the phone.

"Hi, Harris, this is your Captain speaking."

Harris took the cigarette out of his mouth that he shouldn't have been smoking and put it out.

"Hey, Cap. What's happening?" He coughed.

"You're not smoking inside the building, are you?"

"No, no," he lied, fanning the smoke. "Just caught a bit of a cold."

"Well see to it that you do something about that illness immediately." She sat up in her chair. "Anyway, I need a favor, and I want this kept strictly between us."

* * * * *

The day before, thirty minutes after the robbery, the cleaning crew discovered Herm and Tukey bleeding and unconscious inside the motel room. The ambulance came and rushed them to Research Hospital. Anitra was sitting in the emergency room with Shantí when the paramedics brought them in.

The doctors refused to give Anitra any information about what happened to Tukey. Herm was treated for a bump on the head and was released hours later. When Anitra alerted Peko, Peko contacted Tiki, who in turn called Arie. In a matter of hours they were all up there demanding some answers.

By that time, Tukey had regained consciousness. She instructed the doctors not to inform her family that she had been raped. Just roughed up a bit. Except for the robbers and the doctors, no one would ever know the whole truth.

Tukey didn't put up much of a struggle while she was being violated for fear they would hurt her even more. So besides a sore womb, she suffered minor injuries. They treated her for a bump on the back of her head, swollen lips and a bruised forehead.

The doctors released Tukey the next morning. For the next month she would put herself on bed rest with no visitors while she recuperated both physically and mentally. Tukey was a strong black woman, but like any other female, any violation of her private parts could cause permanent mental problems.

When Cody found out, he became enraged and anxious to

get at whoever was responsible for hurting her. He made several attempts to visit her, but was denied entry to her house. Calling her cell was useless as well. All of his calls went to voicemail. After several attempts to contact her, he went on with his life until she was ready to surface.

With the money Tukey had given him, he refurnished his house, bought rims for his truck, attended the Cory Spinks fight with Dulow and started hanging at her club. Anitra had him set up with his table inside the VIP. For Valentine's Day, Tukey sent him an Avianne rose gold chain with a diamond emblem that read "D-Unit" in big letters.

Twila took her ten-thousand-dollar down payment and put some down on a new BMW and bought new furniture.

Dulow gave his wife the Bravada and bought himself a new Yukon. He also splurged on an expensive wardrobe and put a down payment on a new house out in the suburbs.

Dickie copped his ole girl a new Blazer so she would stay out of his truck. He also paid up the mortgage on his home.

Casey didn't buy anything new. He had a crack habit nobody knew about except for his spouse. So the majority of his money went up in smoke.

Tiki was so furious about what happened to Tukey that she wanted to shoot every known jacker in the city. But she was instructed by Tukey to lay low and keep her ears open. With all the dope that was involved, somebody was bound to start talking.

Peko had a suspect in mind. It wasn't a coincidence that Herm had picked her up the night before and gotten her too fucked up to function the next day. If that wasn't enough, somehow her cell phone came up missing. If she would not have been passed out in Herm's bed, she would've been there when her cousin needed her.

* * * * *

Cody had been kicking it in the club for hours. Glancing at

his Avianne, he learned that midnight was nearing. He needed to get home and get some sleep for work the next morning. After he downed what was left of his drink, he motioned for the waitress.

"Yes, Cody."

Cody took out his wallet that held his money and badge and handed it to her.

"There's money in there somewhere," he said drunkenly. "Take it over to the bar and set," he burped, "settle my tab. But first tell the valet to bring my truck around."

"OK." She hurriedly walked away.

When Cody felt himself becoming sleepy, he got up and staggered over to the door. His Suburban was parked and waiting on him.

"Your keys are in your truck, sir," Alf informed him.

After climbing in, Cody pulled off. When he got home, he took a shower, wrapped a towel around himself and stretched out on the couch. A few hours later, he was awakened by the doorbell.

Groggily, Cody stood up and took his time getting to the door. The last person that he ever expected to see was standing on his porch when he opened the door.

"Anitra?" he said. "What're you doing here?"

Anitra held up his wallet. "You forgot this. Thought you might need it for work tomorrow. So I used my expensive gas to bring it to you. The address was on your driver's license."

Cody sighed. "Well, since you used your gas ... you might as well come in and have a drink."

"No thanks. I already had one too many."

"I meant a cup of coffee."

"In that case, I'll accept."

Anitra had been sitting on the living room sofa for five minutes before Cody came from the kitchen with a cup in his hand.

"Be careful, it's hot," he warned her. While he stood watching her drink, he noticed that her hands were trembling. "You get nervous around all men ... or just me?"

Sitting her cup down on the table, she said, "Just you."

Cody was drunk and ready to move on her. If she rejected him and told Tukey, he would blame it on the Moët. But he had a feeling that she wanted him to make a move on her. Why else would she be there?

Slowly, Cody unwrapped his towel and let it fall to the floor. Her eyes rolled down to his impressive set of jewels that dangled in front of her.

"Been a while since you've seen one of those, huh?" he asked. "Go ahead ... touch it."

Anitra's breathing accelerated as she reached out and grabbed it. The tender feel of the thick muscle felt good to her hand, so she started massaging it.

"Yesss!" he moaned. "That's a good girl. You remember what to do with one of those?" She nodded her head.

Cody sucked his finger then stuck it inside Anitra's mouth. "Mmm," she moaned. She began sucking and licking his finger like it was a dick. "*Sluuurrrp!* MMM!"

"That's it," he coached her. "Practice on that, baby."

* * * * *

It was almost sunrise when Anitra finally made it home. Tukey was in the bed facing the opposite direction when she felt the bed sink on one side as Anitra eased into it. Tukey didn't hear her take a shower, but she could smell Irish Spring soap in the air and feel Anitra's legs trembling.

* * * * *

Mi'kelle woke her mother so she could come to the kitchen and eat. She wanted to stay with her mother until she got well. After Tukey took care of her hygiene, she joined her daughter and Anitra in the kitchen.

"Hurry up and eat!" Anitra hollered at Mi'kelle. "You got

to be at school in a minute, and I don't wanna be late getting you there."

Mi'kelle stuffed her face with pancakes. "Finished," she mumbled with a mouth full of sweet dough.

"Mi'kelle," Anitra said, "go spit that stuff out and get your coat. Rose will clean up your mess."

Tukey sat across from Anitra, chewing eggs and watching her suspiciously. Anitra saw the look on her face and did everything she could to avoid eye contact. Anitra tried to devour her food as quickly as she could.

Anitra had finished her last bite when Tukey said, "Why yu got in so late last night?"

Unable to look at the daggers that she knew Tukey was shooting at her, Anitra got up and walked her plate over to the sink like she never heard her.

Tukey dropped her fork onto her plate. "De guilty always choose to plead de fift'."

Anitra came toward her with an angry look on her yellow face. "What are you talking about? What am I guilty of?"

"Yu tell me. First yu come in dis mornin' smellin' like soap dat us doan use. Den yu act like yu didn't hear me when me inquired about ya whereabouts last night."

"That's because I didn't hear you," Anitra said defensively. "You're mad about nothing."

"Me never said me was mad. Did me?"

"You didn't have to," Anitra hollered. "I was at the club doing the books all night. I washed up in the women's locker room before I left. Damn!"

"Like dey say, what's done in de dark ... will soon come tu light."

Anitra chuckled. "You of all people shouldn't say things like that." She grabbed her purse and left to take Mi'kelle to school.

Me doan care if yu are cheatin', bitch, Tukey thought. *Me got some real dick in me life now.*

* * * * *

Tukey sat in the Royal Hide chair with her feet up. Anitra coming in late was now the last thing on her mind. She had to figure out her next move. There wasn't a doubt in her mind that Herm's fat, greasy ass was behind it all.

That one episode was about to cost every drug dealer within the city limits. Tukey had a team of killers with badges that she was about to turn loose. She no longer had love for them, because they had no love for her.

Tukey knew that she wasn't jumping the gun by blaming Herm for what went down. How else would the jackers know that she would be at that location and loaded with dope? When she got knocked to the floor, she saw the dark-skinned guy go through her bags. Not once did they search for, or mention, that they found Herm's money. Nor did the police find it. Why? Because it was never there.

Tukey picked up the cordless phone and called Cody.

"Hello," he answered. Traffic was heard in the background.

"Get prepared tu mek our first hit," Tukey said in a low voice. "Bring some marked bills tu me house tonight."

"I'll be there as soon as I get off."

Next she called Peko, telling her to come over. Since Peko was in good with Herm, she would be the bait that set him up.

Peko answered the door for Cody when he arrived. He tried to come in but she prevented him from entering.

"Her doan want tu be seen, Mr. Policemon," she informed him. "Did yu bring de money?"

Cody peered over her shoulder into the living room. He saw Tiki sitting on the sofa and talking on the phone. There was no sign of Tukey. Anitra had called him earlier and told him that she would be over after she closed the club. As tight as her pussy was, he didn't care at the moment if Tukey wanted to see him or not. He would continue fucking Anitra until Tukey fully recovered.

"I was only able to get a thousand dollars on such short notice," he said, handing it over to her.

"It'll have to do. Tukey will be in touch."

"All right. Give her my regards." He turned to leave.

Chapter 25

That night, Peko called Herm and told him to pick her up from her apartment. When he did, he took her back to his house where she sucked him to sleep. While he was snoring, Peko took a thousand dollars out of his pocket and replaced it with the marked money, just like Tukey had told her to do.

The following day she called Tukey and informed her that everything was set. Herm was inside the house along with two of his boys. He had a gun under his bed and one under the living room couch. She couldn't find any dope, but a lot of people were coming in and out all night, so there had to be some money around somewhere.

After Twila heard from Tukey, she went to the judge and informed him that her narcotics unit had successfully made a purchase from a known drug house. He signed the warrant, where in turn, she handed it over to Cody.

Cody and his men geared up in black trousers, tactical boots, Point Blank vests and tactical masks over their faces. They had to keep their identities concealed so they wouldn't be recognized out in public. With 9mm Berettas on their hips and AR-15s in their hands, they all loaded up in the van. While Casey drove them to their destination, Cody prepped them along the way.

"All right, listen up," he hollered, facing the guys in the back of the van. "This is our first time out the gate, so I don't want no fuck ups." He paused to let his words sink in.

"Now, we've been instructed to take at least one suspect out." Cody pulled three mug shots of Herm out of his pocket, then passed them around. "But not until he's interrogated by me. Is everybody clear on that?"

"Yes, sir!" they all said in unison.

"OK. Now, we've been rehearsing this all morning and I want this to go as smooth as it did when we practiced it. Dulow, you hit the door, followed by Dickie, then me. After Casey enters, Dulow, you're gonna cover the rear. I want all of this done and the three suspects secured in ninety seconds. D-Unit, baby. Let's go get 'em."

Casey pulled up in the front yard and made an abrupt stop. Battering ram in hand, Dulow was the first out of the van followed by Dickie and Cody.

"Police! Search warrant!" Dulow yelled, then knocked the door off its hinges. Dickie and Cody stormed in the house followed by Casey. Dulow went to cover the back door.

When Chris and Kurrupt heard the loud sound of wood being split, they jumped up from the couch and dashed toward the back door. Kurrupt made it out the door.

"On the ground, now!" Dulow shouted. When Kurrupt hesitated, Dulow swept his feet out from under him and apprehended him.

Chris saw that and quickly made a detour down to the basement. Casey locked him down there until Dulow finished cuffing Kurrupt.

Dickie raided the upstairs with Cody.

"Bathroom, clear," Cody said as he waved his gun around.

"First bedroom, clear," Dickie said. He backed out of the empty room.

The door at the other end of the hall was shut. Cody pointed to it and mouthed the words, "Cover me." Dickie pointed his weapon at the door while Cody kicked it open.

"AHHH!" Peko screamed, sitting up on the bed with the covers wrapped around her naked body. She nodded toward the closet door.

Cody slowly grabbed the doorknob, snatched it open and ducked out of the way. Crouched low, Herm pointed his sawed off and fired, blowing a big hole in the headboard just inches away from Peko. Luckily, Herm switched from buckshot to slugs after he shot Kenny, otherwise she would have been hit.

Cody kicked the gun out of his hand. Herm was about to rush Cody until he looked up and found himself staring down the barrel of Dickie's rifle. Herm put his hands up in a surrendering gesture.

"Down on your stomach!" Dickie ordered. Herm put his face on the carpet and locked his fingers behind his head.

Dulow and Casey opened the basement door and pointed their rifles down the stairs.

"Whoever's down there, you'd better surrender, now! There won't be a second warning," Dulow warned.

Chris appeared at the bottom of the steps with his hands up. "It's just me," he said.

"Walk slow," Casey bellowed.

Taking one step at a time, Chris slowly made his way up the stairs. He was two steps away from the top when Dulow kicked him in the stomach. When Chris doubled over, Dulow grabbed him by the head and threw him down on the kitchen floor. Casey cuffed his hands behind his back, then grabbed him by his collar and dragged him to the living room with Kurrupt. Then they began to search the house.

Cody turned to Peko. "You need to leave," he ordered.

With covers wrapped around her, she picked up her clothes and left. Cody slipped on a pair of rubber gloves.

"All right," Cody said, gazing down at Herm. "I'ma ask you

some real simple questions. And I want some real ... simple answers." He removed the stun gun from his utility belt. "I wanna know where the money and drugs are. And I want to know the names and addresses of the guys who robbed Tukey."

"Fuck're y'all cops or hit men?" Herm inquired. "I ain't telling you shit." Cody hit him in the back with the stun gun. "Ahhh!"

"Try again!" Cody yelled. He was enjoying himself. When Herm didn't respond, he hit him with another jolt.

"OK. I give! I giiive!" Herm hollered. Slobber ran out of his mouth while he lay on the floor, burning up internally. He informed them that Duck and Capone did the robbery, then told them where they could be found. Herm also confessed that there were four kilos and about two hundred and thirty thousand in cash under the basement steps.

When he was satisfied, Cody removed the cuffs from Herm's wrist. "Go ahead," Cody said. "You're free to go."

Breathing extremely hard, Herm stood up, wiped his lips and walked out of the room. Dulow was standing at the bottom of the steps when Herm started running down them.

"Drop the weapon!" Dulow shouted. Herm stopped in his tracks with a confused look on his face. *Pow! Pow!* Dulow fired two shots through his face. His big body fell and rolled down the steps.

Four minutes later, Cody stood over Chris and Kurrupt while they were on their knees, brandishing his nine.

"I'ma make y'all a deal," Cody offered. "When the police arrive, y'all are to tell them the exact same story that I'm about to tell you. You do that, and we won't report all of those drugs and money that we found. Try to be cute, and you'll end up in federal prison for a long time." He looked at both of them. "Do we have a deal?" They both nodded. "Good! Casey, take these two outside. All we found was some marked money inside Herman's pocket."

Cody dug the pistol grip pump from under the couch and placed it in Herm's hand. He told Dickie to grab Herm's sawed off because he was taking it with him.

* * * * *

Later on that night, after the D-Unit answered all the questions and handed in their reports, they piled into Cody's truck and drove to Tukey's house. Rose let them in and seated the four of them at the dining room table.

Anitra and Shantí appeared a minute later. On the table sat two hundred and thirty grand and the four kilos that they got from Herm's house. Anitra knew the dope was Tukey's because the bricks were wrapped in red duct tape. Dave's trademark.

"Y'all did good," Anitra said, complimenting them.

Cody snorted. "Always trying to down play us, but that's all right," he said. "Just give us what we come for."

Anitra said, "I'ma give you something all right." She gave them all twenty-five grand a piece, then an additional forty grand for the dope that they recovered. So they all ended up with thirty-five grand a piece.

Before they left, Cody handed Shantí Herm's sawed-off. "Give this to Tukey for me," he said. "And tell her that we got the info on the robbers that she wanted. All we're waiting on is for her to give us the green light."

"OK."

Inside Cody's truck, the four of them laughed and high fived each other. Even though it was their first time, not one of them felt guilty about the murder that they had committed. If anything, they felt more powerful. Like they could do it again.

Cody said, "I'm proud of you guys. We did a thorough job and ended up splitting a hundred and forty g's for one day's work. Now let's go spend this shit. There'll be plenty more in the near future."

"DDDD-UNIT!" Dulow shouted.

* * * * *

Captain Kirby sat behind her desk the next morning, browsing through a travel magazine. Someone knocked on the door.

"Come in."

Debra walked through the door carrying a box and some flowers in her hand. "These just came for you."

"Thank you. Now get back to work." Twila waited on Debra to leave before she read the card that was attached.

> *Dear Captain,*
> *Here's a little something for showing*
> *me such a good time that night.*
> *Love,* A

When Twila opened the box, she found herself staring at thirty thousand dollars. Quickly, she shut it for fear that someone might walk in and see it. Twila smiled as she thought, *Oh my God, I'm rich!* Within the next few weeks, she would purchase a new home and take an expensive vacation to Europe. There were a lot of kinky sex spots over there and she wanted to visit them.

* * * * *

It was four in the morning when the two jackers stumbled out of the club called The Epicurean Phase II. Each one had a bad bitch in his arms. Duck patted his pockets for the keys.

"You looking for these, baby?" his girl asked, dangling the keys in front of him. "I got your money, too, remember?"

"Yeah ... yeah," he mumbled. "You drive." The girl winked at her partner as the four of them walked away.

The girl pulled Duck's rented Cadillac into their driveway. Cody was parked up the street out of their drunken eyesight. He and Dulow watched the small group laugh their way up on the porch and into the house. Soon they saw lights come on.

Twenty minutes later, Cody was ready to go in. They

emerged from their vehicle wearing black carpenter's pants, black hooded sweatshirts and face masks. Both carried Dayton mallets inside the loops of their pants that were reserved for hammers.

Kneeling on the porch, Cody picked the lock while Dulow kept watch. When he heard the lock click, he slowly opened the door. Pulling out his gun, they entered the house.

Laughter could be heard coming from down the hallway. Quietly, they crept down the hall to the closed doors. Cody would take one and Dulow would take the other. On the count of three, both cops snatched open the doors and stormed in.

"Freeze!" Cody yelled.

Capone was in bed on top of the girl. When Cody yelled "Freeze!" he disobediently reached for his gun on the stand next to the bed. A kick in the face by Cody knocked him back onto the bed.

When Dulow rushed into Duck's room, he saw the girl lying on her stomach while Ray ate her out from behind. He looked up with a ghastly look on his face.

"Pull your nose out of her ass," Dulow commanded. "And get the fuck up." He pointed his gun at the girl. "You. Put on your clothes."

The girls were cuffed and locked inside the bathroom. Per Tukey's orders, Cody and Dulow beat Capone and Duck's naked bodies with the mallets until there were no more bones to break. Then they were placed in bed together with their drawers pulled down to their ankles. A note was placed on the dresser that said, "We like to be raped." Their signatures were on the bottom.

The two girls were set free after Cody took their IDs and threatened to kill them if they uttered a word to the cops. Duck and Capone were still breathing when they left.

The very next day, Tukey learned of the incident on the morning news. It was music to her ears while she sat at the table eating breakfast, smiling triumphantly.

So far, every mission that Tukey sent her dogs on was about revenge. Last night's mission would cost her another fifty g's, but the next hit to be carried out would compensate for it all.

* * * * *

White Rich was lounging in his plush Suburban home. He was sitting on the sofa watching cartoons with his seven-year-old son. His eyelids fluttered as he was about to doze off. Then the phone rang.

"I'll get it, daddy," his son said, jumping up. "Hello ... Hold on. It's for you, daddy." Richard Jr. sat back on the sofa.

"Yeah," Rich answered in a low voice.

"Hey, babe. It's Mocha, your favorite flava."

He yawned. "Wha'sup wit' it?"

"Nothing, just trying to get at you on what we discussed."

"What's that?"

She sighed. "You remember those people I told you about? They want ten thousand Ecstasy pills."

"Whoa! Whoa!" he said, trying to shut her up. "You know not to talk to me like that over the phone."

"Oops! My bad. Anyway, they're in town and they want to holla at you."

"I don't meet new people. Besi—"

"I know. That's why I'ma come get it for 'em. Who knows, maybe we'll have time for a quickie."

Rich thought about it for a moment. "All right. Come by the crib."

"OK." She hung up Captain Kirby's office phone. Cody turned off the tape.

Captain Kirby cleared her throat. "I'll run the tape over to the judge and get the warrant."

* * * * *

Rich grabbed his gun and jumped up after he heard screeching tires outside his house. Standing in front of the door, he was just about to peek out when he heard Junior crying. He turned away from the door, walking toward his son.

Dulow ran up on the porch carrying the battering ram, followed by Dickie. Purposely, he didn't yell, "Police! Search warrant!" to identify themselves before knocking down the door. When Rich heard the door fly open, he turned around firing. Dickie took three in the vest before he fell backward.

Cody crouched low, then fired two shots into Rich's body. His son watched in terrified shocking horror as his father's lifeless body crumpled to the floor.

Cody knelt beside Dickie. "You all right?" Dickie nodded. "Good! Casey, call an ambulance. Dulow, let's check out the rest of the house."

While Dickie lay on the ground in anguish, he thanked God that he was wearing a Point Blank vest. Now he would live to choke the shit out of Dulow for putting his life on the line like he did. The only reason why he could see Dulow doing such a terrible thing was because he fucked Tiki.

No cash was found inside the house, but they did find nine one-gallon jugs filled with Ecstasy pills. One of them they would turn in, the rest would be brought to Tukey.

Dulow walked out back and saw a small shed guarded by a vicious looking Rottweiler. After he called for Cody to assist him, they crept toward the shed. The barking dog pulled on his chain, almost choking himself, as he desperately tried to get at them.

Dulow shot him with the 12-gauge pump. The bleeding dog cringed backward, but continued to bark. Cody unholstered a .40-caliber, aimed for the head, then fired a single round into his skull. That was the end of that.

After a search, and digging four feet into the earth, they recovered a fifty-gallon drum. It was filled to the top with bundles of cash. Six hundred fifty thousand to be exact.

The two hundred thousand dollars that they turned in along

with the Ecstasy pills got them all awarded citations. The mayor also gave Captain Kirby a fifty-thousand dollar grant to help fund the D-Unit's operation.

Being that a murder took place during their last raid, the D-Unit was placed on a two-week leave. The superiors thought it would be best if they took some time to clear their heads. Two killings in two raids could start to take a toll on them. Dickie's rib cage was badly bruised. As a result, he would spend his two weeks in bed.

Tukey gave them two hundred thousand out of the four that was left and gave fifty to Twila for her cut. Cody also stole Rich's cell phone for her, which earned him a ten thousand dollar bonus. Now that she had possession of Rich's million dollar line, the pill market was about to be hers.

In just a couple of weeks, Tukey got revenge on the guys who raped and robbed her. She had the biggest Ecstasy dealer in the city taken out and was now about to take over his empire. And she did it all from the comfort of her own home.

Chapter 26

The money shot straight to their heads. Cody traded his Suburban in for a new Escalade, then rimmed and TV-ed it up. He bought a new house out in Lee's Summit. Since his money was long, he gambled big at the boat. When he picked up his check from the police station, he was wearing more jewelry than the average drug dealer.

Money continuously caused problems inside Dulow's home. He, too, bought an Escalade with big rims and TVs. Gambled big. Came home with women's numbers in his pockets. He was doing everything that he shouldn't have been doing. Instead of keeping a low profile, they were doing just the opposite.

Casey gave his wife most of the money. The rest he used to get himself a nice hotel room. Then he bought the biggest rock that he could buy and a couple of crackhead whores and locked himself inside the room. He would remain on cloud nine for the whole two weeks.

While Tukey remained on bed rest, Tiki and Peko worked Rich's cell phone. With all the new out-of-state clientele, money was coming in so fast that Anitra gave up trying to launder any of it. There was just too much of it. Cody was dicking her down so good that she found herself showering him with gifts.

The more distant Anitra became, the more suspicious Tukey became. They hadn't fucked in weeks, even while Anitra was thizzin. And that didn't sit well with Tukey. She had to find out what was going on.

* * * * *

Peko and Tiki raced their two brand new Chrysler Crossfires down Troost headed to No Draws. Peko made it there first. When her car came to an abrupt halt, her Sprewells were spinning so fast that it looked like her car was moving in place. Tiki arrived seconds later.

"Yu cheated, bitch!" Tiki yelled jokingly.

"Unt unh," Peko denied. She broke down shaking her booty in the parking lot.

"Hey!" Tiki joined in. "Do de bump. Do de bump."

Two bad bitches who were entering the club saw them dancing and turned up their noses. Tiki caught them staring and stopped.

"Fuck y'all looking at?" she asked.

"Nothin'," one of them said sarcastically.

Tiki brushed them off. She didn't want trouble tonight. Instead she handed her keys to the valet, then strolled in without having to wait like the rest of the women.

Cody and Dulow pulled up in Cody's Escalade. He hopped out sporting a pink blazer with a button-up shirt, crisp blue jeans and a pair of white and pink Air Force 1's. A toothpick dangled from his lips. Dulow wore the same, only his blazer and his shoes were blue. Cody scanned the line of women through tinted Cartier lenses.

When they walked in, Tiki was the first thing that Dulow saw on the dance floor. She had a drink in one hand and the other wrapped around some dude's neck.

"Look at that ho," Dulow said hotly.

Cody sighed. "You know what your problem is, man?" He put his arm around Dulow's neck. "You be looking for love in all the wrong places." He laughed as he walked away.

An hour later, Cody and Dulow were on the dance floor dancing to The Game's "*How We Do.*" When the song ended he shouted, "DDDD-UNIT!"

Anitra was bringing Big Corn a bucket of ice when she saw Mocha easing her way toward Cody. She stopped where she was to see what, if anything, was about to happen.

Mocha came up behind him. "You gon' back that thang up or should I push up on it?" she said. He smiled, then turned to leave. She grabbed his arm. "Don't be so quick to walk away. C'mon and dance with Mocha."

Mocha held him close. Cody had no choice but to go with the flow. Wearing nothing but a thong outfit, his hand felt all flesh when he grabbed her soft jiggling ass.

Tiera was dressed to kill. She had on a tight, strapless Chanel dress, stilettos and diamond earrings. She was on the floor all up on Kenny, listening to The Ying Yang Twins telling her to "Shake it like a salt shaker." Mocha was making her brown booty clap when Tiera saw Cody.

At first, Tiera didn't believe it was Cody with all the jewelry on. His blazer was open while he held his belt buckle. Man, was he looking good. Finally his eyes met hers. Kenny's head was buried in her chest. Tiera's eyes remained on him while she took the olive out of her martini and slowly swallowed it.

Cody nodded toward the exit. Tiera winked, signaling him that it was all good. He temporarily ditched Mocha and slipped outside. Tiera started fanning herself. Then she told Kenny that she was going to step outside and get some air.

Cody was standing beside his Escalade smoking when Tiera came out. She had a purple mink stole around her.

"That your truck?" she inquired, impressed.

"Yes it is."

"Well, take me for a ride then."

Cody was pulling out of the lot when Tiera reached over,

pulling at his zipper. "Turn a few quick corners, then come back, OK?" She pulled his dick out and began to suck it like Kenny had taught her. When he exploded inside her mouth, she swallowed every drop. Something she had never done before.

The second they pulled back up at the club, Tiera jumped out.

"Wait a minute!" Cody yelled. She turned around. "You just gon'—"

Kenny walked out of the club. "Tiera," he hollered. She looked around and saw him marching toward her. "What the fuck?"

"Chill out, dog," Cody said. "We were—"

"Nigga, was I talking to you?" Kenny said smartly. He grabbed her arm. "You want that nigga back?"

"No, baby," she said innocently. She lifted her head, kissing him on the mouth. She couldn't kiss Cody after sucking Kenny's dick, but she would make Kenny taste Cody's salty semen. "See, baby. I'm yours."

"Just get your ass over to the car."

"I hate it when you get drunk," she said as she did as she was told. Tonight she would receive another beating. That was the price she paid to be with him.

Cody wanted to beat Kenny's ass but thought better of it. Tiera chose to be with him. Her body was under new management, and that was all there was to it. Tiera waved as they drove past Cody in the white Infiniti. Cody would be on her mind all night.

Anitra came outside. "Who you leaving with tonight?" she asked.

Cody grabbed her arms. "Come on, now," he said, pushing her away.

"All right, 'fraidy cat. I'll leave you alone, for now." She snuck a quick kiss, then ran away.

When Cody walked into the club, he had no idea that there were three sets of cameramen snapping photos of him.

Anitra came out of the office an hour later and Cody was nowhere to be found. She was so hot that she jumped in her car and drove out to his crib. Mocha's Mustang was parked in his driveway, but his truck was gone.

"I can't believe I'm doing this shit," she said. She was sitting in her car outside his house, smoking a blunt. "You know what ... you're through with this shit, Anitra. You got a bitch at home, yet you'd rather be somebody's bitch." After she tossed the roach out the window, she sped away. Cody would never taste her pussy again.

* * * * *

"Something's definitely going on between those two," Rocky said, sitting in Tukey's living room. She was looking at a photo of Anitra kissing Cody outside the club. Then another one of her waiting outside Cody's house smoking a blunt. Mocha's Mustang could be seen in the background.

Tukey took a roll of money out of her purse and handed it to him. "T'anks, Rocky."

"Mm hm." He took the cigarette out of his mouth. "Don't trip off them two. You can always call me when you're feeling lonely. Ha! Ha!" He laughed at his own humor.

* * * * *

Rose, Anitra and Mi'kelle were having lunch while Tukey remained in the bedroom. The drill team coach would be there shortly to pick up Mi'kelle for practice. That's when Tukey would confront Anitra about what she had discovered.

The doorbell rang.

Mi'kelle could see her coach through the glass doors. "I'll get it," she hollered. "Mama, I'm about to go. My coach is here!" She grabbed her bag on her way to the door.

Anitra darted from the kitchen to catch up with her.

"Where's my kiss?" Mi'kelle gave her a kiss. "Mmph!"

"Bye, Aunt Anitra. Tell mama I'm gone."

When Tukey heard Mi'kelle leave, she called Anitra up to their bedroom.

"What's up?" Anitra said, walking through the door. Tukey motioned to the pictures that were scattered across the bed. "What the fuck is this?" She looked at them.

"Yu tell me what it is."

Anitra's heart sank to the pit of her stomach.

Tukey grunted. "Didn't me tell yu ... de guilty always choose tu remain silent?" She shook her head in disgust. "It must've been sum't'ing about dat man dat jump-started Ms. Strickly Undickly's hot pussy."

Anitra faced her. "You're right, Tukey," she admitted. "You wanna know what jump-started my hot pussy?" She raised her voice. "When I came home and saw him fucking your brains out in the guest room. When I saw that ... I guess the woman inside showed up."

Outside, Mi'kelle put her bag inside her coach's trunk. Then she realized that she had forgotten her baton. The coach waited while she ran back inside to get it. She had reached the bottom of the staircase when she heard her mother yelling. Being nosy, Mi'kelle tiptoed up the steps to their room and put her ear up to the door.

"You've got a lot of nerve casting stones at me," Anitra said in a cracked voice. Mi'kelle could tell that she was crying. "I'm not the one who killed my daughter's daddy."

Mi'kelle's chin fell to her chest at the same time that Tukey's did. It was at that moment when Mi'kelle finally realized why her grandma had so much hatred for Tukey. Mrs. Banks never told Mi'kelle how she felt, but she could feel the tension in the air when they were around each other.

"Me didn't kill Keith, bitch! So talk what yu know," Tukey said in defense.

"OK, you just put the gun in his hand that did."

Tukey's bottom lip quivered. "Bitch, if yu ever ... ever ... mention dat in me house again, yu getting de fuck out."

"You don't have to threaten me, 'cause I'm leaving," Anitra said. "Your ass is headed for doom and I'm not about to let you take me down with you."

Mi'kelle had heard enough. She ran down the stairs as fast as she could. When she got inside her coach's car, she sat back in the seat crying her heart out.

The coach asked, "Mi'kelle, what's wr—"

"Drive!" Mi'kelle shouted. "Just take me away from here."

The longer Tukey stood there watching Anitra pack her bags, the angrier she became. She stormed over to the dresser and yanked open the drawer.

Tukey picked up a dildo and hollered, "Doan forget dis!" Then threw it upside Anitra's head. "Or dis." She held up an anal dildo, then without warning, slung it at her also. "Yu de one who turned me out on dis shit! Now yu want tu be a woman, huh?" Tukey cocked her arm back, ready to throw another dildo at her.

"Don't hit me again," Anitra warned. "I'm not playing, Tukey."

"Ahhh!" Tukey screamed, then threw it at the mirror, shattering it. "Hurry up and get de fuck out!" She stormed out of the room.

After Tukey left, Anitra picked up the phone and called Cody.

"Hello," he answered. Mocha and Naughty could be heard chatting in the background.

"Mph!" Anitra snorted. "You really know how to run through a clique, don't you, Officer?"

"Anitra, lis—"

"Save it! I just called to tell you that Tukey knows about us." She hung up.

Chapter 27

Two Months Later

Since their breakup, Anitra had moved into a spacious loft in the downtown area. She used some of the money that she had stashed away and began investing in old houses that needed to be rehabbed. Her plan was to get twenty of them, then start a real estate company. Whenever she became horny and was in the mood, she would call up the Captain for a little bondage. Anitra found that beating the shit out of Twila was a great way to relieve stress.

Mi'kelle had shut Tukey out of her life. She didn't want to be around her. She wasn't there when Tukey called and she hid whenever Tukey came over. She didn't discuss with her mother what she had overheard, she just wanted Tukey to feel like she was being shut out of her life. Not knowing why Mi'kelle was acting the way she was would taunt Tukey for a long time. She was hurt and confused all at the same time. Later, Mi'kelle would drop the bomb on her by unveiling her mother's secret.

To occupy her mind, Tukey focused on getting money. She had Tiki, Peko and Shanti traveling from state to state selling pills to their new clients. Within the next year, she planned to open another club in Lawrence, Kansas. There were a lot of pills to be sold in the small college town, and she wanted to supply them.

The D-Unit was still assisting her with transporting dope from LA, but she was paying them less and less every trip. Now she would only give them a fourth of what the dope was worth after they raided a house. The whole D-Unit was feeling the effects of Cody fucking Anitra.

*****

Cody and Dulow were in their squad car patrolling Woodland Avenue. Neither had spoken too many words to the other. Cody was mad about how Tukey was playing him on the pussy and the money tip. Dulow was tripping because his new lifestyle was causing problems at home.

The white Infiniti with the sparkling rims that was coming their way got Cody's attention. As the car drove past, he caught a glimpse of Kenny in the driver's seat. Paper Boy was riding shotgun. They fit the description of the suspects involved in the Amoco shooting a while ago. Cody made a U-turn and began to tail them.

*****

"I got some bitches coming by tonight," Paper Boy informed Kenny. "You chilling at the spot or going home to wifey?"

"Depends on who's coming. If it's Tasha and Nicky, I'm going home to wifey. But if it's Disirea and Octavia, I'm staying."

Paper Boy passed him the blunt. "Well, be prepared to come up with a good lie 'cause it's the latter."

"I ain't gotta tell her shit. I bring home the pig."

"You sucka."

Cody tailed them all the way to their spot without being detected. He watched from the corner to see what they had going on, if anything. Cars were coming and going like it was a car wash. It was just what he had suspected. A drug house.

From Mocha they learned that Kenny copped his work from Tukey. So they watched them until the day she delivered their package. That night they would be raided.

* * * * *

Paper Boy was on his knees, directly in front of the front door, shooting dice with Kenny and Dewey. He was shaking the dice when he heard someone outside yell, "Police! Search warrant!" A second later the door came crashing in on him.

"On the ground, now!" Cody hollered.

Kenny and Dewey looked up and saw four high-powered rifles pointed at them. Paper Boy was holding his sore head.

"I knew I should've took my ass home," Dewey said.

Kenny lay down, locking his fingers behind his head.

"Unt unh!" Cody said. "Get up!" Dulow came out of the dining room with a chair. They sat him in it and cuffed him to the chair, then started beating him savagely. After ten minutes of getting hit, kicked and slapped in the face, Kenny fell over in the chair. "Get up!"

Dulow picked Kenny and the chair back up. Cody wrapped a plastic tie around his neck and tightened it around his throat. Kenny's loss of breath kept him from screaming. Dulow pulled a piece of paper and a pen out of his pocket, then uncuffed Kenny's hands.

"Sign it," Dulow commanded. When he hesitated, Cody tightened the tie around his neck.

Cody kneeled, looking Kenny in his red eyes. "You gon' cooperate, muthafucka, or you and your partner here are going down for a double homicide."

"Don't tel—"

"Shut up!" Dickie said, kicking Paper Boy in the mouth. Dewey looked stunned, wondering what the fuck was going on.

"OK," Kenny mumbled. He took the pen and scribbled his

name.

"That's a good bitch," Cody said, rubbing Kenny's head. He cut the tie from around Kenny's neck, then took his mask off. "You know what you just signed?" Kenny shook his head. "It says here that you agree to be our stool pigeon. You are to provide the D-Unit with any information that you have and learn about anyone who deals narcotics. If you do not comply, you'll be prosecuted for obstruction of justice." Cody chuckled. "You fucked my bitch, Kenny. Now I'm fuckin' you."

"Fuck you!" Kenny spat.

"Unt unh." Cody slapped him across the face. "Rat mutha-fucka."

They confiscated fifteen kilos, two guns and eighteen grand in cash from them. Inside the van, Cody addressed his crew.

"All right, listen up," he commanded. "From now on, anything we seize in a raid that we don't turn in belongs to us."

"What about Tukey?" Casey inquired.

"Fuck Tukey," Cody simply said. "She don't give a damn about us or if our families eat. From now on the D-Unit is a self-contained unit. Nobody, especially a bitch, will have control over us." He peered at his men. "Now, we'll use Kenny as our snitch to lead us to our scores. I'm working with Mocha on locating buyers for the dope we seize. Is everybody with me on this?" They all nodded. "Good."

* * * * *

The next day, Mocha sat inside The House of Vogue barbershop waiting on Fuzzy and Black to finish getting their heads cut. When they finished, they all stepped outside to discuss business.

"So what's up with your boy you keep bragging on?" Black asked, rubbing his head. Fuzzy leaned against his BMW.

Smacking on gum, Mocha said, "He has fifteen bricks in his possession right now and he's ready to deal."

Fuzzy asked, "What's the price tag?"

"Fifteen apiece. Plus a small finder's fee for me."

Black and Fuzzy looked at each other. Fuzzy nodded, then Black said, "We'll take it." He stepped to Mocha and gently removed her shades from her face. "But if shit don't go right ... you better disappear. Understand me?"

Mocha snatched her glasses. "I wouldn't involve myself in a faulty deal, Mr. Black."

"OK," Black said. "Make it happen."

Cody was inside his patrol car, watching from the parking lot of the Kentucky Fried Chicken next door. Before Mocha hopped into her peach-colored Mustang, she gave him a thumbs up.

* * * * *

Peko was driving down Blue Parkway in Tukey's Dodge Magnum talking to Eight Ball on her cell phone.

"I need to come your way," Eight Ball said.

"Ya only callin' because Rich ain't 'round, mon."

"Damn! How you know about Rich?"

She giggled. "Doan even trip. But check dis, rude boy. Since ya pissed on me like dat last time, de price has gone up."

"What? Bitch is you—"

Peko hung up. Thirty seconds later, Eight Ball called back.

"I'm sorry, Peko," he said. "I'll tell you what, I'ma come down there to y'all's club and we can discuss it. Cool?"

"Yeah, dat's cool. Me got a frien' name Shantí dat me want yu tu meet anyway. Her got dat killa pussy."

"In that case, I'm hitting the highway now."

Cody was pulling out of One Way Rim and Body Shop in his Escalade when he saw the familiar-looking rose-pink Magnum drive by. Peko was driving it.

"I know she ain't the bitch who shot at me," he said to himself. "Aw, yeah. It's on now." He pulled out four cars behind her and followed her home.

Peko kicked off her shoes and was just about to make a booty call when she heard a knock at the door.

"Who is it?" she hollered.

"Cody!"

Peeking out the window, she saw him looking around suspiciously. Just to be on the safe side, Peko put her Bulldog .44 into her pocket and pulled her T-shirt down over it.

Cody wore a friendly smile on his face when Peko opened the door. "I was in the neighborhood, so I dropped by."

She shot him a look that said, *And?*

"You gonna offer me a drink?"

"Sure, come in." She stepped aside.

"A glass of ice water should quench my thirst," he said.

Peko was reaching for the ice tray when she felt Cody come up behind her. She spun around and found him staring at her.

"Wha—"

Cody seized her neck and squeezed. The glass fell.

"You don't remember me, do you bitch?" he said in a strained voice. "Remember the night when you shot at my police car?"

"Fu ... fu ... fuck ... yu," she stuttered.

"That's exactly what you're about to get." When Cody laughed, he sent a chill up Peko's spine. His face looked like it belonged on the devil. He stopped laughing after he felt the barrel of her gun poking his stomach. Then he heard the clicking sound of the hammer cocking back. He loosened his grip.

"Nigga, get ... ya fucking ... hands off me," she said slowly, "'fore me blow pig shit all over de wall."

Slowly, Cody released his grip and backed up. By rights Peko could have shot him for attacking her inside her home, but there was too much dope and money in her house to cause a scene.

Cody cracked a weak smile. "I was just trying to scare you, Peko. We've gotten too cool for me to trip on that bullshit."

"Trip ya ass de fuck out dat door."

"All right, I'm leaving. Just don't do anything you'll end up regretting later. I'm a cop, remember?"

Peko watched him drive off the grounds before she closed her door and locked it.

Chapter 28

Captain Kirby was busy typing up a report when a group of tall, suited white men barged into her office. A jolt of fear shot through her after she peered up and saw the four stone faces staring down at her. Two were from Internal Affairs, one was from the IRS and the last was the Prosecutor, Richard Hulagan.

"May I ... help you, gentlemen?" she asked nervously.

The heavyset man wearing the cheap suit, who was from the IRS, opened his briefcase and took out some papers. "Yes, you may," he said. "If you look at these papers you will see a paper trail of over seventy thousand dollars that you spent over the last couple months. None of which had been reported to the IRS."

"I ... wh, can assure you that I can explain all of that," she stuttered.

One of the men from Internal Affairs stepped forward and barked, "You'd better, or your ass is gonna be up shit creek."

"Yes sir, Mr. McDonald," Twila said, getting up from her desk. Out of her file cabinet she took out a folder and six small cassettes.

"First off," she began, "I should inform you that Sergeant Cody Brown and myself have been intimately involved for the past few months, during which, Mr. Brown took it upon himself to shower me with cash and expensive gifts. When I inquired where he obtained the money, he said that he won it gambling while he was in Vegas."

McDonald grunted, then asked, "Didn't that strike you as odd, Captain?"

"Yes it did," she informed him. "That's why I ordered Lieutenant Harris to plant listening devices in the D-Unit's van."

"And you came up with …" Hulagan asked, anxious for something to prosecute.

Twila placed one of the cassettes inside her tape player. For the next hour they sat and listened to the D-Unit talk themselves into an indictment. Then she opened the folder and passed around some pictures that Harris took while he was surveiling them. They saw photos of Cody in the club, with strippers, getting in limos, his new home and they saw various pictures of Dulow, Dickie and Casey as well.

McDonald said, "Dave, show the Captain what we have." Dave opened his briefcase and tossed some photos on her desk. "As you can see, we've been surveiling Sergeant Brown as well." They were not just photos of the D-Unit, but of Tukey and her crew as well.

Hulagan said, "He came to my attention after he up and changed his testimony in the middle of a drug hearing. That's when I became suspicious and alerted Internal Affairs."

The IRS man said, "And that put us on the trail of a Ms. Tukey Tosh. After we did a little research, we found that she has spent over one million dollars on homes, cars, clothes, jewelry and a club."

"How did she manage to slip under y'all's radar?" Twila inquired, hoping that she was out of the hot seat.

He said, "A few years ago, the feds were investigating her child's father for tax evasion and conspiracy to sell narcotics. After he died, the feds closed the case." He shrugged. "Three years later she surfaces with his money. Now we need to focus on busting her and Mr. Brown."

"Leave it to me, gentlemen," Twila said. "Dead or alive, I'll bring them in by the end of the month."

"You'd better," Hulagan threatened. "Because if you don't ... I guess we'll have to reopen the case on you. I mean, who knows ... maybe Sergeant Brown will implicate you."

"Don't worry," she assured them. "Give me thirty days."

Hulagan set his watch. "Your time just started."

Twila watched their backs as they walked out of her office. "Niggers," she said to herself. "Always gotta fuck up a good thing."

* * * * *

"Man, that shit was raw," Black said to Cody. They were shooting pool inside Club No Draws. Mocha and Dacari were sitting at the table next to them, drinking and talking.

Cody sipped on his cognac. "Just remember," he said, "I'ma have it when don't nobody have it. You hear what I'm saying?" He was tipsy and feeling good.

Tukey stood inside her office, staring at them through the two-way mirror. What the hell were Cody and Black laughing and chatting about? She didn't know that they even knew each other let alone had anything in common.

Tiki walked in. "Gurl, guess what? Me just seen Fuzzy comin' out of de bathroom. Him said dat dey're gettin' dey dope from Cody now."

That explained a lot. Cody hadn't been calling or inquiring about their next hit and his spending habits hadn't slowed. First the situation with Peko, now this. His ass needed to be dealt with.

"Tiki, tell Cody dat de boss wants to see him," Tukey said in a low voice. "And deal wit' Mocha for me."

Mocha had her arm around Cody's waist while he chatted with Black. Tiki tapped him on the shoulder.

"De boss wants tu see yu," she informed him.

"The boss, huh?" he said, laughing. Mocha peered at Tiki with glassy eyes. "In that case, I'd better go see what she wants." He looked at Black. "Order us another round and rack 'em up. Be right back."

Tukey was standing next to the conference table when Cody walked in. To be disrespectful, he took a seat in her chair at the head of the table.

"What's up ... boss?" he said sarcastically.

"Me hear yu movin' ya own stuff now."

"Come on, girl. I would never go behind your back and do that," he said loudly. "You should know me bet—"

"Dat's not what Fuzzy says."

Cody smiled bashfully. "Well ... I guess you got me. So what?"

"So what? So yu just gonna cut me out of sum't'ing dat me put toget'er?" She put her hands on the table. "Ya square ass wouldn't be shit if not for me."

With a serious look on his face, Cody stood, towering over her. "Don't you ever raise your voice at me again," he said through clinched teeth. "I'm the police, bitch! I make the law around here, not you. You bitches can't move without me saying so. You started it, Tukey." He lowered his voice and continued, "You started cutting me off after you got robbed. You didn't take my calls, hell, I couldn't even see you, but you wanna bark orders." He put his face directly in front of hers. She could smell the liquor on his breath. "Then you started with the money ... the money." He laughed and shook his head. "Why?" She said nothing. He put his hand in between her legs and said, "Is it because I fucked your gay lover?"

Full of rage and anger, Tukey swung her fist at Cody, but he caught her arm. "Control your temper before I mop this floor with your ass, bitch." He dropped her arm. "Also, the D-Unit is no longer under your command. There's a new Sheriff in town, and his name is Cody Brown." He stepped around her on his way to the door. He stopped in the doorway and turned around. "Hate it or love it, the underdog's on top."

"Me shoot disobedient dogs, Cody," she said coldly.

"Well ... you bet not miss." They glared at each other for a moment, then Cody left.

* * * * *

Mocha flushed the toilet in the women's restroom. When she opened the stall door, she found Tiki and Peko standing there glaring at her.

"Shall us wait until yu wash ya hands, or shall us get started now?" Tiki asked courteously.

"Tiki, ple—"

Tiki stole her in the face, cutting her off. Peko clutched a handful of Mocha's weave and dragged her out of the stall. Four girls were standing outside the locked restroom door, listening to Mocha scream for help.

* * * * *

Captain Kirby stood over Cody inside her office while he viewed the pictures of Tukey that McDonald had left her. She failed to inform him that he, as well as herself, were also under investigation. As far as he knew, Tukey was the only person under watch.

"So what now?" he asked.

"Now we rid ourselves of Ms. Tosh before she gets indicted and rolls over on everybody."

"And how do you suppose we do that?"

"We raid the club and make sure that she dies in the process." She sat on the edge of her desk facing him.

"I'm with it. But let's hold out until she gets another shipment of drugs in. A truckload of drugs will be delivered to her club, most likely at night. Then we'll raid it. We can retire on all the shit that will be in that truck and there'll still be enough to turn in to our superiors." He placed his hand on her thigh. "And I'll personally see to it that she gets shot during the raid."

Twila removed his hand. "Good. The warrant is on your desk. You've got three weeks ... so make it fast."

The warrant that was placed on Cody's desk by the Captain was a fake. Her signature, as well as the judge's, was forged by Lieutenant Harris. That way, after the shit hit the fan, she could deny any involvement in the bust.

* * * * *

Sixteen days later, Tukey and Shantí pulled up in the back of her club. Tiki and Peko had shut it down an hour ago after the truck arrived from LA. She let the top up on her SSR, then lifted up the doors.

They were about to enter the club when Shantí stopped Tukey. "Hold up real quick," she said. She dug a ring box out of her pocket and flipped it open.

"Damn!" Tukey exclaimed as she looked at the beautiful diamond ring.

Shantí had a big grin on her freckled face. "I'm gonna propose to Derrius tomorrow," she said excitedly. "I wanna know what it feels like to be married before I die."

Tukey hugged her. "Congratulations in advance."

"Thank you."

On their way inside, Tukey offered to send them on an expensive vacation as a honeymoon present. To Tukey's surprise, Dave and three of his men were sitting in her office with Tiki and Peko. Dave had followed the truck in a rental car to make sure that it made it.

* * * * *

Mocha had called Cody two hours earlier and tipped him that the truck had arrived. Now the D-Unit was posted around the corner, gearing up for the raid. Cody informed them that they had the green light to kill.

Dave and his goons were shooting pool, laughing and drinking Dom while Reggae music played out of the system. He set fire to a Jamaican spliff.

Tukey and her girls were inside her office counting the money that the club took in. She had already checked out the stuff inside the truck.

* * * * *

Captain Kirby was in the garage at the station gearing up with six members of another task force. Their mission was to get to Club No Draws and bust a group of renegade cops, the D-Unit, who were allegedly committing robbery in the name of the law. Since the cops were armed and presumed dangerous, they also had the green light to do what they had to do. Twila had it timed just right. She would give Cody a sufficient amount of time to raid the club and kill Tukey before they would come in behind them.

* * * * *

"Police! Search warrant!" was yelled, then the club door came crashing in. Dave and his men were too drunk and the music was too loud for them to hear Dulow when he identified themselves before they entered. So when they heard the crash, they instinctively went for their weapons. That's when the gunfire erupted.

The shots took the D-Unit by surprise. But instead of retreating, they stormed in firing their high-powered rifles wildly. Dickie could've easily taken the opportunity to kill Dulow with friendly fire for getting him shot, but at that moment his main concern was making it out of there alive.

When the girls heard the commotion, they immediately put their evacuation plan into effect. Tukey and Shantí both grabbed the conference table and slowly lifted the heavy wood over on its side. Then Tiki and Peko knelt down and removed the carpet, exposing a big hole in the floor. It had a stairwell that led to a basement that led out back to where their cars were parked.

"Let's go! Let's go!" Tukey hollered.

The D-Unit took out Dave's three men. Dave himself ran

inside the strippers' locker room. While the rest of the team went after him, Cody went to find Tukey.

Captain Kirby and her team arrived on the scene.

"Let's go get'em!" she commanded.

Tiki shot the lock on the basement door and they bailed up the steps to the alley where her Crossfire and Tukey's SSR were parked. Tiki and Peko jumped into the Crossfire.

"Hurry up!" Peko yelled at Tukey and Shantí.

When Tukey hit the button on her key ring her doors automatically lifted. They had just entered the truck when Cody came running out of the back door. Tiki hit the gas, causing her tires to smoke up the wheel wells.

Cody dropped the rifle and unholstered his .40-caliber. When Tukey hit the gas, the back end of the truck spun sideways putting Shantí in the line of fire.

Pop! Pop! Pop!

Tukey ducked her head as the bullets tore through her truck. Cody was running behind them, emptying his clip.

Dulow, Dickie and Casey were hunting for Dave when they heard the task force come in screaming, "Police!" Since they had a legitimate warrant to be there, they stopped hunting Dave and went to see what was going on. Just in case, they went with their guns drawn.

"Freeze!" the second team yelled when they saw Dulow and the rest of the D-Unit come out of the strip club. When they didn't drop their weapons, they opened fire.

Captain Kirby heard gunshots out back and automatically assumed that it was Cody.

"Check on those three," she commanded. "I'm going out back." In the alley, Twila saw Cody crouched in a shooting stance, shooting at the fleeing vehicle. "Freeze, Cody!" she ordered with her weapon drawn. He had turned around halfway when she fired three shots at him. One bullet struck him in the thigh, another went through his arm and lodged in his ribcage.

The other grazed his neck. Before she could fire another round, two members of her team had made it out there to assist her.

Tukey was flying up Holmes Road. "Damn! Damn! Damn!" she hollered as she beat on the steering wheel. "Shantí, us gotta ge ..." When she looked over, she saw Shantí's chin on her chest. Blood was leaking out of her head.

"Nooooo!" Tukey cried out. It hurt her deeply to see her best friend's lifeless body sitting next to her.

Tukey stopped dead in the middle of the street. Wrapping her arms around Shantí's bloody body, she cradled it like a child. Tears ran down her cheeks while snot bubbles popped out her nostrils. Closing her eyes tight, she recited a prayer for Shantí, hoping that she would be admitted into heaven.

Peko had already alerted Rose to load everything she could inside Tukey's Hummer and bring it to the hideaway house where Tukey used to creep with Lateka.

* * * * *

Anitra learned about Shantí's death on the morning news. She also found out about Dulow, Dickie, Casey and the three unknown subjects that were killed in a police raid. Cody was shot and taken to Research Hospital where he was listed as in critical condition. Large amounts of drugs and money were seized and the police were on a hunt for one Ms. Tukey Tosh. Tiki and Peko were being sought for questioning.

There was no mention of him, but Dave had escaped through a window. At that very moment, he was on a bus back to Los Angeles.

Chapter 29

A week later, Tukey sat on the living room couch in her hideaway loading the sawed-off that Cody had given her after he knocked off Herm. It was a gift from him that she wanted badly to give back to him.

Tiki and Peko sat around the kitchen table smoking trees, awaiting Tukey's next move. The three of them had disguised themselves by cutting their hair and running the clippers over it with a number four guard. When it was all over, they planned on fleeing to Denver, Colorado. Tukey heard that blacks were on the rise in Denver, legitimately, so her flamboyant lifestyle wouldn't make her stand out.

But first, Tukey had business to tend to. She had to set fire to the trail that the police were on. Then she would wait around to kill Cody. Her conscience wouldn't be clear until he no longer walked the earth. She owed it to Shantí for getting her involved in this mess.

There was a knock at the door.

"It's me, Rocky," he said. Tukey still peeped out to verify that it was Rocky before letting him enter.

Rocky had been sent on a mission. That mission was for him to install a hollowed-out metal door on her safe house. He would fill the hollow door with gasoline, douse the house with gas, then leave.

On the table, Rocky placed three false driver's licenses and social security cards for them to use in travel.

Rocky put a hand on her shoulder. "You're sure you want to go through with this?" he inquired.

"Got no ot'er choice," she said, reaching for the phone. "Me on de run now." She dialed Anitra's number.

"Hello," Anitra answered.

"Hi," Tukey said timidly.

"It took you long enough to call," Anitra yelled at her. She sighed. "What you need me to do?"

Tukey cracked a smile. Anitra knew her too well.

* * * * *

Captain Kirby had bitten her fingernails down to the nubs. Tukey was on the run with the DVD of her and Cody had survived her failed attempt to murder him.

Twice, Twila contemplated boarding a plane to another country but she didn't want to act too soon. Tukey had enough money to run forever. Cody was another matter. After he recovered, he would be indicted. That's when he would roll on her. If Twila could somehow get rid of him, her problems would temporarily be over.

Debra peeked her head in. "Captain, you have a visitor."

Anitra appeared in the doorway. "Hi, Captain."

"Anitra," she replied, surprised. "Shut the door and have a seat." She sat. "I hope you got some good news."

Anitra said, "I can't solve your Cody problem, but I can solve your Tukey problem and give you your DVD." Twila smiled and Anitra continued. "But Tiki and Peko would have to be cleared of any future charges."

"How do I know that Tukey won't talk?" she quizzed. "And how am I supposed to convince my superiors that Tiki and Peko should walk away scott free?"

"Because they are gonna call and tip you to Tukey's whereabouts. It's Tukey they want, not them. And trust me, Tukey won't talk. When it's over, she will be thought to have been killed. Dead women can't talk."

"And then you'll turn over the DVD?" She nodded. "Then it's a deal."

Ten Days Later

"Yu ready?" Tukey asked. She was sitting inside a rental car, talking to a replica of herself. She had searched and found a tall, dark crackhead, had two platinum crowns put in her mouth and put a dreadlocked wig on her.

"Yes, I'm ready," the woman replied.

"Let's go over de plan again."

"I know what I'm supposed to do, Tukey. Just have my money ready after this is over."

"Me put fifty t'ousand dollars in ya mom's mailbox dis mornin' for yu."

The woman frowned. "Tukey, why you do that? Damn! Now mama's gon' think she can control it."

"Yu doan need it in ya possession noway. Now go 'head."

Fuming, the frail woman stepped out of the car, slung her purse over her shoulder, then proceeded to walk. Tukey drove off. She walked three blocks up to the address that she was searching for.

Captain Kirby and her crew watched the frail woman from a park on the other end of the block. She was glancing around as if she thought she was being followed.

"She's a lot thinner than in the photograph, huh Cap?" one of her officers said.

"Can't eat good on the run," Twila said convincingly. She picked up her CB. "It's her, people. Let's move in!"

The woman spun around and saw all the police cars speeding in her direction. They hopped out with their guns drawn.

After throwing her purse in their direction, she broke and ran inside the house.

Tukey was standing on the side of a house that sat directly behind the safe house with a gun in her hand. When she heard the door slam, she fired two shots into the fender of Twila's car.

"Shots fired! Shots fired!" Captain Kirby yelled.

All of the officers immediately started discharging their weapons. The house was full of fumes from the gas that Rocky doused the house with, so when the bullets struck the metal front door, the sparks caused the fumes to ignite. Then, *boom!* The house exploded.

After the Fire Department came and cleared some of the smoke and debris, Debra picked up the purse that the woman threw, then took it to the Captain. Inside they found Tukey's license, credit cards, social security card and some miscellaneous items.

* * * * *

" ... the suspect, Tukey Tosh, is presumed to be dead," the news anchorwoman reported. "Now, in other news. A sk—"

Tukey shut off the TV. Now that she had thrown them off her trail, it was time to take care of Cody.

Anitra pulled into Russell's Car Wash and parked behind Twila's BMW. Twila had her hand out before Anitra got inside her car good. She handed her the DVD.

"Thank you," Twila said gratefully. "I can't believe that Tukey is gonna just let Cody get away." She was hoping that Anitra would leak some information.

Anitra shrugged. "She just wants to get away."

Twila lit a cigarette and took a few drags. "My superiors want me to charge you with something," she lied.

A shocked look appeared on Anitra's face. "For what?"

"For what? How about conspiracy, money laundering, aiding and abetting, you name it."

"What did you tell 'em?" Anitra asked worriedly.

Twila cut her eyes at Anitra, then said, "That depends on what you tell me."

Four Days Later

Tukey had been hanging around the house while Rocky hung out at the hospital, trying to find out when Cody would be released. He had come around days ago and the police were anxious to get him down to headquarters to be interrogated.

Tukey missed Mi'kelle badly. Since Mi'kelle was now staying with Mrs. Banks, Tukey was hesitant to call. She didn't feel like dealing with her bullshit, but she wanted her daughter to know that she was alive, despite what the news may say.

"Hello," Mi'kelle answered. She hadn't even seen the news. The police contacted Arie about Tukey's death, but she already knew otherwise.

"Mi'kelle, it's Mama. Me alive," Tukey said.

"So," Mi'kelle replied bluntly.

Tukey sniffled as her eyes began to water. "Mi'kelle, please. Me really need yu right now. Ya b—"

"And I need my daddy, but you killed him. I wish you would join him," she spat before she hung up.

The phone fell out of Tukey's hand. "Oh me God!" she cried. "Oh me God! Please kill me, Lord! Please! Me doan wanna live no mmmmore." She began to sob.

Anitra came out of the bathroom and saw Tukey balled up on the couch crying. She knelt down beside her.

"Tukey, what's wrong?" she asked, concerned.

Tukey sniffled. "Mi ... Mi'k ... she knows about Keeeith." She started sobbing uncontrollably. "Me baby."

"Oh my God!" Anitra said, putting her arms around her. The phone rang. She dug under Tukey's leg into the couch and retrieved it. "Hello."

"Anitra," Rocky said. "I'm up at the hospital. My contacts

informed me that Cody will be snuck out of here at midnight because they want to avoid the media."

"I'll tell Tukey."

"None of the other officers have been alerted because they want to keep a lid on it. There'll be one uniformed cop and Cody. This'll be her only chance."

"I know." Anitra hung up. "Tukey, that was Rocky. He says that Cody is being released tonight, so if you want to do this, you need to pull yourself together."

* * * * *

Captain Kirby was sitting in a bar guzzling down her third shot of whiskey. Her Cody problems weren't settled yet and she feared the outcome. Her cell phone rang.

"One more round," she ordered before she answered it. "Hello."

* * * * *

Hours later, after Tukey collected herself, she loaded the sawed-off double barrel. "Call Tiki and Peko and find out what's tekin' dem so long tu get here wit' de vans." She was about to walk out the door when Anitra stopped her.

"Tukey!" she yelled. "B ... be careful."

* * * * *

Tukey was sitting low in her Magnum, parked on the street across from the hospital. Through binoculars she could see a police car pull up and park outside the front entrance. A medium-sized, pale-faced cop with a cap on entered the building. Tukey sat down the binoculars, then tightened the straps on her gloves.

Rocky was standing at the nurses' station chatting with Naughty. Since the closing of No Draws, she started working as a CNA. He was busy bidding on her pussy when he saw the officer walk out of the room with Cody in cuffs. Rocky alerted Tukey that they were coming out.

After Cody and his escort stepped off the elevator, they

were greeted by Captain Kirby. She flashed her Captain's badge.

"Officer Cole," she said, reading the name on his badge. "I'm Captain Twila Kirby. I've been sent to relieve you of your prisoner, Cody Brown. You are to stand by and call someone to pick you up."

"But ... I ..."

"But what, Officer?" she asked firmly. "You're gonna stand here and challenge a superior officer's authority?"

"No ma'am," he replied respectfully.

"Good!" She took his hat off his head, balled up her ponytail, then placed it on hers. "And the keys, too."

From across the street, Tukey saw what appeared to be the same officer bring Cody's limping body out to the car and put him in the back seat. She cocked the shotgun. Her plan was to hit them with one shot apiece, then disappear into the night.

Twila's plan was to let Tukey kill Cody, then she would kill Tukey. It would be perfect. She would kill a cop killer and expose the fact that she wasn't deceased. She could justify her relieving Officer Cole of Cody by telling her superiors that she received a call from her informant telling her what was about to go down, then she acted on it the best way she knew how.

Cody didn't speak until they were inside the car.

"About to take me to jail, huh?" he asked.

"It's your own fault Co—"

"Bitch, you set me up! Yeah. My lawyer told me that you were the first on the list."

Quickly, Twila leaned over the seat and pointed a finger at him. "You were the one who changed your testimony during a drug hearing. That's where this all started."

"Well, don't think I'm going down alone," he said in a serious tone. "I've already informed my lawyer that I will cooperate to the fullest, so you and Anitra better get together and run to the edge of the earth." He laughed. "Now hurry up and get me to the station."

Twila adjusted the mirror so she could see his face. "I don't think you're gonna make it that far, Cody." She chuckled, then drove away.

"What the fuck you talking about?" he asked suspiciously. She ignored him. "Twila? Twila?"

Pulling out of the parking lot, Twila drove past the median and made a left onto Meyer Boulevard. She caught a glimpse of Tukey parked on the side of the road. There wasn't any traffic around that time of night, so everything was set to go as planned. Twila stopped at the red light about ten yards away from where Tukey was parked.

"Twila, what are you planning to do to me?" Cody inquired. He looked like he was constipated.

Tukey crept her wagon alongside them with her window down. Twila turned to face Cody.

"You believe in ghosts, Cody?" she asked bleakly, then nodded her head in Tukey's direction.

Slowly, Cody turned his head to the right. Tukey leaned out the window, pointing the shotgun at his face. He had about a half a second to figure out that he was about to die before Tukey blew half his face off. Twila wiped the blood from her eyes with one hand while she unholstered her gun with the other.

Tukey pulled up about a foot and aimed the gun at the front window. She hesitated when her eyes locked in on Twila's face. Her hesitation gave Twila enough time to duck down in the seat, missing the next slug that Tukey released.

When the Captain came back up, she had a .38 pointing in Tukey's direction. Tukey ducked and hit the gas just as the chamber released its first rounds. *Pop! Pop!* The Captain fired at the fleeing vehicle. The Magnum's powerful Hemi V8 engine went from zero to sixty in 6.1 seconds. Twila was in pursuit.

Tukey had just crossed Swope Parkway into Swope Park when a bullet from Twila's gun struck her back tire. The car spun out of control, spinning around until it finally crashed into a light pole. She shook her dazed head. She had a cut on her forehead and her lip was bleeding. Two more bullets entered her car. After the gunshots ceased, Tukey squeezed from between the airbag and the seat out of the car. Twila's patrol car entered the park at full speed. The lighthouse was the only thing in Tukey's view. Another shot was fired over her head as she ran inside the building.

Tukey stood on the side of the door, breathing heavily, while she waited for Twila to enter. Twila, with her gun drawn, slowly inched inside. Tukey kicked her in the stomach, then the knees, causing her to fall over. While Twila was sprawled out on the hard floor, Tukey closed the door. By the time she turned back around, Twila was lying on her back with the gun pointed up at her. Without delay, Twila pulled the trigger.

Tukey flinched after she heard the empty gun click. It took a second for her to regain her composure. By that time, Twila tossed the gun and was back on her feet.

"You're not leaving here alive, you black bitch!" Twila kicked her in the stomach, then punched her in the face. Tukey fell back up against the door. When Twila locked her fingers around her throat, Tukey kneed her in the crotch, then hit her in the eye. She grabbed Twila and the two began to tussle.

The fighting women fell to the floor, Tukey on top of Twila. While Tukey squeezed her throat, Twila eased a knife out of her boot.

"Oow!" Tukey screamed after Twila poked her with the cold steel. She rolled off of her, then back-pedaled up against the heater vent. *The heater vent*, Tukey thought. She had just remembered where Tiki told her that she had stashed the gun that night when she shot at Cody.

Twila stood up, taking the time to wipe the blood from her lips. "I told you that you wasn't gonna leave here alive, nigger bitch," she said. She held up the knife as she inched toward her. She smiled when she saw Tukey digging inside the vent. "Ain't nothing in there that can save you."

Twila was about a foot away from her when Tukey pulled out the chrome revolver and pointed it toward her face. Twila's grin turned into a terrified frown. *Pow! Click! Click!* The one bullet that was left in the chamber lodged inside Twila's forehead.

Sirens could be heard nearby when Tukey limped out of the lighthouse. From where she stood, she could hear the bling tone of her phone playing. As quickly as she could, she hurried over to the wagon and dug her phone out of the seat.

"Freeze!" Tukey whirled around to find an officer standing there pointing a gun at her. "Drop the phone and lay down on the ground. Slowly."

Tukey's heart was beating out of her chest. If she wasn't determined to kill Cody, she wouldn't have been in this situation. Now it was over. A double homicide would be added to her already long list of drug charges. Tukey got on the ground and placed her hands behind her head.

Car lights could be seen speeding in their direction. The cop shielded his eyes with his hand until the car stopped beside him. Tiki got out of her car with Dickie's stolen badge in her hand.

"Hi, Officer," she said, walking up on him. "Me name is Detective Edwards. Dis woman yu have here is a fugitive dat me have been following all de way from Kingston, Jamaica. Her wanted for multiple homicide and ya just apprehended her for me."

The baffled cop regarded the woman curiously. Tiki walked completely up on him. "Let me check out that badge," he said suspiciously. Tiki handed it to him. After taking a good look at it, he could clearly see that it was not a detective's badge. "Wait a minute. This is an officer's ba ... Ahhh!"

Tiki hit him with the stun gun that she got when she broke into Dickie's truck. His body collapsed on the ground, shaking.

Quickly, she kicked the gun away from him, then hit him again.

Surprised and happy at the same time, Tukey got up and embraced her heroic cousin.

"Not time for dat now, gurl," Tiki said. "Let's go!"

They weren't gone a minute when two more patrol cars drove up from the other side of the park and spotted the officer lying on the ground.

"How did yu know how tu find me?" Tukey inquired.

Tiki pointed to the walkie-talkie that she had stolen from Dickie. "Me heard it on de radio. Den when me showed up at de scene, me followed de cop over tu de park. Me had a feelin' dat Dickie's t'ings would come in handy one day." She smiled. "So, tell me what happened?"

After Tukey finished telling Tiki the story, she said, "How did her know yu was gonna be dere tonight? It doan mek any sense."

"Sure it does," Tukey said as she stared out her window. "Me been hoodwinked."

* * * * *

Anitra was sitting on the bed, tapping her foot nervously when Tukey and Tiki arrived. Stopping in the bathroom first, Tukey cleaned herself up. When Anitra saw the bedroom door open, she was surprised to see Tukey standing there stone-faced.

"Tukey!" she shouted as she stood up. "You made it."

Tukey embraced her and their lips locked as they kissed each other wildly. After they undressed each other, Tukey took the strap-on harness that she used to hit Lateka out of the dresser drawer. It confused Anitra to see Tukey putting it on.

"No, baby. Let me."

"Me doin' de fuckin' dis time," Tukey stated. "Yu seem tu like it when Cody does it."

Anitra reluctantly lay on the bed and spread her thin legs. Her throbbing pussy was dripping wet. Tukey grabbed her by the ankles and entered her. Anitra moaned from the orgasmic, painful pleasure that she was receiving. Soon the painful pleasure turned into just pain after Tukey started hitting her hard and rough.

"What are yo—"

Tukey seized her throat, cutting off her words. Anitra held Tukey's wrists tight, trying to break free, while Tukey continued to pound her mercilessly.

"OW! OW! OW! OOOOW!" Anitra screamed. Her cries encouraged Tukey to drill her with even more force. "Ple ... e ... e ... se!"

Blood was streaming out of her womb when Tukey pulled the thick, bloody dick out of her. Her chest was heaving with anger while she glared down at Anitra curled up on the bed, quivering.

"Ummmm!" Anitra bawled like a child. "What's wrong with you!?"

"Bitch, yu know what's wrong wit' me," Tukey said loudly. "Yu told Twila dat me was gonna kill Cody tonight. Didn't ya?" Crying, Anitra shook her head. "Yes ya did. T'at's why ya was never charged wit' not'ing. Yu was in cahoots wit' dat bitch."

"No! I swear I wasn't, Tukey," Anitra cried. Her pussy felt raw. "She threatened me that they were gonna charge me if I didn't tell 'em that you planned on killing Cody." She paused. "I told her that you didn't ... and ... and if she didn't believe me then she could take me to jail."

"Den why de fuck was her out dere tonight!? Huh? Yu said dat Rocky told yu dat didn't no ot'er officers knew."

"That is what he said. Please, Tukey!" she pleaded. "You gotta believe meee. The only thing I ever did to betray you was fuck Cody."

Tukey stared at her long-time friend regretting what had to be done. Her eyes began to tear at the horrible thought of Anitra dead. But it was her own fault. She chose to betray

Tukey and Tukey was almost killed and arrested as a result. So what had to be done, had to be done. Cody had deceived her and was murdered on sight. It was only right that Anitra meet the same fate.

Slowly, Tukey turned away and left the room.

"Tukey! Tukey!" Anitra painfully yelled at her back. After Tukey was gone, she put her head in the pillow and continued to sob. She was in too much pain to move.

The room door creaked as it opened, but Anitra didn't look up. Tiki walked over to the edge of the bed, leveled the Bulldog .44 at the back of Anitra's head and closed her eyes. When Tiki heard Peko turn the stereo up, *Pow!* She pulled the trigger.

* * * * *

The next morning, the girls packed the money into the two vans along with their personal items. Tiki and Peko got in one of them and hit the highway for Colorado. Tukey would give them a couple hours head start, then she would follow their trail. She chose to split her money up just in case one of them got pulled over on the highway.

Rocky arrived twenty minutes before Tukey was set to depart. She had cried four times and avoided going into the bedroom where Anitra's cold corpse lay lifeless.

"Ran into some trouble last night, huh?" Rocky asked.

"Yeah. As a matter of fact, me did. Me t'ought yu said dat it was a male officer dat picked Cody up last night?"

Rocky frowned. "It was. You can ask Naughty. We was standing at the nurses' station talking when he brought Cody out of the room in cuffs."

Tukey thought for a moment. "Well, Anitra must have tipped her off after yu called. Den somehow dat bitch managed to intercept him wit'out yu seein' anyt'ing."

"I don't know," Rocky said nonchalantly. "What you gon' do now?"

Tukey stared at a letter on the table. It was the note that she had left Keith that encouraged him to commit suicide. She was in the room next door when he shot himself. Afterward, she went back inside his room and got the two letters that she left him, then she disappeared.

"Me have ta go by me dawta's grandma's house tu confess sum't'ing tu me dawta ... and den me ... me gonna say goodbye tu her." Tukey was on the verge of tears. After a few seconds, she wiped her eyes then handed Rocky an envelope stuffed with cash.

Rocky gladly accepted the money and stood. "Well, good luck, Tukey." She nodded. Rocky left without another word.

After another ten minutes of sobbing, Tukey rose, grabbed her bag, then glanced around the house to make sure that she wasn't forgetting anything. She saw a picture on the table of herself, Shanti and Anitra at the club on Halloween. She picked it up, looked at it and smiled.

"T'ug bitches 'till us die," she said, then put it in her bag. Pulling out her lighter, she set fire to the curtains. As soon as she got a nice flame going, she turned to leave.

Her cell phone rang.

"Hello," she said, putting her hand on the doorknob.

"Have yu left already?" Tiki asked.

"Me walkin' out de door now." She opened the door. "But first m—" Tukey's eyes widened.

Pow!

The force from the blast knocked Tukey back up against the wall. She coughed up blood as her body slid to the floor.

"Tukeyyy!" Tiki yelled after hearing the blast. "Tukeyyy!"

Tukey took a couple slow, deep breaths, then gazed up at her assailant through dying dilating pupils. She half smiled when she saw who it was standing over her, pointing an old pistol at her face.

You're either gonna get us killed or put in jail, Tukey remembered Anitra saying to her. And she was right.

Pow! Pow!

The killer glared down at Tukey's grotesque corpse splattered against the wall. Then politely closed the door and left.

Chapter 30

"Tukey should've been killed by that Captain lady last night," Rocky said. He was sitting behind his desk while the killer made out a check for his services. He fired up a cigarette. "I really hate that you had to get your hands dirty. Bad thing about it is ... Tukey really believed that Anitra was the one who snitched her out. Hell, it was obvious that I'm the one who called the Cap'n." He paused. "Oh well, at least now it's over."

The killer handed Rocky the check.

"You know, you really didn't have to refinance your house to pay me, but I thank you for your kindness." The killer left Rocky's house for home.

* * * * *

Mi'kelle was sitting on the couch when she saw the front door open up. "Grandma, where have you been all day?" she inquired, looking up at Mrs. Banks.

ORDER FORM

Triple Crown Publications
PO Box 6888
Columbus, Oh 43205

Name: _____

Address: _____

City/State: _____

Zip: _____

TITLES	PRICES
Dime Piece	$15.00
Gangsta	$15.00
Let That Be The Reason	$15.00
A Hustler's Wife	$15.00
The Game	$15.00
Black	$15.00
Dollar Bill	$15.00
A Project Chick	$15.00
Road Dawgz	$15.00
Blinded	$15.00
Diva	$15.00
Sheisty	$15.00
Grimey	$15.00
Me & My Boyfriend	$15.00
Larceny	$15.00
Rage Times Fury	$15.00
A Hood Legend	$15.00
Flipside of The Game	$15.00
Menage's Way	$15.00

SHIPPING/HANDLING (Via U.S. Media Mail) $3.95 1-2 Books, $5.95 3-4 Books add $1.95 for ea. additional book

TOTAL $_____

FORMS OF ACCEPTED PAYMENTS:
Postage Stamps, Institutional Checks & Money Orders, all mail in orders take 5-7 Business days to be delivered.

ORDER FORM

Triple Crown Publications
PO Box 6888
Columbus, Oh 43205

Name: _____

Address: _____

City/State: _____

Zip: _____

		TITLES	PRICES
		Still Sheisty	$15.00
		Chyna Black	$15.00
		Game Over	$15.00
		Cash Money	$15.00
		Crack Head	$15.00
		For The Strength of You	$15.00
		Down Chick	$15.00
		Dirty South	$15.00
		Cream	$15.00
		Hoodwinked	$15.00
		Bitch	$15.00
		Stacy	$15.00
		Life	$15.00
		Keisha	$15.00
		Mina's Joint	$15.00
		How To Succeed in The Publishing Game	$20.00
		Love & Loyalty	$15.00
		Whore	$15.00
		A Hustler's Son	$15.00

SHIPPING/HANDLING (Via U.S. Media Mail) $3.95 1-2 Books, $5.95 3-4 Books add $1.95 for ea. additional book

TOTAL $_____

FORMS OF ACCEPTED PAYMENTS:
Postage Stamps, Institutional Checks & Money Orders, all mail in orders take 5-7
Business days to be delivered.

ORDER FORM

Triple Crown Publications
PO Box 6888
Columbus, Oh 43205

Name: _____

Address: _____

City/State: _____

Zip: _____

	TITLES	PRICES
	Chances	$15.00
	Contagious	$15.00
	Circumstances	$15.00
	Black and Ugly	$15.00
	Hold U Down	$15.00
	In Cahootz	$15.00
	Dirty Red *Hard Cover Only*	$20.00

SHIPPING/HANDLING (Via U.S. Media Mail) $3.95 1-2 Books, $5.95 3-4 Books add $1.95 for ea. additional book

TOTAL $_____

FORMS OF ACCEPTED PAYMENTS:
Postage Stamps, Institutional Checks & Money Orders, all mail in orders take 5-7 Business days to be delivered.

Dirty Red

From the author of *Imagine This* and *Let That Be the Reason*,
Urban lit icon and independent publisher Vickie Stringer conceives
the most mischievous and malicious urban heroine of all – Red.

In a scorching tale of love, lies, loss and the unconquerable spirit
of a woman scorned, we meet Red in the trenches of her game – on
the toilet of her boyfriend's apartment, faking a pregnancy.

A connoisseur of deception with a provocative femininity, Red's
dirty ways win her a closet full of Gucci bags, a deluxe condomin-
ium full of baby accessories, a new car and a book deal. But when
Red's cons backfire and she winds up truly pregnant by her inmate
ex-boyfriend, Bacon, Red finds herself in more trouble than she's
ever known.

Drama unravels when Red's picture-perfect scandals fall apart due
to the power of – surprisingly – love.

Vickie M. Stringer is the publisher of Triple Crown Publications,
one of the most prevalent African American book publishers in the
country and abroad. She has been featured in multiple magazines
and newspapers such as *The New York Times, Newsweek, Essence*
and *Black Enterprise*. She lives in Columbus, Ohio with her son
and newborn baby.